PRAISE FOR MARILYN ARNOLD'S PREVIOUS NOVELS:

"These novels touched me deeply, leading me, along with Delia McGrath, through an ever-widening range of emotion. As Delia grows and moves beyond her narrow world of career, she broadens her spiritual horizons and opens her heart to others. Her heart changes, and so does mine."
> —*Carol Lee Hawkins, chair of several BYU women's conferences*

"*Desert Song* is evidence of a maturing in Mormon literature. The levels of meaning, the importance of the land, the engaging sentences, the vitality of contemporary concerns—all make this an important book. And it is delightfully readable."
> —*Douglas Alder, past president, Dixie College*

"*Desert Song* is SO good! I couldn't put it down and had to read most of it twice because after reading it to myself I then had to share it with my husband. I was just going to wait and let him read it himself, but couldn't hold myself back. . . . What a page-turner!"
> —*Kristine Twiggs, St. George, Utah*

"You wrote my feelings in your books. . . . I wanted you to know how much both *Desert Song* and *Song of Hope* have meant to me. Just the little extra push to get me on track again."
> —*Sandi Hardy, Cedar City, Utah*

"Perhaps the Mormon novel for which we yearn—at once good Mormonism and good fiction—has arrived in Marilyn Arnold's first novel, *Desert Song.*"
> —*Richard H. Cracroft, BYU professor of English and director of the Center for the Study of Christian Values in Literature*

"I read *Desert Song* in two days—for a very slow reader like myself, that's record time! As I read along, I found myself wanting to underline certain phrases so I could go back to enjoy them again and again."
> —*Louise Crosby, Bloomington, Utah*

SKY
FULL *of*
RIBBONS

OTHER COVENANT BOOKS BY
MARILYN ARNOLD

Desert Song, a novel

Song of Hope, a novel

*Sweet Is the Word: Reflections on the Book of Mormon—
Its Narrative, Teachings & People*

SKY
FULL *of*
RIBBONS

a novel from the author of
Desert Song *and* Song of Hope

MARILYN ARNOLD

Covenant Communications, Inc.
Covenant

Cover image (sky) © PhotoDisc, Inc.

Published by Covenant Communications, Inc.
American Fork, Utah

Printed in the United States of America
First Printing: January 2000

07 06 05 04 03 02 01 00   10 9 8 7 6 5 4 3 2 1

ISBN 1-57734-605-x

To those whose eyes marvel at rainbows,
and whose hearts aspire toward
the Hand that makes them.

I do set my bow in the cloud,
and it shall be for a token of a covenant
between me and the earth.
GENESIS 9:13

CHAPTER ONE

It was precisely 8:50 a.m. when two perky, elderly women parked their faded brown 1978 Ford LTD below the clock tower atop a stately granite office building east of town. The sturdy edifice, which contrasted sharply with the LTD's sagging front bumper and peeling vinyl roof, was evidently intended to inspire public confidence in the law firms and title companies it housed.

That the car took its repose on a slant, while the building and its parking lanes sat square with the world, did not appear to trouble the vehicle's occupants in the least. With some effort, they pushed open the heavy sedan doors and hoisted their compressed, waistless bodies out. A youthful onlooker might judge them to be anywhere between seventy and ninety.

"First thing I do when I get my inheritance," puffed the driver, tugging at her aqua polyester skirt, "is get me a snazzy new vehicle with the easiest opening doors on the planet."

"Not me," replied her passenger, likewise tugging at an aqua polyester skirt. "First off, I'm going to Hawaii!"

"Not without me?"

"No, 'course not. When have I set foot outside the Cheyenne city limits without you since my Clarence and your Henry died?" The two tripped across the soft asphalt toward the building. It was late summer, but the day in Ogden, Utah, had heated up early.

"Think there'll be enough for a car *and* Hawaii?"

"My land, yes. After all, how many bona fide first cousins did Cousin Archibald have? Just us and Aunt Vera's two, and that sorry pair wouldn't be anybody's favorites."

"I've never been one to count my chickens 'fore they've hatched, but I have to say I like our prospects."

"Only problem is, *his* money all went to *her* first, though as I've told you before, I fail to see the rhyme or reason to it."

"And as I've told you, he made out that will right after they tied the knot, and he never changed it. Lucky for us they never had children."

"And that her close kin are deceased, ever' last jack one."

"She had only us Plumms to leave it to."

"If she hadn't gone and died of a heart attack, we might've gotten right friendly with her."

"Well, we did our part. We showed up at Cousin Archibald's funeral, at no small inconvenience to us, what with our car trouble and all. Thanks to that standoffish Polly woman who gave us a lift, we even made it for the viewing."

"Well, at that time his bereaved widow was in jail for killing him, if you recall, and wouldn't have given a plugged nickel to know if we came or not."

"If I recall! Wasn't I appalled enough to suit you? Though I can't say I blame her for dispatching him, what with him joining up with the Mormons and all." The two women—obviously twins in their identical skirts and aqua-checked knit tops, and their tightly permed, lavender-tinted, thinning white hair—entered the tiled foyer. One wore brown-rimmed spectacles, the other blue.

"There it is," cried Golda, the sister in blue-rimmed glasses. "'Phileon Q. Magleby, Attorney at Law. Please walk in.' Wonder what the Q stands for. Quincy maybe, like in John Quincy Adams?"

"Maybe 'Quantity,' as in *money*," Rosa giggled.

Just then the door behind the women opened and a rather tall, tanned man in a khaki western-cut suit and hat walked in. He was seventy and maybe then some, but he had the vigorous stride of a young man.

"Well, well. Look who's here," the newcomer exclaimed in mock surprise. "The reading of a will has brought the Plumm sisters to Mormondom."

The startled twins, widowed now, but Plumms before their marriages, hurriedly adjusted the expressions on their powdered and rouged faces. Golda was the first to find her voice. "Why, if it isn't

Anthon Clemmer! We hardly recognized you, what with your fancy suit and all."

"And minus a bottle?" he chuckled.

"We never blamed you," Rosa said defensively.

"For the drinking or the counterfeiting or the leaving town," Golda blurted out. "That spendthrift wife of yours would've driven any man to drink."

"Why're you here?" Rosa asked a little suspiciously.

"I was summoned by the good Mr. Magleby, though why is a mystery. Maybe Merinda Plumm left some instructions for me, a final English assignment," he grinned. "Maybe she wanted me to publish her memoirs. I had some business in Salt Lake City yesterday, anyway. No trouble to come on up to Ogden."

"We expect she left us some cold cash," Golda bragged.

"Hush!" cautioned Rosa. "We shouldn't be talking that way in front of strangers."

"Well, ladies, I'm hardly a stranger, since we're from the same town. Your Cousin Archibald's wife Merinda taught me high school English, you know. I even lost part of a tooth in her defense one night." Anthon Clemmer lifted his upper lip to reveal a newly crowned front tooth. "Just got a shiny white cover for the remains, in fact."

"I remember yours used to be gold, like my name," Golda said.

"My gracious sakes, enough of this gab!" Rosa cried impatiently. "Let's go in. We won't find out anything if we don't go in."

"You're absolutely right. Allow me to hold the door," Anthon offered with exaggerated gallantry.

"Oooo, you were always such a gentleman," Golda cooed.

"And a scholar," Rosa added coyly.

A somber middle-aged woman in a white dress ushered the Plumms and Anthon Clemmer into the presence of one Phileon Q. Magleby. The attorney wore a severe gray suit and tie, with a magenta handkerchief in the pocket and a silver arrow tie clip. His round glasses pinched hard against his nose, and his white hair, parted on the left, was impeccably trimmed and combed. All in all, Anthon decided, he was Merinda Plumm's sort of lawyer. Elegant and slender, he arose ceremoniously from behind a massive mahogany desk when his three visitors entered.

Already seated in the room were "Vera's two," the Plumm sisters' cousins, Albert and Francis, and their mousey wives. The cousins greeted each other like opponents squaring off for a cockfight, and Anthon Clemmer delighted in the shocked expressions the sight of him produced on the otherwise dull faces of the late Vera's pudgy, nearly bald sons.

"All the principals appear to be present," Phileon Magleby declared. "Shall we get on with the matter at hand?"

"Oh yes, sir," said Rosa.

"Please do," chimed in Golda.

"I don't see what this has to do with me, but here I am nonetheless. I guess your letter of notice piqued my curiosity," Anthon said.

The Plumm sisters smiled at each other. They loved to hear Anthon talk, especially in public. He didn't sound like other people they knew in Cheyenne. He sounded more intelligent, more like their in-law, Merinda. Only he sparkled and she didn't.

"Oh, this business has a good deal to do with you, Mr. Clemmer," the lawyer said in an imperious tone that made Albert and Francis shift in their chairs.

"Well, get on with it," Albert said, with an evil glance at Anthon.

"Very well. Shall we go ladies first?"

"Oooh yes, do!" Golda cried, knocking her flowered handbag off what little lap she had. She retrieved it without taking her eyes off the attorney. Rosa, in the meantime, was busily molding her face to reflect her anticipated new station in life. She tried arching one eyebrow and curling her lip. Anyone seeing her might think she had colic.

"I'll read directly from the will, so as not to be misunderstood," Magleby began, taking his seat behind the desk. "These are Merinda Plumm's words, in the will she revised just over a year ago: 'To the sisters Rosa and Golda,'"—Rosa gripped her sister's hand—"'cousins of my late husband, if I should chance to survive him, ten thousand dollars each.'"

Golda turned bright pink, while her sister went white. Both women's handbags thudded to the carpet. The brothers Albert and Francis smirked with satisfaction, now fully expecting to receive the bulk of the estate. Phileon Magleby made a quick visual survey of his audience, then returned to the document at hand.

"'To the brothers, Albert and Francis, also cousins of my late husband, five thousand dollars each.'" The attorney paused while the news sank in.

"That's . . . that's all?" stammered Francis. Rosa couldn't resist a snicker, even though she had fared little better.

"That's all, yes, pertaining to the four of you. It isn't, however, all of the bequest. Allow me to read on. 'To Anthon Clemmer, who as a boy took a beating for my sake, I leave the balance of my estate.'"

"Wha . . . what is this!" Francis and Albert cried in unison, jumping to their feet and storming the mahogany desk.

"You . . . you did this!" Albert fairly screamed at the man sitting calmly before him. "You put her up to it, told her what a great joke it would make!"

"No, I'm afraid she thought of it all by herself," replied Magleby dryly, removing a tiny fleck of lint from his left sleeve.

Although stunned for a moment, the pear-shaped Plumm sisters soon saw the comedy in the situation. Merinda had put one over on the Plumm family in the end, especially Albert and Francis and those dreary wives of theirs. As if wired together, Rosa and Golda revolved from the drama at the desk to Anthon Clemmer, the beneficiary of Merinda Plumm's final revenge against a philandering husband.

It was rumored that early in their married life Archibald had, as the local talk put it, "fooled around" considerably. When that got old, or he did—the town gossips weren't sure which came first—he got religion. It was hard to say which offended Merinda most, the debauchery or the religiosity. But in the end, it appeared, she gave her husband's money to the only knight in shining armor who ever pranced across a page of her life story. And until this minute, Anthon had not realized that she even knew what he had done.

What Rosa and Golda saw when they finally turned to Anthon Clemmer was a man nearly capsized with laughter. The incredulous Cheyenne printer was thoroughly enjoying Merinda's unexpected triumph and the temper tantrum erupting at the desk. It hadn't really dawned on Anthon that he had just inherited what was, given the distress of Aunt Vera's boys, probably a sizable sum of money.

Anthon's laughter infected the widowed twins, who had married jolly brothers, and they chortled merrily along with him. When they thought about it, the twenty thousand they would get between them would take them to Hawaii and buy a car besides, if they settled for something conservative. Maybe one of those friendly little Neons. Money didn't really mean any more to them than it did to Anthon. Large sums of it were beyond their comprehension anyway.

"She can't do this! You'll be hearing from us!" Albert threatened as he grabbed his briefcase and his wife's arm and slammed out the door. Francis and his stunned spouse were only a few steps behind.

"They can contest the will from now till kingdom come," Magleby assured the others. "It will stand up in any court. Merinda Plumm even took the trouble to have herself certified sane at the time. If they're smart, they'll save their money."

Anthon didn't bother to ask how much the estate amounted to. He simply took the packet of documents that Magleby handed him and invited the Plumm sisters to join him in a celebratory bowl of butter pecan ice cream, which invitation they enthusiastically accepted. And as the sisters spooned the cold confection between their disappearing but still painted lips, Anthon told them about the night he had tackled young Merinda's husband as the fellow rushed from a brothel. Those were the days when Cheyenne was still a small town, he reminded the sisters. The older and stronger Archibald had given his youthful assailant a sound beating and broken the boy's front tooth in the process.

"It's a real live fairy tale, that's what it is," Golda sighed.

The reading of the will was Friday morning. Two weeks later, Anthon Clemmer was on the road once again, rattling south in a weathered green Ford Econoline van. Polly McGrath knew who was in it the minute the metal monstrosity lumbered into her unpaved driveway, giving the chickens and dog reason to move faster than they cared to in the afternoon heat. Summer was never in a hurry to leave the southwest desert, and that included Smithville, Utah.

Polly had seen the unfortunate vehicle once before, even ridden inside it from Smithville to Las Vegas, against her better judgment, a few weeks back. She had let the wandering poet-hijacker talk her into it. To make matters worse, his overgrown bait box on wheels had no air conditioning. Polly had spent most of the trip—Anthon was trans-porting some printing equipment—wondering where the last vestige of her waning senses had gone to. After all, hadn't he kidnaped her at what she assumed was gunpoint on their first encounter at a freeway rest area earlier in the summer? And in broad daylight? Now here he was again.

Anthon himself thought he must have lost his mind. What was it about this unyielding, cranky, straight-talking woman that drew him like a moth to the flame? Heaven only knew. One thing was certain: she would be totally unimpressed by his new circumstances. In fact, he probably wouldn't even tell her that Merinda Plumm's estate was worth around two million dollars, much of it in liquid assets, and that she had left nearly all of it to him. More than likely, Polly would only hmmph disdainfully and ask him if he had driven all the way from Cheyenne to the bottom corner of Utah just to toot that horn. *Well,* he thought, *she isn't the only one unimpressed. After all, it was two or three days before I got around to reading the bottom line in Magleby's big manila envelope.*

No, it wasn't bragging rights that brought him to the old two-story, yellow frame house on Spring Road. It was the woman. He liked her. He suspected he even loved her, though for the life of him he couldn't figure out why. She hadn't spoken more than ten civil words to him since the day they met. But she hadn't turned him over to the law, either. And she had seen to it that he made it on the road to Cheyenne. "I was an hungered, and ye gave me meat, . . . I was a stranger, and ye took me in, naked and ye clothed me," he recited to himself. She was a hard woman, but there was something soft about her, too.

Polly McGrath was just doing up her lunch dishes when she saw the old van rattle to a stop outside her window. *What now?* she thought. *Am I going to have to enter a witness protection program to escape this ne'er-do-well from Wyoming? If only Jed were alive, I could turn the itinerant felon over to him. The two of them could talk philosophy in the barn till the cows came home.* But Jedediah McGrath wasn't alive. That was just the trouble. His sudden stroke and subsequent death in early summer had left her hollow and worn. And vulnerable, she reminded herself. Not that the rest of the summer had been uneventful, either. Jedediah McGrath was scarcely cold in the ground when she met up with this same Anthon Clemmer on Interstate 15.

Just days later, her youngest child, Delia, and her son Ronald J. and grandson Miles went off and tried to get themselves killed in a flash flood in some Godforsaken desert gulch. Then there was Torry—whose real name was Jennifer, Polly grudgingly admitted—the temporary "boarder" Delia brought home from the hospital because she had nowhere else to go. No sooner had Polly grown accustomed to having the foul-mouthed eighteen-year-old around than the miscreant who had deserted the girl came back, scooped her into a beat-up yellow truck, and half-killed her in a highway accident. All in all, it had been quite a summer. An exhausting summer.

And now Delia was back in Jefferson, Wisconsin, on crutches, starting a new school year at the university. If English teachers didn't have enough sense to stay out of slot canyons in flash flood season, how could they expect rational behavior from their students? And then there was that Hector Gabrielson Delia had taken up with some years ago. Polly didn't trust a man who wore a beard in this day and age. The Lord's anointed had started shaving their chins decades ago, and that was good enough for Polly. However, it was just like her stubborn daughter to prove that she had left the Church by taking up with some faithless academician in a beard. That it was a short, well-trimmed beard was beside the point.

By contrast, that easygoing BLM fellow, Gordon Foster, was more to Polly's liking, even if he did draw a federal paycheck. He wasn't a Mormon either, not yet anyway, so she couldn't be accused of prejudice on religious grounds. Furthermore, she had to lay some blame on him for Delia's shattered right leg and Miles's broken collarbone. Hadn't Gordon organized the fated hiking expedition? But Gordon hadn't shown his face around the McGrath acreage since the bearded professor of ancient languages turned up and whisked Delia back to Jefferson, and Polly thought she knew why. She had hoped Gordon might at least come by now and then to check on Jed's two horses.

With exaggerated annoyance, Polly wiped her hands on the dish-towel, tucked a strand of wavy gray hair behind her ear, and met Anthon Clemmer at the back stairs outside. She wasn't going to expose Jed's things to this hooligan one more time if she could help it.

Her husband's telltale levi jacket and straw cowboy hat still hung on nails above the washer on the back porch. Likewise, his cocoa mug and pocketknife still sat on the big oak table in the kitchen.

"What's your excuse this time?" Polly demanded of her visitor as she descended the stairs.

"Does a man need an excuse for calling on his lady fair?" Anthon responded.

"There's no lady fair at this address, and certainly not one you could call yours. I see you've fixed that tooth. You don't whistle your words anymore."

"I see you've mellowed since my last visit," he chuckled, scratching the ears of the collie who came loping over to him. "At least the dog is glad to see me," he added.

"Which just goes to show how little sense this particular dog has."

"I bring world-shattering news. I've decided to retire, and I thought you should be the first to know."

"Retire! Since when have you been anything *but* retired? What happened? Things take a downturn in the counterfeiting and kidnaping business?"

Anthon laughed heartily at her reference to his earlier indiscretions, the first of which landed him in the state penitentiary for an extended visit. It was one of several misfortunes that led to his becoming a knight of the road when he should have been filing for social security benefits and polishing his golf game. His "career" as a bold desperado had lasted about ten minutes. It fizzled miserably when he more than met his match in the person of Polly McGrath, newly widowed and too full of grief to be frightened for long by the likes of him.

"Why should I care what you do, in any case?" Polly added as an afterthought.

"Don't you know that in some cultures when you save someone's life, you become responsible for that person from then on? I consider that you saved my life, figuratively at least, and now I'm yours forever. I'll throw in the van for good measure."

"Hmmph. Where'd you get that nonsense? The only thing I want of you is your permanent absence."

"Now, is that any way to talk to an old traveling companion? Especially an old companion who might become a neighbor."

Polly's head jerked toward Anthon. "What do you mean, *neighbor*? I thought we had too few jackrabbits and too little sagebrush to suit you."

"There's enough cactus to make up the difference," he grinned. His gaze left Polly's face and traveled out toward the river, where gigantic cottonwoods cut lacy patterns out of the bluest sky he had ever seen. To the right of trees and river, Coral Mountain rose in brilliant contrast to the strong gray granite of the mountains across the valley to the left. At the foot of those mountains, bright pink sandstone humped and swirled in petrified splendor, and a red-tailed hawk circled lazily overhead. "I guess the time I spent in Arizona softened me. The prospect of Cheyenne winters puts a shiver in my thinning blood," Anthon said, turning back to Polly.

"Well, hair-raising trips with bad-smelling criminals put a shiver in mine."

Anthon winced, laughing. "Tell you what. You come looking for a piece of property with me. That way you can influence me to buy something a good way from you. Otherwise, I might end up in your backyard."

Polly was alarmed to think Anthon might actually do it, though where he would get the money was a mystery. He and his cousin must have made their little printing business pay big of late. The last thing she wanted, she told herself, was this wandering troubadour entertaining her with his rhymed nonsense for the rest of her natural life. Even Cheyenne apparently wasn't far enough away to keep him out of her hair. What if he actually moved to Smithville? The thought was enough to give her the hives.

If only Jed hadn't died, she wouldn't be at the mercy of this buffoon who could talk a normal person to death in a matter of hours. The trouble with Anthon Clemmer was that normal people couldn't tell when he was serious and when he wasn't. In all likelihood, he was putting her on about moving to southern Utah. It wouldn't be the first time he had said something merely to get a rise out of her.

At that moment, Polly heard another vehicle in the drive and fervently hoped it was a stranger, someone asking directions to the nearest petroglyphs or some such. How could she possibly explain this man in a pearl-buttoned cowboy shirt and boots to a friend or relative? He couldn't be mistaken for the irrigation man; he was dressed for dry ground. Polly had never mentioned her two previous encounters with Anthon to anyone, and now here he was and here they were, whoever it was. All she needed was for Jed Junior, her oldest son, or Hannah, her oldest daughter, or Arva Plimpton, her nosiest neighbor, to get wind of this visit and she'd never hear the end of it.

Polly's first impulse was to hide him in the barn. She also realized, in a flash of circumspection, that it was time for her to destroy the idiotic little verse he had penned for her when they went their separate ways in Colton, Utah, last June—after he had abducted her and she had fed and clothed him and put him up in a motel room for the night. At the opposite end from her room. What she had wanted then, and wanted now, she insisted silently, was space between herself and Anthon Clemmer. The more the better. The crumpled verse was still tucked above the visor of her aged Chrysler Imperial—though why she had, on second impulse, rescued it from her auto trash bag was beyond her.

Polly recoiled from the prospect of explaining herself, especially to one of her older children, who now thought it their bounden duty to run her life for her. Jed Junior and Hannah were the worst, and Paul came a close third. Victor, the youngest of the older four, was okay; and Ronald J., with whom she had begun a second brood, was a peach. And Delia? Well, Delia wasn't so bad in the bossiness department, but she had a Ph.D., and cynicism was her specialty. She was madly in love with irony and employed it every chance she got. Smithville, Polly was sorry to say, provided Delia limitless opportunities to ply her trade.

Ronald J. was the only one of Polly's children to have made his home in Smithville. If the truth be known, except for her sister Dorothy, Ronald and his family were the only surviving flesh and blood relatives that Polly found wholly to her liking. She loved the others, and tried to love their spouses, but most of them were rather stuffy and presumptuous. And their children seemed self-absorbed and distant.

Delia wasn't stuffy, Polly admitted, but she was hard to talk to. And she had her own opinions, most of them unreasonable, about everything. Delia would probably get a kick out of the Anthon business, but a person never knew where she stood with Delia. Mother and daughter were terribly different, though at times Polly wondered if they weren't also terribly alike. Different or alike, for years they had been at odds most of the time. Especially about the Church. Delia was thirty-two, and she was finally showing signs of coming around. In Polly's view, it was well past high time.

Two vehicles on the gravel generated more excitement than the mixed-breed collie had enjoyed in weeks, and he left Anthon to greet the new arrivals. His yip of pleasure confirmed Polly's fears: the caller was someone he knew. Polly gripped the railing on the back steps and mentally rehearsed her lines. Meet Mr. Clemmer, a friend of Jed's who called by on his way through from Wyoming. Meet Mr. Clemmer, a distant cousin who is looking to retire in this area. Meet Mr. Clemmer, who stopped to inquire if our little farm might be for sale. All of them sounded phony.

Lying had never been one of Polly McGrath's strong suits, for the reason that she rarely practiced it. She had trouble getting her tongue around an out-and-out lie. When pressed, she could on occasion fumble through an edited rendering of the truth. Nine-year-old Effie, Polly's granddaughter, was first to round the corner of the house, with the collie rejoicing beside her. A few steps behind the dog was Ilene, Ronald's wife, with a fresh loaf of bread in her hands.

"Here, Grandma, new bread!" Effie cried, taking the wrapped loaf from her mother and holding it high away from the dog. Effie stopped short when she saw Anthon.

Ilene rescued the bread and handed it to Polly. "We baked today and brought you a loaf. I see you have company, so we won't stay."

"Don't leave on my account," Anthon smiled. "I came unannounced, but I refuse to leave until I've tasted that bread. I can smell it from here."

Polly was trapped. "All of you come in," she said stiffly. "I'll find some jam and milk. No school today, Effie?"

"I got out early for parent-teacher confrontations."

"She means 'conferences,'" Ilene laughed, then turned to Anthon. "I'm Ilene, wife to Mrs. McGrath's son, Ron. Any friend of hers is a friend of mine." Ilene had a way of defusing even the most combustible situation.

"Glad to meet you. My name's Anthon Clemmer."

As they crossed the back porch to the kitchen, Anthon noted that Jed's belongings were still in evidence and concluded that Polly was more lonely than she would ever let on. He didn't relish wrestling with a ghost, and wondered if Polly McGrath would ever look twice at any man alive.

"I saw the Wyoming plates on your van," Ilene said as she poured milk for Anthon. "What brings you to our part of the world?"

Polly shot Anthon a warning glance, and he elected to humor her, for now. "I'm interested in acquiring some property where it rarely snows, and where when it does, the stuff arrives vertically instead of horizontally," he said, hoping Polly appreciated his charming little charade. "Mrs. McGrath and I have mutual friends, Rosa and Golda Plumm Epstein. I'm hoping she might advise me."

"Didn't you say that Arva Plimpton was intending to put her place up for sale, Mother McGrath?" Ilene asked.

"Did I? I don't remember," Polly said blandly, concealing her agitation. "I don't think that's the sort of place Mr. Clemmer is looking for. More jam, Effie?"

"No thank you, Grandma. Can I have a cookie?"

"Aren't you going to reward me for my good behavior?" Anthon teased after Ilene and Effie left.

"I'll reward you by not calling the sheriff," Polly snapped.

"Nice daughter-in-law you have. Pretty, too."

"She'll do."

"Tell me about the property she mentioned. Is it nearby?"

"Come outside and I'll show you."

Anthon surmised that Polly mainly wanted to get him out of the house, but he followed her obediently.

"See that fence line beyond the barn? Arva's property starts there. It's bigger than this, and I expect it's getting to be a worry. She's been a widow for several years. I didn't tell you about it because you make a habit of preying on defenseless widows."

Anthon laughed. "If I had any sense, I'd stick to the defenseless ones. So far I'm running one hundred percent the other type," he said.

Polly scowled to let him know she did not appreciate his humor.

"Well, I think I'll pay the Widow Plimpton a call. Want to come along to protect your neighbor from the big bad wolf?"

"I guess Arva can take care of herself. As I think about it, you're the one who might need the protection." Polly smiled ever so slightly, made an about-face, and marched up the back steps. "Supper will be ready at six," she said without turning around. "See that you're not late."

Anthon chuckled as he climbed in the van and drove onto Spring Road. Polly McGrath was indeed a woman to be reckoned with. He thought he'd like to meet her youngest child, this daughter who taught English and hiked dangerous canyons. From what Polly had said about her, he supposed she had a stubborn streak as formidable as her mother's. A man who married either of them would have his hands full, Anthon added to himself. But the prospect sounded better to him than the dull pleasures of television and couch potato aerobics.

The battered mailbox by the next gravel lane had seen better days; the name on it was illegible, and the red flag was bent and hanging. Anthon turned in, then followed a barbed wire fence for fifty yards and halted before a square, saggy brick house. Brittle pull-down shades hung at an angle across two windows, and an old four-legged kitchen range leaned toward the door on the crumbling concrete side porch. The official "front" steps to the whitish building were on the other side, but it was obvious to Anthon that the only entrance anyone ever used was this one.

He knocked on the peeling white enamel door, then half-sat on the corner of the range to wait. Before long, he saw the lace curtains inside the door window part, and a pair of eyes peer left and right through the gap. Then the door opened, and the short, square, dyed and permed Arva Plimpton stepped out. Anthon stood, and Arva jumped two inches off the ground.

"Didn't mean to startle you, ma'am," Anthon said, taking off his cowboy hat.

"Oooo," Arva sighed, gripping the door casing with one hand and grasping her lower throat with the other. "Where'd *you* come from? You the roto-rooter man?"

"No, ma'am, though I have done a little roto-rooting in my day."

"Well, if you're not a criminal on the loose, c'mon in. If you are, then kill me out here and get it over with. If I'm gonna die, I prefer to do it in the open air where I can at least breathe. I just read in the paper that a man in Salt Lake City has died of an overdose of black licorice candy. He gobbles two and a half pounds of the stuff in one sitting, and his heart quits, just like that." Arva snapped thumb and finger for emphasis. "Blood pressure goes up, arms swell, windpipe clogs, and he's gone." Arva Plimpton put both hands to her throat and gagged.

Anthon laughed and sat down on the top step. "I'm too old to be much of a criminal, and I don't have an ounce of licorice on me. You're safe."

"Well, then, state your business," said Arva, plopping herself down beside him, but not too close.

"I'm a friend of Mrs. McGrath, next door," Anthon began, but saw his mistake immediately. On the instant, Arva Plimpton was all ears.

"I didn't know Polly McGrath was entertaining gentlemen friends these days, what with Jedediah in the ground only three months," she said in a sugary voice, giving Anthon the once-over and wondering what a hunk of man like this saw in a starchy woman like her neighbor. Suddenly Arva remembered that her hair was maroon this month, and dearly wished that Beverly had achieved true auburn when she mixed the colors last time. Even too orange would have been better than maroon. Arva was torn between wanting her caller to stay, so she could pump him for details, and wanting him to go so she could get on the phone and spread the news.

Anthon tactfully ignored Arva's comment. "I understand that your place may be for sale," he said in his most businesslike voice.

Arva wasn't fooled. She eyed his van. "You don't look like a land speculator to me," she said slyly.

Anthon saw her gaze travel to the rusted green Econoline. "Well, as it turns out, I am," he lied. "I've just come into a little money, quite unexpectedly, and I'm looking to invest it in something solid, like land. Something compatible with the new Lexus I've just ordered." When her eyes lit up, Anthon saw his second mistake. He never should have mentioned the money. It would get back to Polly by nightfall that Mrs. McGrath was entertaining a wealthy gentlemen caller from Wyoming—and she, by all standards of decency, still in widow's weeds.

Anthon decided that the situation called for extreme measures. He casually sidled closer to Arva. "Truth is," he said engagingly, "I hardly know Mrs. McGrath myself. But some friends of mine in Cheyenne met her once. She was a place to start, is all. Her daughter-in-law was there when I stopped, and she mentioned that the comely widow next door might be looking to sell. I rushed right over."

Well, that changed everything. Arva regretted a little that she wouldn't have a good story to tell about Polly, but what she might have to tell would more than compensate. She covertly checked the third finger on her visitor's left hand and found it bare. What would Polly think when she, Arva Plimpton, snatched this lovely fellow from under her nose? Come to think of it, Polly probably wouldn't even notice, Arva concluded sourly.

It was hard to get the best of Polly McGrath because she never would compete with anybody. Arva didn't call Polly uppity, though some did. Arva just wished Polly would let her hair down a titch, maybe even tell a little white lie once in a while, or kick the dog, or use the wrong verb. Polly hadn't even cried hard at Jed's funeral, though Arva could tell she needed to. For the release. Polly never released, so far as Arva knew.

"Grandma has a boyfriend!" Effie shouted as her father came in the door that evening.

"What's this?" Ron McGrath turned to his wife, who was drilling Effie on her spelling words.

"Does not!" eleven-year-old Wilson yelled from in front of the computer where he was surfing the Internet. He had just turned eleven and was feeling the distinct advantage another birthday gave him over his younger sister.

"How do you know? You weren't there! Mama and I saw him. He was big and had cowboy boots," Effie insisted.

"The truth is, Grandma had a *visitor* who happens to be a male of her generation," Ilene corrected with an indulgent smile. "Apparently, they have mutual friends in Wyoming and he looked your mother up. He's thinking to buy property here."

"Frankly, I'd be glad if she did have a boyfriend. She's alone too much. I think she broods. She needs something to take her mind off Dad, get her away from the place."

"Why don't you call and invite her over for supper? I made lasagne, and there's plenty."

"Will do." Ron plucked a cherry tomato off the salad in the center of the table and went to the phone in the den. A few minutes later he returned with a puzzled look on his face. "She says no thanks, that she has 'other plans' for dinner. She didn't explain, and I didn't dare ask."

"So maybe Grandma *does* have a boyfriend," said Ilene mischievously.

"Hnnnh! Fat chance!" Wilson muttered.

"What's this about Grandma?" asked thirteen-year-old Sabrine, who was just coming in from soccer practice.

"Nothing, nothing at all," said her father. "Get washed up for supper. Where's Miles?"

CHAPTER TWO

Delia McGrath, assistant professor of English at Jefferson University, had just finished her first day of the fall term, and she was exhausted. Before taking the freight elevator in pre-historic Brandon Hall to the third floor cubby that just barely passed muster as an office, she steered her aluminum crutches into the more commodious first floor office of her friend and colleague, Angie Turner, full professor. It had been quite a summer.

"I could write a book chronicling events of the past several months," she told Angie, flopping into the nearest chair, "except no one would believe it. Too far-fetched."

"I'd believe it. I lived some of it," Angie reminded her. "I'm still living it." Angie was referring to the discovery of a malignant tumor in her left breast and her subsequent radical surgery. Chemotherapy had also taken a heavy toll, and she wasn't yet finished with the periodic chemical invasions. At best, the long-term prognosis was iffy; the cancer had been well-advanced before it was detected.

One obvious consequence of all this medical activity was the substantial reduction in girth of the notoriously plump Angie. "Look at me," she complained good-naturedly, pulling at the jacket that hung loosely on her diminished but still ample frame. "I'm wasting away to nothing. I put on my old slacks, and I look as though I'm being eaten by a couch. If I'm not careful, *Shape* will be photographing me as next month's cover girl."

"And the *National Enquirer* will be after me. They specialize in freaks and catastrophes," Delia said.

"Which is your category, freak or catastrophe?"

"Take your pick," Delia replied, weakly waving her right leg, which sported a hard-used fiberglass cast.

While Angie went for coffee, Delia mentally rehearsed the summer's litany of traumas. Her list sounded like Armageddon. Things had started out on a high note that spring, when Delia drove to her parents' home in Smithville, Utah, for spring break. While backpacking through Chinta Canyon on the Utah-Arizona border, Delia had uncovered an old leather pouch containing four metal sheets which appeared to be inscribed with ancient writings.

The events that followed might have led a superstitious person to suspect that the ill-fated packet carried a curse. Not only were the pouch and its contents later stolen, but before the summer was over, Delia's father had died of a stroke, her tennis partner had been shot to death by her estranged husband, Angie had been diagnosed with breast cancer, and Delia had nearly lost her own life. She was lucky to have come through a flash flood with no more than a broken leg and some painful scrapes and bumps.

And that wasn't all. Now her longtime friend and sometime love interest, Hector Gabrielson, was probably going to bail out and remarry his former wife. Then there was Delia's frightening run-in with the implacable Horace Rostrand, one-time chair of the department committee on promotions and tenure at Jefferson. Even with His Arrogance (Angie's term) out of the picture, a victim of heart failure, in a figurative as well as a physical sense, the matter of Delia's candidacy for a permanent faculty position was far from settled.

On the plus side, she conceded, were Angie and Howard Turner's resilience and the entrance into her own life of the nutty, irresistible, invincible Gordon Foster. God's gift to lizards and horny toads, as he put it. The trouble was, he was in Smithville, Utah, and surrounding territories, halfway across the country. And even if he weren't, despite their desert connection and their genuine feelings for each other, they would still be worlds apart. She happened to be a teacher of English, while he was a salty river runner who now worked the southwest desert of Utah and northern Arizona out of a dusty BLM pickup truck. Although they had finally confessed their love, she couldn't help wondering if their particular East-West "twain" could ever really meet.

Other things had changed, too. Delia had actually attended church a few times—voluntarily. She couldn't say just now whether or not that was a wholly satisfactory development, but one thing she knew: the summer's events had been spiritually unsettling for Polly McGrath's youngest child, and the Church seemed to offer an anchor to a soul that had been drifting for more than a dozen years. Now that she had gone a few times, Delia was more comfortable attending church services in Jefferson than in Smithville; but even so, she could feel her iron-willed mother silently monitoring the situation across the miles.

It wasn't just her mother Delia could sense, either. She supposed the whole family—except for RonJay and Ilene—were having their say about their younger sister's possible return from "apostasy," and she hated it. Whatever she did in matters of religious observance, Delia preferred to do on her own, without a gallery of blood relatives superintending. Her father had been different from the rest of them. He never judged her, and he seemed willing to wait for her to come around, however long it took. When he died, she lost a defender and a buffer as well as a beloved father.

Angie interrupted Delia's ruminations. "Here's a Coke for you. I've noticed that you take your caffeine cold rather than hot these days."

"Yes, it's an old Mormon custom. I'm getting acclimated gradually. One day I might go cold turkey and strictly de-caff my way through life, except in products made of chocolate, of course. Even reformed saints have limits to their piety, after all."

"Is that what you are, a reformed Mormon? Are you going to become intolerably self-righteous?"

"Maybe, maybe not. I haven't decided yet. However, you might find me quite lovable as a practicing Christian."

"Well, you can go ahead and practice all you want on Howard and me. I don't know whether to credit the broken leg, the cancer, or the Mormons, but you haven't nagged me about my eating habits or tried to force carrot juice down my throat in months. I almost hate to finish chemotherapy for fear you might take up the cause again."

"I'm waiting for you to get your strength back, then look out. No more cream puffs without critical commentary."

Angie began sorting through the stack of memos and announce-ments that had accumulated on her desk. "To change the subject from the sublime to the ridiculous, what does Lyle have to say about your tenure prospects? Will the department give you more time?" Lyle Parry was chair of the English Department.

"I think so. Funny thing, now I'm not sure I want a permanent position here anymore."

Angie looked up. This was news. "Can't say I blame you after what Horace put you through. But he is gone, rest his soul, and he was your only real hurdle. The others on the committee—except me, of course—will be putty in your hands."

"And you?"

"Oh, I can be brought around for a dozen or so cream puffs." Angie sighed and stood up, sliding some books and papers into a worn canvas bag. "C'mon, I'll drive you home. We can pick up Howard and the cream puffs on the way."

Delia's evenings and weekends were longer and lonelier now. No jogging, no tennis, no research trips to the library, no impromptu visits to the Turner home, no Gabe dropping by to go for frozen yogurt or a walk along the lake. The professor of ancient languages had been a given in Delia's life ever since she moved to Jefferson. How could she just blot him out? Maybe she should have married Hector Gabrielson when she had the chance. Well, it was too late now. Denise wanted him back, and it appeared he was willing.

Delia sat on her little condo patio that evening, staring at nothing, sipping orange juice and listening to the golden lab next door chew noisily on some toothsome dog delicacy. Off in the distance, a raven sounded its guttural cry as the air slowly turned a dusty rose and the sky overhead thickened.

Words from an old Joni Mitchell song tracked through Delia's mind. "Don't it always seem to go that you don't know what you've got till it's gone. . . ." She realized that the words applied equally to herself and to Gabe's former wife. In more rational moments, Delia knew that if Gabe and Denise were to call the whole thing off, she wouldn't change her mind and say yes. But tonight, she was feeling sorry for herself—wallowing in self-pity, her mother would have said. It wasn't specifically Gabe she was missing. He was part of it, but there was something else. She couldn't give it a name.

Delia wished she could lace on her running shoes and head for the park. This was a ten-lap night, definitely a ten-lap night, minimum. With sudden determination, she got up and hopped inside. Ignoring the stack of books she intended to consult before meeting classes tomorrow, she jammed a house key into the pocket of her levi cut-offs, pulled on a long-sleeved T-shirt, tucked her crutches under her arms, and made for the front door.

She was pretty good on the walking sticks now, and her leg hurt only when it hung vertically too long. Physical exertion, Delia decided, was the best cure for spiritual malaise. But her inescapable lurching gait these days was a far cry from the swift, sure strides she used to take along this route in the days when she was a well-tuned machine, taut and strong.

Feeling defeated by the time she reached the park, Delia clenched her teeth and pushed all the harder, planting the crutches far ahead of her and lunging forward on her left foot, touching lightly on her right. Instead of doing laps, she went beyond the park, swinging the metal crutches almost spitefully. Street signs floated past under bluish lamps, none of them registering in her conscious mind. At last Delia realized that she was in unfamiliar territory, a good distance from home. She could hear the belt route humming in the distance, but she couldn't see it from the street near the river where she found herself.

A stab of panic raked through Delia's abdomen. The timorous stars gave small comfort, and she had passed the last pale corona of the last street light. The pavement appeared to end ahead, and she could just make out a dirt road winding on toward the willows that lined the river. *I must be near where the beltway crosses the river,* she thought, trying to create a mental map that would lead her back to Monroe Boulevard and the Morningside condominiums.

The air had cooled at least ten degrees, and her T-shirt was damp with perspiration. Delia's arms and left leg ached from the effort, and her right leg was beginning to throb. She laughed ruefully to remember a friend who as a child used to walk in one direction until she was too tired to go on, and then had to make the return trip. *I need to rest before I start back,* Delia thought. *What possessed me to come clear out here?*

Several yards off the street, she made out the dark form of a large fallen tree and hobbled toward it, grateful to get off her feet and elevate them. Delia had never been what her childhood playmates called a "scaredy-cat." She knew that sometimes Polly McGrath had wished she were. Polly's youngest child left a good many samples of her delicate flesh on barbed wire fences, barn rafters, boulders, and tree trunks around the McGrath place before she reached puberty and turned her attention from horses and bicycles to boys and books.

But tonight that child felt vulnerable and exposed. She wished she could close her eyes, count to ten, and open them to find herself safely at home. Before the hiking accident, Delia had been reasonably confident that she could outrun a pursuer should one fall in behind her some dusky night. But now, she knew she couldn't outrun anyone, not even Begonia Slopek, her somewhat elderly neighbor with a bad leg. *If only Begonia and Elmer Roy would come rumbling up in Begonia's aged Pontiac convertible,* Delia thought, *I'd get in and never walk alone at night again.*

As if in response to Delia's wish, a pair of headlights appeared, only they didn't belong to Begonia's Pontiac. Delia just managed to crouch behind the tree before the long, dual beam licked across it. Heart pounding, she watched the departing vehicle—a pickup with amber lights defining the cab roof. As the truck rumbled by, she noticed that the left taillight was out. Probably a couple of kids heading for the river, she told herself—"to watch the whale races," an earlier generation would have said. She didn't know what the younger set called a necking party these days, but assumed the current terminology was less innocent.

After a short rest, Delia knew that, tired or not, she had to get home—or at least to a telephone—on her own power. She decided to head for the beltway and look for a convenience store. There was a crumpled dollar bill in her pocket. A few houses, ramshackle but occupied, began to appear, and Delia relaxed a little. As she passed one house with a cracked front window showing a bare-globed lamp, the rickety door banged open. Delia's spine turned to ice.

"Git outta here, you!" a male voice croaked. "You wanna git yourse'f kilt?"

Heart thundering, Delia picked up her pace. Out of the corner of her eye, she saw a shaggy gray head framed in the lighted doorway. An unseen cur barked menacingly from somewhere behind the speaker. At last, Delia reached the dying remnant of what had been a tall privet hedge and stepped behind it to catch her breath. Just then, headlights appeared from the direction of the river. It was the same truck, on its return trip. Curious despite her fear, Delia risked a better look.

The pickup was full-sized—maybe a Ford, four or five years old—with a king-cab. Out-of-state plates, she thought. A driver and at least one passenger. Delia wanted only one thing: to get out of there and find safety. Lights, people, cars, well-tended houses. Adrenalin pumping, she raced toward the beltway sounds. Everything was a blur. When she finally rounded a corner and saw the beltway lights, she nearly wept with exhaustion and relief. Ten more minutes and she was inside a Circle K, getting change for the pay telephone outside, next to the door.

Whom should she call? The Turners? Gabe? One of her Relief Society visiting teachers, Mary Beth Archer or Susan Fines? When Delia thought about it, she really didn't have that many people she could call, and that was a disturbing thought in itself. She settled on Gabe, Denise or no Denise. No sense sounding a general alarm, and Gabe already knew she was a lunatic. He would lecture her briefly, but then he would drop it, whereas Angie and Howard would scold ceaselessly.

Delia was grateful when Gabe answered the phone. She asked him to come for her; he asked where. That was it. With Gabe one was free to explain or withhold explanation, and one never had to lie. He was an exceptional human being, as she had known all along. Why, then, hadn't she been able to fall in love with him as she had with Gordon? Why, she asked herself, was *loving* such a different feeling from being *in love?* She had no answer and doubted that anyone did.

Wishing to avoid the scrutiny of the Circle K's employees and customers, Delia elected to wait for Gabe outside. As she leaned next to the phone, shivering with cold, two men who looked to be in their late thirties swaggered out the door bearing two greasy servings of thickly breaded, deep-fried chicken and a six-pack of Blatz beer. They wore misshapen baseball caps, jeans with wide belts, and soiled undershirts; and both sported two or three days' beard growth on their surly faces. As they passed the dented ice bin next to the telephone, the shorter one turned back to Delia.

"Say, little lady. You look cold. W'yntcha come along with us? We'll keep you warm."

Delia merely glared at them.

"Shut up, you fool," the taller one growled at his partner. "Let's get outta here."

The two men strode around the corner of building, and moments later, a bronze Ford king-cab pickup with one dark taillight roared past the pumps. The truck bore Illinois plates, and Delia knew it was the vehicle she had seen. She wondered, briefly, what had taken that ungainly pair to the river. She concluded that they must have been looking for a shortcut to the highway.

Several minutes later, Gabe pulled up in his Nissan Pathfinder. He jumped out and helped Delia into the passenger seat, still a trick with a full leg cast. Inside the vehicle, he reached over and took her hand. "Are you hurt?" he asked.

"No, just tired and sore. My arms are ready to drop off. Thanks for coming."

"Any time. You know that. You training for the Special Olympics, or just out tempting fate?"

In her relief, Delia was able to summon a laugh. "Sleepwalking, I think. I'm not even sure how I got here."

The next morning, Delia was still a bit shaky when she met her first class, Introduction to the Short Story. As a rule, Delia preferred to stand while she taught, so she could move about and see faces better. The shattered bone in her right leg temporarily changed all that, however, and she now had to sit most of the time. When she entered the classroom, the students eyed her crutches, cast, and backpack. She offered no explanation, having grown so accustomed to the gear herself that she would have felt undressed without it. Delia greeted the faces of the strangers before her and marveled privately at the fact that within a few weeks she would know most of them better than she knew her own family. Just now it didn't seem possible, but it would happen. It always did.

Delia handed out the class syllabus and introduced the course, then turned to the day's subject: the standard elements of fiction, with particular reference to the short story. The students dutifully pulled out their brand-new notebooks and began taking copious notes as Delia spoke of plot, character, theme, point of view, setting, tone, and the like. It was, after all, the first meeting of the term for Tuesday-Thursday classes, and the young people in front of her were at least making like students. Their good intentions would wear thin, or even dissolve entirely, with the lure of football, sailing, and beer parties, Delia knew; but for now, these nineteen-year-olds were virtuously doing what their high school counselors termed "applying themselves."

Toward the middle of the hour, a young man with a shaved head and three rings in his right ear raised his hand. Delia nodded at him. "Maybe . . . there's like, maybe there's a story right here, teacher, and you're not telling it," he challenged her.

Every head popped up from every notebook. The general run of students both admire and fear anyone audacious enough to take on the instructor, the authority figure, the dispenser of grades.

"How's that?" Delia responded, surprised. "What story?"

"Of your leg, man. You keeping us in suspense on purpose? I bet that story has some cool plot. Like, 'stead of tellin' us about some story some dude made up, whyn't you tell us a real one?"

Delia laughed, and the class relaxed. It was okay; she wasn't offended. "I wouldn't know where to begin," she said.

"Jus' start at the beginning, where that thing you called the 'risin' action' starts."

Delia turned to the others. "You really want to hear it?"

Heads nodded vigorously and notebooks slammed happily shut. Delia had more than a vague suspicion that she had been conned, but she smiled and stood up. Maybe it would be a good ice-breaker. Hopping around the desk, Delia leaned back, half-sitting on it. "All you see is a cast," she said, raising the leg slightly and knocking on it with her fingers. "There is indeed a whole story behind it."

She hopped back to the old wooden chair, dragged it out from the desk, moved it close to the front row of student desks, and leaned forward on it, her hands resting on its high back. Delia didn't tell why she, Gordon, her brother Ron, and his son Miles happened to be in Slingshot Gulch on the day a dangerous flash flood roared through the deep, narrow slot canyon. But she took the students in their imaginations through the experience—the spectacular wilderness setting, the thunder in the distance, the onset of rain, the sudden wall of roiling water, the rope and juniper that saved three of them, the sandbar and snag that saved young Miles, the night spent on a narrow ledge of rock, the dawn and rescue by helicopter.

The students' eyes were riveted on Delia. It was plain that they were listening intently. "What . . . what did you do on that ledge while you waited for morning?" a young woman in heavy makeup asked at last, her jaws working a rather large wad of gum.

Delia paused. "Mostly, I prayed," she said softly.

An almost tangible hush blanketed the room. "You mean, like, to God?" one student whispered at last.

"Who else?" Delia responded.

In an obvious effort to rescue an awkward situation, a husky fellow in a Green Bay Packers ball cap broke the spell: "To get back to what you said before, does your story have a theme?"

"You tell me."

Emboldened, a young woman in round, gold-rimmed glasses asked if the female character in the story was dynamic or static, according to Professor McGrath's earlier definitions of those terms. In other words, did the character change in any significant way during the course of the narrative? Delia stared out the window for a good ten seconds, then turned back to the class as the bell rang. "I think we could safely say that the female character changed," was all she said.

The rest of the week was a jumble of classes and meetings, and by the middle of the second week, it seemed to students and faculty alike that there had never been such a thing as summer break. Delia found she could manage the logistics of travel to campus via bus and crutches, and preferred to get there by her own devices. A longish denim wrap skirt became her uniform of choice; it was easy to wear over her cast, it was washable, and it was virtually indestructible. Occasionally, she caught a ride home.

Delia loved autumn in Jefferson. Already the air carried a distinct nip evenings and mornings, though the days were warm and golden. Soon enough it would be winter, but not yet, not yet. Sometimes after classes, Delia made her way to the lake's edge, a distance Polly McGrath would have judged to be merely "a hop, skip, and a jump" from Brandon Hall. There, the desert child would sit on the damp, mulchy grass in the humid air and watch sails of every hue catch the breeze as their crafts skimmed lightly across the blue, blue waters of Lake Winauka.

She imagined herself springing to her feet, throwing crutches to the four winds, and literally inhaling autumn through her nostrils. To bound along the fragrant, wooded lake shore to Picnic Point would be the highest happiness any mortal could desire. Delia also thought of her father as she carefully extracted the inner core of individual grass stems and chewed on the sweet white tips. It was a trick Jedediah McGrath had taught his little daughter years ago with the spindly spring grasses near his small barn in Smithville. The sandstone desert was his landscape, but he would have appreciated the beauty of this place just the same. Delia longed to take his sinewy, calloused hand and show him where some of the shore birds nested.

Saturday morning, two weeks into fall term, before Delia was even remotely ready to face the day, some heartless soul began ringing her doorbell. Her first impulse was to bury her head in her pillow and ignore it. Her second impulse was to shout curses down the stairwell in the direction of the front door. When Delia first returned home from Smithville, she had slept in the den downstairs, in deference to her fractured leg and the problems presented by a narrow set of stairs. As she got stronger and the leg became more manageable, however, she began sleeping in her upstairs bedroom again. Which was fine, until someone rang the doorbell in the early morning. Which someone just did again, even more insistently.

Must be important, Delia thought, and unearthed herself from the sheets. Gordon had called last night, and they had talked until pretty late. It was their Friday night date, he said, so he was allowed to keep her up later than usual. She smiled to remember it. She also remembered that it was an hour later for her than for him. Hurriedly wrapping herself in a terry cloth robe that resembled a "before" picture for a Tide commercial, Delia grabbed her crutches and made for the stairs. When she reached the midpoint, the bell rang again.

"Hold your horses! I'm coming!" Delia ran her fingers through her sunbleached, easy-care hair and opened the door to greet the offender.

"Hello, dear. I knew you'd want me to wait, so I did."

Whatever gave you that idea, Delia said to herself. To her sprightly little neighbor in the white knit top stamped with balloons of every color, Delia said nothing. She only smiled blankly and ushered into her front room one Begonia Slopek, senior citizen; former inmate of the Arizona State Penitentiary ("it was all a mistake"); bottle-blonde enchantress (ask Elmer Roy Tracy, senior citizen hailing from Mississippi and enamored of said enchantress); owner of one good leg and one not so good leg; and also owner of one large, faded blue Pontiac convertible (with automatic transmission) that was decidedly a senior citizen in the kingdom of combustion. Which automobile was the only vehicle of Delia's immediate acquaintance that she could actually enter on the driver's side (by dropping in from the open top) and drive (with her left leg).

Begonia *could* drive, in a manner of speaking, but it put the whole town at risk. She was too short to see over the steering wheel. Moreover, she had a tendency to take the hide off any objects, moving or stationary—animal, mineral, or vegetable—that came within range. Range being about fifty yards in all directions. Delia's own car, a very experienced Subaru wagon with a standard transmission, sat next to the Pontiac, its battery dead, its owner unable to get behind its wheel, much less operate its clutch and gas pedals in tandem.

"Have you had breakfast?" Begonia asked all too innocently. As if she couldn't see that she had jerked her neighbor out of a sound sleep and brought her to the door in an ill-tempered muddle. "D'ya know what I said to myself when I woke up this a.m.?" Begonia continued.

Delia replied that she hadn't the foggiest.

"I said that today's Saturday, the day when they fix up all those tasty little food samples in the grocery stores. I said to myself, a good half of those freebies are breakfasty things—y'know, sausages, egg substitutes, juices, prefabricated waffles with some fancy new syrup. Why not eat breakfast on the house, I said, and why not take Delia with me?"

Some time back, Begonia had struck a mutually beneficial bargain with her neighbor. Delia could use the Pontiac when she needed it in exchange for chauffeuring Begonia on occasion. The arrangement had enabled Delia to manage a few errands, but she had drawn the line when school began. Delia refused to tie up Begonia's car by driving it to the university. So with the start of fall term, Delia hadn't seen much of her neighbor. *And I could have lasted another hour or two,* she observed silently.

"Is Elmer Roy accompanying us?" Delia asked.

"Oh dear me, no. He likes to sleep late. I wouldn't dare call him this early."

Delia rolled her eyes. "Well, I'll need a little time to get showered and dressed. As you can see, I'm not exactly in street clothes."

"Yes, I see that. Oh my, yes. You get dressed. Take your time." Begonia looked Delia over, then added, "Why don't you let me take that robe home with me, dear? I'll pop it in the washer with my towels this afternoon."

"Thanks for the offer, but I can handle it. See you out front in forty minutes or so."

Not too many months ago, Delia's Saturday morning routine would have called for a pot of coffee to wake up her brain and set her on her feet for the day. It was mainly the aroma she missed. Did her mother appreciate her sacrifice? Not likely, since she had never tasted the stuff. Being hooked on morning coffee was just one more sign of spinelessness, in Polly McGrath's view.

On her way to the stairs this Saturday morning, Delia took a detour to the utility closet, where she stuffed the maligned terry robe into the dry bowl of the washing machine. "With Begonia around, who needs a mother?" she muttered, making her way upstairs in the oversized T-shirt that served her as a nightgown.

Re-entering her bedroom, Delia punched the TV remote control, and the nine-inch portable that sat on a low, unfinished chest of drawers crackled noisily to life. Saturday morning was about the only time she paid much attention to local news, and then only channel three carried it. The other Wisconsin channels, she had discovered long ago, were into Saturday morning cartoons in a big way. Entertainment for the kids so Mom and Dad can sleep in. *I must introduce Begonia to Saturday morning cartoons,* Delia told herself.

A breaking story caught her attention as she tidied the pale yellow comforter on her bed. The body of a young adult male had been discovered in a shallow grave by the river on Jefferson's west side early this morning. Two fishermen noticed a fresh mound behind some willows and kicked the dirt off one end of it. They uncovered a human foot and notified police.

Delia stopped to watch. Behind the on-the-scene reporter, she could see what looked like the beltway spanning the river. The body, the grim-faced reporter said, had apparently been there for several days, perhaps weeks. No identification had been made yet. The body might be that of a transient, the reporter speculated, since the homeless sometimes hung out along the river beneath the beltway overpass.

A police detective came on camera for a brief interview. Cause of death is unknown at this time, he said. There are no visible lethal wounds. The victim, a male in his late teens or early twenties, was wearing expensive designer jeans and deck shoes, and a Ralph Lauren polo shirt. He didn't appear to be a transient. Too well dressed. His wallet, if he had one, was missing, and he wore no jewelry.

"Any leads?" the reporter asked.

"Not yet. Our first job is to find out who he is and notify the family. Then we'll follow leads and look for motives."

Delia felt shock register in her stomach. The events of her ill-conceived night journey cut into her consciousness. She saw again the pickup truck and its occupants, who looked capable of anything. The scene by the river seemed familiar, though she couldn't say for certain, and she knew she should call the police. But she didn't want to. She didn't want this thing intruding in her life, which was complicated enough.

Heartsick over the death and troubled over her possible implication in the affair, Delia wasn't sure she was up to cruising the grocery aisles at Kroger's and the A & P with Begonia, looking for handouts.

She clicked off the television, secured a green trash bag over her cast, and stepped into the shower, letting the pounding spray pelt her face and clear her head. In a matter of weeks, she expected to bid farewell to both cast and Hefty. That day couldn't come soon enough.

"Mind if I take a little side trip first?" Delia asked as she cranked the ancient Pontiac engine to life.

"Ooo, no! I love adventure!" Begonia cried. "Don't tell me where we're going. Surprise me!"

The air was cool as they left the condo parking area and pulled onto the street. It occurred to Delia that soon Begonia would have to raise the top on her convertible—assuming that it had a top, of course. When the weather turned cold, Delia would no longer have access to the driver's seat by dropping into it and angling her fractured leg across the drive shaft. The old Pontiac was what Begonia called "the cat's meow" for Delia because, in addition to an open top, it had the gear lever on the steering column instead of the floor. *Maybe I'll be able to sit down and slide across from the passenger's side,* Delia thought.

Then her mind returned to the morning's news story. If the dead person was a student, his death would reverberate through every dormitory and classroom in the university, traumatizing the whole student population. And at least one representative of the faculty population. The more Delia thought about it, the more it seemed likely that the body was found in the same area where she had wandered that eery Monday night nearly two weeks ago. Delia hadn't followed the dirt road on to the river, but she was certain she hadn't been more than half a mile from it. An odd sensation crawled up the back of her neck.

Delia drove past the park and, after several miscues, found her way to the street she had followed that night. A roadblock at the last intersection before the pavement disappeared told Delia what she wanted to know.

Begonia was no dummy. "Is this where that lovely boy in the new shoes was found?" she asked.

"I think so."

"S'pose we can sneak around the back way for a closer look?"

"There isn't a back way, unless you want to swim the river."

Begonia giggled. "Time was when I could've," she said, then grew immediately serious. "I didn't think you were the sort who followed ambulances and fire trucks, dear."

"Normally, I'm not." Delia turned around, squealing the tires, and headed for Kroger's.

Begonia was dying to ask her neighbor why they had driven to the crime scene this morning, but she could tell by the set of Delia's jaw that she'd best keep her questions to herself. Begonia sighed softly and began silently counting white cars. She frequently tested the theory that there were more white cars on the road than any other color. She, Begonia Slopek, wouldn't be caught dead owning a white car. Too blah, she told anyone who asked her opinion on the matter. Almost her only disappointment in Delia was that the girl owned a white vehicle. Of course, the Subaru was so weather-beaten and yellow that it hardly qualified as white.

CHAPTER THREE

Sitting there on her porch, passing the time of day with Anthon Clemmer, Arva Plimpton told him he was more than welcome to have a look-see around her property, such as it was, and he took her up on it. He ambled about, checking the condition of the barn and tack house and sizing up the acreage while Arva bobbed along behind him like a beach ball caught in an ebbing wave. She chattered about this, that, and the other thing, but she was thinking all the while. Arva was torn between wanting him to buy her farm so she could move into town, and secretly hoping he might opt to take the place and her too. As a kind of bonus, like at Albertson's. Buy one, get one free.

If he did that, she'd have a man on the premises, but then she wouldn't be able to move into town either. Women she knew in the Pleasant Hours senior residential complex had raved on about their sewing circle and their literary group. Not that Arva liked to sew a whole lot—Relief Society quilting about did it for her. And the last book she read was the one written a number of years ago by that woman who claimed to have returned from the dead.

The writer vowed she had met Jesus on the other side, and she came back converted. She then proved the value of the experience by writing it up and selling several million copies. Plowing through those pages, however, had cured Arva of any inclination to read books, maybe permanently. Even a nonliterary person like Arva could tell that the book was a composite of bad sentences and worse doctrine. She had been grateful to come out the other end in one piece. Still, the idea of a literary group was appealing on the surface of it, even if the experience itself might give a person the willies.

And then Arva had to admit that she would hate to throw this delectably eligible man into Polly McGrath's clutches. Not that Polly would have him, even if he was inclined. It was obvious to anyone with a grain of sense that he wasn't Polly's type. He laughed too much. And he had hinted that he had a "past." Arva's neighbor wasn't the kind to consort with anyone tainted by even the tiniest smirch on his name.

Arva's late husband used to say Polly had a steel rod for a backbone. He was surprised, he said to Arva on more than one occasion, that Polly McGrath had consented to do what people had to do to bring children into the world. She was fussy about little things, too. Why, Jedediah McGrath swore to his dying day that when he first asked to come courting, Polly made him shave his already nicely groomed beard before setting one foot on the premises.

Not that Polly wasn't a good woman. She just wasn't someone a person could cozy up to. If Jedediah managed it, and apparently he did—six children's worth—he was all who did. It wasn't that Arva didn't like Polly. Polly had no loyaler friend than Arva Plimpton, Arva liked to say. It was just that Polly didn't have much *give* to her. She was born knowing what she thought about everything. As for herself, Arva sometimes didn't know what she thought till she said it. Sometimes it was a huge surprise to her what actually came out of her own mouth.

Anthon Clemmer was indeed interested in buying Arva Plimpton's place, but he wasn't entirely settled as to his own motives. He suspected that proximity to Polly McGrath, and not the desert's semi-friendly weather, was his primary reason for pursuing this real estate venture. But if anyone should ask, he could certainly justify a move on grounds of climate. After all, half the senior citizens of northern Utah and southern Idaho had discovered the pleasures of living in a town where blizzards and slippery roads, not to mention snow shovels, were only fading memories. There was something to be said, too, for golfing in February, if not in July.

One fellow Anthon met at the Red Lobster said he left his hometown of Billings, Montana, with a snow shovel tied on his minivan. It was his weather vane, he said, and he had vowed to drive south until someone asked him what that thing on his van was. When he got that question, he would know he was far enough. Well, he got it in Smithville, and here he was. And here he intended to stay, the fellow declared. The printer from Cheyenne saw the man's point. He himself wouldn't mind contributing to the graying of Smithville. As for the Mormons who inhabited the place, Anthon figured he could keep an open mind about them. If they could stand him, he could stand them.

In what he called his saner moments, however, Anthon knew it was a mistake to pursue this woman. She was the kind who would give a starving man a handout, but wouldn't give a thriving man the time of day. It was just his luck, he chuckled to himself, that he happened on Polly McGrath when she was newly widowed, and that they met—*collided* was a better term—under such "prejudicial" circumstances. Now, if she had lost her mate several years ago, like the Plumm sisters and Arva Plimpton, she might have been more amenable to a little Cheyenne-style courting. At least after the shock of their initial encounter wore off. On the other hand, if he hadn't been desperate and dirty, and she hadn't just buried her husband, they wouldn't have met at all.

Satisfied that he had pretty well seen Arva's place, Anthon took his leave of Polly's neighbor and bounced down the long lane, whistling. It wasn't yet the appointed hour for supper with Polly, so he drove on toward the river. As he pulled up alongside a massive, thick-barked cottonwood tree, a great blue heron lifted its heavy, sculptured body out of the reeds along the shore. The man almost felt the slow beat of the huge black-tipped wings in his own chest, as if the effort were his own.

A favorite poem from high school, William Cullen Bryant's "To a Waterfowl," sprang to his mind. When he closed his eyes, he could see Merinda Plumm, once his teacher and now, surprisingly, his bene-factress, reading it to a class of mostly unimpressed seventeen-year-olds. He remembered how light from the window near which she stood had etched her hair and cheek, and how her voice had softened with the lines that spoke of faith engendered by the bird's divinely guided flight. How was it, he mused, that the poem's message never took hold of her in a personal way?

As for himself, Anthon had no doubt that there was a higher power. Oddly enough, he had felt its presence most surely on certain nights in the Arizona desert, when he hadn't so much as a warm coat, much less a roof. While his erstwhile companions snored beneath their cardboard covers, Anthon had studied the stars and composed his own stories about the constellations. Now and then, the lament of a mourning dove or an owl punctuated his thoughts. Those years of homelessness and physical deprivation—years when he was what Polly McGrath would have called a tramp—were not easy, but they had deepened him. They had wrested him from the shackles of material frenzy and spiritual decay.

In the end, however, want had driven him to extremes, and he had accosted a woman at a freeway rest area—jabbing a wrench in her side and calling it a gun. A wave of gratitude swept over him. What if that woman had been anyone other than Polly McGrath? She had refused to take him seriously as a criminal, shaming him instead, and had therefore saved his life.

Opening the door of the van, Anthon strolled to the water's edge. He smiled as a few napping frogs did quick nosedives from sandstone boulders and pocked lava rocks into the shallow pools near the shore. The intense heat of summer was beginning to abate in this part of the world, and he could almost feel the imminence of fall. In a few short weeks, the cottonwoods would flame up golden against the sky and cliffs, changing the whole complexion of the landscape. Even the aggressive, water-guzzling tamarisks were beautiful when they traded their dull bluish wands for burnished bronze.

Anthon asked himself why he had never been moved to worship in a formal way. He had attended Bible school as a youngster, and had wiggled through Methodist Sunday services beside his mother until his middle teens. But since then, his only devotions had been expressed under the arched beams of the firmament, or with his pencil. Polly McGrath, he knew, was a church-going woman. He was struck with a desire to know what she believed and why she believed it. Her strength had to come from somewhere.

Polly McGrath never doubted for a minute that the otherwise unpredictable Anthon Clemmer would turn up for supper, and on time, too. She had astonished herself by inviting him. Once he sat down anywhere, it was like moving mountains to dislodge the man. The last thing she wanted was for Arva Plimpton to see that poor excuse for a van plugging up the driveway all evening. Arva was not the sort to keep her observations to herself, and she specialized in embroidering the messages her eyes delivered to the lump of gray matter inside her skull.

Polly did not want the Wyoming wanderer around, either, if Ron and Miles should come by to take the horses out. It was bad enough that Ilene and Effie had seen him. She wasn't about to have him become a fixture in her life, by way of the Plimpton place or any other place. She invited him to supper because she was a decent woman and it was the decent thing to do, after he had driven all the way down here from Cheyenne in that faded green rattletrap.

As she set two plates on the big oak table, Polly heard tires on the gravel drive and the scurrying of chickens. Not only on time, but early, Polly said to herself. She didn't turn from her work when she heard feet on the back steps.

"You can smile again, I'm back!"

The voice was familiar, but it wasn't Anthon's. Polly looked up, startled. "Gordon Foster! What brings you here?"

"The smell of pork chops, what else?"

Polly was glad to see Gordon, though she sorely regretted his timing, what with Anthon due any minute. She thought that Delia's going off with that Gabrielson fellow on short notice might have been a hard pill for even an agreeable man like Gordon to swallow. It was all speculation, however, because Delia never discussed her men friends with her mother, and her mother rarely asked. Polly had to admit that Gordon was a bureaucrat and that she liked him anyway. What Polly didn't like was having to admit his government connection. From her father she had inherited a fierce antipathy toward the abstraction called the federal government, its regulations, and its employees. Minions and parasites, Parley Appleby had termed the latter.

Delia had once tried to convince her mother that the government shouldn't be seen as the enemy, that in a democracy the government reflects the people. It's what we make it, Delia had insisted, or what we by our neglect or greed let it become; the people give it its character. It's no worse than the people are. Polly wouldn't hear such nonsense, and Delia had let the matter go. But Polly knew she hadn't changed her daughter's opinion; she never did.

Then along came Gordon Foster, a living rebuttal to Parley Appleby's notion, though of course Gordon was pretty low in the federal hierarchy, maybe too low to count. Polly settled the dispute satisfactorily for herself by concluding that Gordon was the exception that proved the rule. The nice woman at the post office, Polly had to concede, was another.

Gordon's quick eye noticed the two place settings on the table, and Polly saw his glance.

"You expecting me, or some equally handsome fellow?" After the words were out, it crossed his mind that perhaps when alone, she set a place for her dead husband. He wished he had kept still.

Polly flushed briefly and turned away. "Just a fellow from Wyoming come to Smithville looking at some property. We have mutual friends."

Seeing her discomfort, Gordon changed the subject. "Well," he said, "I'm planning a brief trip to bring solace and comfort to the youngest of the McGrath children. I figure she's pining away back there with only students and hungry mosquitoes to keep her company."

"When are you going?"

"Thursday. Just for the weekend. I imagine a few days of me will make Jefferson look a whole lot better to our favorite English teacher. But I intend to plant a stink bomb in the bearded scholar's Pathfinder. At the very least."

"You have my permission," Polly said, then caught herself. "Delia always comes home at Christmastime," she added hastily.

"Glad to hear it. Maybe you'll let me hang my stocking in your parlor."

"It's not likely to be very festive around here this year."

Gordon read her meaning. It would be her first Christmas in many decades without Jedediah McGrath. "Delia apparently left a couple of books here by mistake. She asked me to bring them when I come," he explained.

Although it violated all her rules of hospitality, Polly did not invite Gordon to stay for supper, and she desperately hoped he would leave before the minstrel of freight trains and viaducts returned. "I saw them on her father's desk," she said. "You can get them. They look like Greek to me."

"She said they're reference books. Not exactly recreational reading, I guess."

Polly wanted to ask Gordon how her youngest and most difficult child was doing. How she seemed. Polly had spoken with her daughter a few times since Delia had returned to Jefferson, but Polly was not, as she put it, a telephone talker. Especially long distance. In the back of her mind she could always hear the meter running, clicking off the quarters. People who knew her, however—people like Arva Plimpton—would say she was not much of a talker, period, phone or no phone.

And those tinny, irksome answering machines that had displaced living conversation across the globe put her off completely. By the time Polly suffered through the sometimes inane, sometimes incomprehensible recorded message and the ear-shattering beeps, she was too exasperated to speak. It was some comfort to Polly that Delia didn't like the devices either. Nevertheless, Delia had purchased one—as a concession to her friends, she said. Polly refused to say one word to it. And if she ever got e-mail, Polly vowed, it would not be in this life.

"I think her leg is coming along," Gordon offered. "I'm glad to hear she expects to be out of the cast by Halloween."

"Yes, that is good news."

Gordon, who was rarely ill at ease with anyone, fell silent. "Well, I'll go find those books," he said.

"Yes, do. Call me if you need help."

Polly's heart sank as Anthon's head passed under the kitchen window. Gordon would return and find him.

"Hey," Anthon called as he burst onto the back porch. "Whose vehicle is that blocking the driveway? You seeing someone behind my back, Mrs. McGrath?"

"Hush, you old vagabond! You want the neighbors and everyone else to hear your foolishness?"

The neighbors didn't hear Anthon Clemmer, but Gordon Foster did as he entered the kitchen from Jedediah's makeshift den.

"Now really, Polly McGrath," Anthon teased, "don't you think he's a mite too young for you? I'll bet he doesn't entertain you with poetry, either. In my experience, these young bucks lack poetic souls."

Gordon grinned. "Hi, I'm Gordon Foster, and you might be surprised to hear how much poetry there is in my everlovin' blue-eyed soul."

"Pogo!" Anthon shouted joyfully. "How does anyone under fifty know lines like that from good ol' Pogo Possum?"

"Some youngsters cut their teeth on Dr. Seuss; I cut mine on Pogo. My dad collected every book Walt Kelly ever produced."

"Only thing anybody knows of Pogo these days is, 'We have seen the enemy and he is us.' Most of them who quote it have no idea where it comes from. Will you look at that, Polly! A soul-mate, right here in your kitchen."

"I'm looking."

"You must stay to supper, young man. I've got you blocked in with my van anyway. What do you say, Polly, is there enough food to go around? By the way, I'm Anthon Clemmer, and I'm mad about this woman. I aim to court her till I drop."

Gordon laughed and sat down. "Are you mad about him, too, Mother McGrath?"

"There are only two mad persons in this room, and I'm not one of them," Polly said, half-smiling in spite of herself. "Of course there's enough. Wash up, the both of you."

After supper, Anthon and Gordon—and Polly, after much persuasion—retired to the screened front porch. The sun disappeared earlier these days, but it was still streaming at a low angle into the bright red and pink oleander blossoms that bordered the drive, and the air was pleasantly warm. Polly dusted the porch chairs before she would let the men sit in them. Gordon remembered a good many happy hours on that same porch during the summer, when he used to come over and while away evenings with Delia, Jennifer, and Polly.

Sometimes the missionaries dropped by—Elders Kirk and Hochtel—to teach Jennifer. They all thought her name was Torry, then. She was a tough case, and Gordon had marveled at the young men's patience. He also found it quite remarkable that Delia and her mother would take the injured girl in, open their home to her, and she so belligerent and unappreciative. And he remembered the Sunday Jennifer's old boyfriend kidnaped her while the McGraths were in church. After the fellow deserted her, he decided he wanted her back. It was a miracle she survived the subsequent accident that killed the roughneck and his co-conspirator.

"What do you hear from Jennifer?" Gordon asked as he sank into the familiar straw-bottomed chair.

"She has written a time or two," Polly replied. "She still has a lot of healing to do. In her head as much as her body."

For several minutes Anthon stayed discreetly out of the conversation, which act of self-control Gordon was in no position to appreciate fully. Finally, at the first lengthy pause, the garrulous king of the road addressed Gordon with a knowing grin. "What's a hot-blooded youngster like you doing with a couple of old fogies on a Friday night? Shouldn't you be off wooing some princess?" he asked.

"As it turns out, the only princess I care to woo lives in Jefferson, Wisconsin, just now. Besides, I'm not all that young. Ask the kids I coach in soccer. They think I'm over the hill."

Anthon laughed. "Aha, the plot thickens. Well, if the daughter is anything like the mother, you're in for quite a ride. When this gorgeous creature here consents to marry me, in about ten or twenty years, I'd guess—however long it takes me to wear her down—we'll be related. Who knows, one day I might be singing cowboy songs to your babies. And introducing them to Pogo Possum and his swamp pals."

Polly cleared her throat and announced that she had imbibed her limit of Wyoming's overspill, and that having reached the saturation point, she would take her leave and do up the dishes. Which chore was a pleasure by comparison, she added. Both men offered to help, but she wouldn't hear of it.

"Gordon," Polly said as she reached the door, "when you feel the need for something resembling intelligent conversation, you can escape this madman and go talk with the chickens."

Anthon laughed out loud. "See how she is? How could a man resist her?"

Polly washed dishes by hand. She had said more than once that an automatic dishwasher was about as low on her priority list as anything she could think of. Such a machine, she argued, interfered with the education of the young and the memory flexing of the old.

As Anthon and Gordon watched night overtake them, each told the other the story of how he had happened into the life of a McGrath woman. Anthon chuckled frequently and made no excuses for himself, and Gordon liked that. Gordon had to wonder, however, how Polly would handle it if Anthon did indeed buy the Plimpton place. It was obvious that she was anything but ready to consider "keeping company." Gordon wanted to advise Anthon to lie low until Polly was through with her grieving, but he held his tongue. He seriously doubted that Polly would ever come around, anyway. Clearly, Jedediah McGrath, alive or dead, was the love of her life. She accepted no substitutes.

Gordon couldn't help wondering, too, how the older McGrath children would respond to a man like Anthon if Polly should decide to surprise them all. Delia had told him something about her three oldest siblings—Jed Junior, Paul, and Hannah—and Gordon suspected that a liaison between their mother and a man once convicted of a felony would send the lot of them into orbit. And even Victor and Ron might be alarmed at first.

As for Delia, Gordon didn't know. She might have mixed feelings about someone displacing Jedediah McGrath, yet at the same time she would thoroughly enjoy watching the others fuss and fume. Delia had on one occasion told Gordon that she thought her mother too rarely did anything spontaneous or foolish, that she almost wished Polly would lose her head, just once, and prove she was human. It was plain to Gordon, however, that Delia knew nothing of her mother's adventures with Anthon Clemmer on the interstate system.

That wasn't all Delia didn't know. Or anyone else, for that matter. Polly was working over the whole outlandish business in her head as she washed and dried the dishes. She had told no one about the automobile breakdown that had marooned her for several days in Ogden, on her return trip from calling on her sister Dorothy in Logan. Nor did anyone know of her inexplicable obsession with the case of Merinda Plumm who, at eighty-five, had poisoned her eighty-seven-year-old spouse. People who knew Polly would have been shocked to learn that she had actually visited the elderly assassin in the Ogden jail, and visited her more than once. And that on her way to Logan Polly had conveyed Rosa and Golda, cousins of the deceased Archibald Plumm, from Colton to Ogden for his funeral.

Although Polly was surprised at herself, she had long since attributed the whole bizarre episode to temporary insanity, induced by grief and distress over Jedediah's death. But then, too, there was the trip to Las Vegas with Anthon Clemmer a good many weeks later—on the day Delia departed for Wisconsin and left Polly face to face with an empty house. Oh, the man was persuasive, all right. That must have been part of it. But there was no gun in her ribs on that occasion.

She, Polly McGrath, a sensible woman with gray hair in a bun and numerous grandchildren, had, of her own free will and choice, actually boarded the same green Ford Econoline van that now sat, leaking oil most likely, in her driveway. And she did it, she reminded herself, with the same man who at their first meeting had tried to scare her out of her wits by masquerading as a murderer and commandeering her automobile. And now, what does he do but turn up again, looking for property, he says; and what does she do but feed him? It made no sense at all.

Sunday morning, Polly was not what you'd call overjoyed at the prospect of going to church. Arva Plimpton would be lying in wait for her, she knew. Polly surmised that Arva hadn't seen the Econoline in her drive Friday evening, or she would have hotfooted it over to Polly's doorstep first thing Saturday morning. And if she had hotfooted it, she would likely have bumped into Anthon, who had stopped by on his way out of town. Polly was relieved to see him go, and couldn't for the life of her comprehend why he felt the need to inform her of his comings and goings. Polly assured herself that she in fact couldn't care less, and that she enjoyed his goings a far sight more than his comings.

Just as the worship service was beginning, Polly slipped in the back door of the meetinghouse chapel, spotted Arva's maroon permed head, and sat as far as possible from it. She managed to avoid Arva in Sunday School class as well, but Relief Society was another story. Arva corralled her the instant Polly walked into the room, and followed her to her seat.

"I'm sure Mr. Clemmer liked my place," Arva panted at Polly's elbow, "and he's got the shekels to buy it."

"What makes you think that?" Polly scoffed. "A man who drives around in that wreck of a van can't be too well-heeled."

"Oh, he's well-heeled all right. And well-toed, too. When he knocks on my door, his name rings a bell, but I can't rightly put my finger on it. I mull at it, and this morning it hits me. Out I go to the garage and haul in my stack of old newspapers. I save 'em. Not as long as you, Polly, but I save 'em. And there it is, in the 'state news' section two Saturdays ago. Not last Saturday, mind you, the one before that."

Polly decided that if Arva and Anthon hit it off it was because they were both sound machines. Either of them could talk a person into the grave faster than anyone else alive. "Has this story a point?" she demanded. "The meeting is about to begin."

"Don't rush me, Polly. I've got to lay the groundwork. There I am, flipping through the pages, and my eye lands on this here headline: 'Plumm Estate Settled.' Why would my eye land there, you ask. Well, I wondered that myself. Then it comes to me. Generally, my memory is real good. I don't suffer from memory loss, short term or long, the way so many do. I'm real blessed that way."

Polly gave an inadvertent cough, as if Arva's words had stuck in *her* throat. Still, she was more than a little curious in spite of herself.

Arva continued. "Plumm's the name of that awful woman who killed her husband and inherited all his money. You remember? We talked about it over that quilt at homemaking meeting a while back. *You* even said something. That's why it stuck in my mind. You were in your bereavement, but you said something. For the life of me, I can't recall what it was, though."

At that point in Arva Plimpton's verbal exposition, the woman conducting the meeting stood up, looked straight at Arva's busy mouth, and said sweetly, "Sister Plimpton, would you offer the opening prayer?"

Arva jerked her head toward the table at the front, looked back in mute appeal to Polly, who ignored her, and helplessly nodded her head and stood up. Then the woman said just as sweetly, "Not till after the opening song, Sister Plimpton." Arva sank bewildered to her seat. In a compassionate impulse, Polly very nearly patted Arva's arm, but caught herself in time. It didn't pay to encourage Arva. She'd read too much into the gesture. For her, a pat on the arm could signify that Polly regarded them as blood sisters from here to eternity.

Somehow Arva got through both song and prayer, but with the rest of her story stopped up inside her, Polly could tell she was miserable throughout the class period. Arva cut off in the middle of a story was like someone with a mouth chock full of soda crackers hearing a side-splitting joke in a circle of polite company. The teeth and lips must be kept closed while the pressure of an immense guffaw builds, sending partially chewed cracker fragments into every available cavity in the head. The suffering is extreme, and Arva suffered. Oh, how she suffered. She was a kernel of popping corn in hot oil, an overfilled balloon, a shaken-up bottle of seltzer. She was ready to burst.

Polly could feel Arva's agitation scrambling her own insides. She had some cause for agitation herself as she awaited Arva's uncorking, though she wouldn't let Arva know it for all the tea in China. There was no point in guessing at the supposed connection of the newspaper article to Anthon Clemmer. Arva was sometimes so far out in left field that it didn't pay to conjecture. The link might be so remote that only Arva could forge it. When the meeting finally ended, Polly made a beeline for the nearest exit, with Arva right at her heels, taking two steps to Polly's one, all the way to Polly's old Chrysler Imperial.

"Guess who got nearly all that horrible woman's money?" Arva finally blurted out as Polly searched for her keys. "Anthon Clemmer, that's who! He got the blood money! Upwards of two million dollars!"

Polly gasped involuntarily. If she ever read the paper, or paid much attention to the television news these days, she might have heard about it. She used to watch the news sometimes—the evening news and *Jeopardy* were about all she watched any time—but since

Jed's death she hadn't even bothered with those programs. The world more or less went on without her.

"Why on earth would Merinda Plumm leave her money to him?" Polly stammered. "She might as well have left it to the canary."

"I don't recollect mention of any canary, Polly. All's I know is what I read in the paper, and the paper had what I regard as a logical explanation."

"Logical, I'll bet. By whose definition?" Polly interjected.

Arva ignored her. "The woman's lawyer said Anthon had 'defended her honor' once. 'Defended her honor,' whatever that means, were the words the man used. Anthon did whatever he did when he was a high school student in her English class. Isn't it exciting? And romantic? And to think he was at my house only two days ago. And yours, too, Polly. He was at both our houses, a millionaire. Think I should call the newspaper so's Alta can put it in her column?"

Polly only rolled her eyes, and Arva went on. "Anyways, Mr. Clemmer told me he'd come into a little money—a *little*, mind you—but he didn't go into the particulars. It makes me all shivery, him being a hero and rich. Isn't it just like him to go and do something noble and grand?"

Yes, like print counterfeit bills and abduct helpless women at gunpoint, Polly muttered crossly to herself. She had no patience with what she called "the goose bumps school of response to practically everything." The minute Polly got home, she searched through the tall stack of unopened newspapers on her back porch and pulled out the Saturday issue Arva had cited. For some reason, Polly hadn't canceled her subscription, though she had scarcely looked at a paper since Jed's stroke in June. It was now September, and not early September either.

Her son Ron regarded the pile as a fire hazard, and had offered to haul the whole works to the recycling center, but she had said not yet. Now she leaned over the kitchen table, turning pages. There it was, just as Arva said. Polly devoured the article, noting that the sisters Rosa and Golda were to receive ten thousand apiece and two male cousins five. So Anthon Clemmer was a rich man. It didn't change anything, Polly hmmphed to herself. He was still a clown who had never grown up, who laughed for no reason at all and at any time at all. She had to admit, however, that even though his laugh didn't sound any better, it looked better since he got himself a new tooth.

That evening, Polly received a phone call from Hannah, her third child. Hannah was active in the Church, like all of Polly's children except Delia, and for that Polly was grateful. At the same time, Hannah wore on a person's nerves in a way that Delia didn't. Hannah was what Miles and Sabrine, Ronald J.'s two oldest children, would call "radical hyper." Hannah lived in what Polly described as organized fury. Polly wondered how Hannah's husband and children stood it. The McGrath home had relaxed about six notches when Hannah married and moved away for good.

Polly couldn't count Hannah's university years as away time because until she married during her junior year, the girl still blew in and out of the house like Mother West Wind, upsetting the natural disorder of things. Hannah planned every detail of her life months in advance, and she researched every purchase she ever made—from water softeners to fingernail polish. Her husband Lester, Polly concluded long ago, was either a saint or brain dead. She knew he left on business a lot, and figured she knew why. If Hannah's children hadn't developed incurable neuroses, it wasn't because their mother hadn't tried.

"Hello, Mother. I'm glad I caught you."

"Hello, dear. Where else would I be?"

"Yes, of course. Well, I'm calling about Thanksgiving." Hannah generally got right to business.

"It's still September."

"Yes, of course, but we all like to know what our plans are."

"Some of us seem to, yes."

"I've talked with Jed Junior, Paul, and Victor. They all expect to be with their in-laws that day. That leaves you, Ron, me, and the children. Ilene's parents are so far away. I don't suppose Delia will be out, will she? It's just as well, since she doesn't have children, or mingle. What if we all gathered at the old family home this year? We could divide up the work."

Polly didn't appreciate the reference to the *old* family home, but she let it go. Otherwise it would become what Delia called an "issue," and Hannah would explain herself on into the millennium. Polly also knew that "divide up the work" meant Hannah would plan the menu down to the last olive and make assignments. The rest of them would do as they were told. Polly was conscious of the fact that she was being a little unfair, but then it was so easy to be unfair with Hannah.

The girl meant well, and she ran a tight and tidy household. "Uptight and tidy," Delia would have said. Polly predicted that the stack of newspapers on the porch would disappear ten minutes after Hannah arrived. She found herself wishing that Delia were coming, too. Hannah and Delia together, Jed used to say, were offsetting penalties.

"Well, what do you think, Mother?" Hannah was still talking.

Polly replied absently, "That'll be fine, dear. You work it out with Ronald J. and Ilene and let me know." Polly wagered she would have her marching orders within the week.

Monday after work, Gordon Foster dropped by to see Ron and Ilene. He hadn't been around their place since Delia left town, though he had said hi to Ron at a little league soccer game or two. His being on the outs with Delia had kept him away from her family. But with the tiff mended, he had an urge to see them all again. He also wanted them to know he was flying out to see her later in the week.

"Gordon, Gordon!" Effie squealed, and ran across the yard to throw her arms around him. Wilson came up and gave him a high-five. Hugging, he had told his mother numerous times, was for girls. It was yard cleanup time, and Ron was pruning shrubs with long-handled clippers while Wilson and Effie broke the stems and stuffed them in a big bag for the city's mulching machines. Gordon fell in beside them, holding the bag for the cuttings.

"Glad to see you," Ron called. "What's up?"

"I'm flying out to see the English professor this weekend. Anything you want to send her?"

"Maybe some of Ilene's fudge. Is there such a thing as fat-free fudge? Delia's such a nut about what she'll eat."

"I think she's relaxed her standards considerably since we nearly drowned her in Slingshot Gulch. In the matter of health risk, fat grams don't hold a candle to roaring walls of water. Or maybe swallowing several gallons of said water gave her a new perspective on nutrition."

"Glad to hear it. Things are friendly with you two, I take it?"

"Depends on how you define 'friendly,'" Gordon grinned. "I lean more toward a term like 'rapturous' myself, but then I always did exaggerate a little."

"Are you Aunt Delia's boyfriend?" Effie asked, fingering the beeper attached to Gordon's belt.

"I hope so, youngun'. Who's your boyfriend?"

"Don't got one," Effie said, ducking her head.

"*Have*n't one," Ilene corrected as she approached the group. "Stay for supper, Gordon? We've missed you."

"Well, I don't got no other plans, so maybe I will."

"Yay!" Effie cheered. "Mama, Gordon's Aunt Delia's boyfriend. He said so."

"Never you mind." Ilene took Effie's hand.

"Grandma's got a boyfriend, too," Effie informed Gordon.

"So I understand," he said, winking at Wilson, who grinned back.

Ron and Ilene looked at each other, and Ron hurriedly found another subject. "Anything new on the theft of the plates Delia found in Chinta Canyon?"

"Not that I know of. The trail's pretty cold by now. I think the feds have concluded that the sheets and inscriptions were fakes anyway. I'm afraid my friend Max Blohm—the skeptical professor— is to blame for that. Delia says she might want to go in again for another look."

"Think her leg will be strong enough by spring?"

"I don't know, but whenever she decides to go, she'll make it strong enough."

Ron nodded knowingly. "Just for fun, let's stay out of Slingshot Gulch this time."

Tuesday morning, Polly McGrath's telephone rang before she had cleared up her breakfast things. Arva Plimpton, who else?

"Polly, you'll never guess!"

"Try me. Your pig had a litter of calves."

"Polly! get serious. It's in the paper. Go get your paper."

"Why don't you just tell me and spare me the trouble."

"It's about Anthon again. He's giving those cousins—the women, not the men—a bunch of the money! The three of them are going off to Hawaii together to celebrate."

"Good riddance," Polly said, and hung up the phone.

CHAPTER FOUR

Making a breakfast out of free samples at the grocery store that Saturday morning in late September gave new meaning to the word "piecemeal." What a pair the two of them made, Delia thought, as she swung along beside the sprightly Begonia Slopek decked out in her balloon-print top. At Kroger's they began with minuscule lumps of fried Jimmy Dean sausage on aisle one and ended with runny NuLaid yolkless scrambled eggs on aisle eight.

The A & P, their next stop, seemed to be serving up every kind of dip known to mortals. For the tortilla chip crowd there were salsa, guacamole, and refried beans in skimpy, one-gulp portions. For the dietary purists, there were tiny celery and carrot sticks in little plastic cups. The veggie dip choices were all pastels, in taste as well as color, but they were sour cream, mayonnaise, and cream cheese nonetheless. Even if Delia had felt like eating, which she didn't, none of the artery-cloggers Begonia tested that morning would have been her foods of choice. Admittedly, she was not the fat-free fanatic she used to be, but she still shuddered at the sensation of grease coating the roof of her mouth.

Regardless of the dubious offerings, it was always a party when Begonia was around. She so relished a bargain, and she loved being out in the world, rubbing elbows with humanity. *Let's face it,* Delia said to herself, *Begonia is a people person and I'm not. Give me a few forgiving friends, a lot of landscape, a library of books, a college class-room, access to live musicians and theater, and I'm happy.*

"Isn't this fun, dear?" Begonia exulted, dipping a finger of chicken into some tangy barbecue sauce. "And to think it isn't costing a cent!"

She then employed the toothpick that had speared the chicken to probe the spaces between her various molars and crowns. "Don't you want to try this chicken?"

Delia smiled in spite of herself. The frozen chicken strips waiting for the skillet appeared to be composed of small scraps of fowl stuck together, like pressed wood chips. She wondered which would taste better and be more nutritious in the long run, pressed wood or laminated chicken. "You eat up," Delia replied. "I can't swallow solid food before ten or eleven a.m. My throat refuses to accept anything but liquid or fruit."

All the while Begonia was frolicking from aisle to aisle and table to table, chatting with the servers and collecting their coupons and recipe handouts, Delia was working over the morning's news story in her mind. If it turns out that the slain fellow disappeared Monday night of last week, then . . . . But of course, Delia rationalized, the body wasn't necessarily dumped by the river that night. It could have been brought there days later. Even as she articulated the thought, however, dread welled up in her and wouldn't let her believe it.

In an effort to settle her mind on the matter, Delia vowed not to jump to any conclusions until the coroner's report set the time of death. Then she went ahead and jumped anyway, only to be visited again by her rational self. *People must get lost and take that road by mistake all the time, just as I did,* she reasoned. *And some people merely like to see a river at night, or show a friend a favorite fishing spot. The truck I saw was just one of many vehicles that have visited the river in the last two weeks.* But all the logic in the world wouldn't shake those evil-seeming men loose from her head. They were bolted to her brain.

Finally, Begonia pronounced herself stuffed, to her silly gills, she said. Delia noted, however, that as the two of them passed the bakery section on the way to the exit, Begonia's hand shot out and snatched three doughnut samples from the glass counter top. She very nearly had to stand on tiptoe to reach them.

"I just couldn't resist, dear," she giggled apologetically. "Y'see, I was born with this raging sweet tooth. Inherited from my daddy. His people all ruined their natural teeth on sweets. Went to the grave toothless, every one of them. Their dentures were bequeathed to the next generation along with their cats and pocket watches. Thanks to fluoride in this day and age, I've managed to keep a few of my originals." Begonia popped a sugar-coated delicacy into her mouth. "Wait'll I tell Elmer Roy what he missed," she said, smacking her lips with pleasure. "That'll teach him to sleep in on Saturday mornings."

When Delia got home, there was a note on her door from Susan Fines, one of her Relief Society visiting teachers. Delia hadn't seen either Susan or Mary Beth lately, but she knew they wouldn't let the month pass without a visit. *If the world should end, it wouldn't stop those two,* Delia mused. *I fully expect them to deliver their message en route to glory. In my case, they may have to make a temporary detour in the other direction.* Delia had missed church last week, and she realized it would be very easy to slip back into her old habits. *Better go tomorrow,* she thought. *Maybe I can borrow Begonia's car, or con her into going with me. Wouldn't that be a picnic?*

The note said that Susan and her fourteen-year-old son, Edward, were headed for the high school courts to hit tennis balls. It was an invitation: "We have your rolling chair, so come join us." *And how will I get there?* Delia wondered silently, even a little bitterly. She had enjoyed "chair tennis" with the Fines family once before, and knew it would improve her disposition, but she hated to borrow Begonia's car. She crumpled the note in her hand and jammed it in her pocket. The unidentified body found by the river was a thorn in the soul.

Delia also felt some anxiety about Gordon's coming out Thursday, even though she wanted to see him. How would it be to have him here, on midwestern rather than desert turf? Would he hate it? Would he like her less in this setting? Would she like him less? She didn't want any snags in their relationship just now. On her way to the refrigerator for a carton of skim milk, she punched the playback button on the telephone answering machine and kicked off her scruffy left Birkenstock sandal. Next year she would have to destroy her left leg so she could even up the wear on her footgear.

Howard Turner's voice broke into her revery, sounding played out even in metallic reproduction. Angie was feeling pretty punk after her final chemotherapy treatment yesterday, Howard said. Could Delia cover for her Monday? Howard would bring over the class text and other materials, if that was okay. *Looks as though I get to brush up on British Medieval literature this weekend,* Delia ruminated. *Well, it'll keep me off the streets.*

Howard, Delia knew, was more worried about Angie than Angie was herself. How would it feel to love and be loved like that, Delia wondered. She shut off the machine and flopped on the couch with a book, stretching her legs the length of it. When Howard arrived with Angie's class materials, Delia could see the wear in his face. "Want to go for a little walk, let off some steam?" she suggested.

"No, no," he protested, "I should get back to Angie." Tears threatened, and he removed his glasses and pinched the top of his nose with the thumb and forefinger of his right hand. "This process has been so doggoned hard on her, and she's been such a good sport about it."

"And you feel helpless," Delia said.

"And I feel helpless," he nodded. "And . . . ," he paused, adding quietly, "what if it's all for nothing?"

Delia had asked the same question silently a hundred times. Indeed, what if it is? She had no answer to give. Howard put one arm around Delia, gave her a squeeze, and shuffled out the door. Delia followed him down the walk on her bare foot and crutches. As she stood watching his station wagon pull away, the image of Polly McGrath bent over her husband's marble replica broke across Delia's mind. *Devotion. It is called devotion,* she said.

The unexpected conjunction of Howard's anguish with her own poignant memory gave Delia another perspective on her mother's feelings. Jedediah and Polly McGrath hadn't been openly demonstrative like Howard and Angie Turner, but Delia had come to realize that their love went just as deep, shone forth just as powerfully, had an indefinable luster all its own. In answer to a sudden, sweet ache, Delia went inside and dialed her mother's number. After two rings, she hung up. *Not now,* she told herself. *Maybe later, or tomorrow.*

The next morning, Delia got herself organized and went to church. Susan's seventeen-year-old daughter Lucia had called "Sister McGrath" Saturday night and volunteered to pick her up.

"Please, please, don't 'sister' me yet," Delia pleaded, laughing, when Lucia arrived in a Ford Taurus. "Give me another twenty or thirty years before consigning me to that title. It makes me feel terribly old. Break me in gently."

"Mother told me I was not to call you by your first name, not yet anyway. She said you're a professor, and it would be disrespectful," Lucia explained.

"Well, I'm not a professor on the weekends, so you can call me 'Delia' when we're out of your mother's hearing."

The rest of the Fines family were deboarding their minivan when Lucia drove into the meetinghouse parking lot. Nine-year-old Amy ran over to Delia and shyly stroked one of her crutches. "Can we play tennis again soon, Sister McGrath?" she begged. "I liked chasing balls for you that day."

"You bet we can," Delia smiled down at her. "Let's set it up with your mom." It appeared that the title of "Sister" was going to be a permanent fixture, and that she'd better get used to it.

Suddenly Delia wished she were walking into church services with RonJay's Effie skipping along beside her, now chasing a butterfly, now smiling up at her with a face full of sunshine. It occurred to Delia that she had never once attended Sunday services with Ron's family, and a cavity opened behind her ribs.

Even as she half-walked, half-hopped toward the meetinghouse door, Delia was visited with another ghost from her past, a little girl in plaid ribbons singing "I'll be a sunbeam for Him" at the top of her lungs. In front of that little girl, gangly Sister Blauser waved her arms vigorously, her eyeglasses jumping on a loose chain around her neck as she mouthed the words for the children, stretching her red painted lips across her protruding front teeth. That was back in the Middle Ages, before the wandering child left both Smithville and the Church. How long since that song had chanced through Delia's consciousness? She'd hate even to guess.

Delia tried to focus on the talks and the Sunday School lesson, but her mind kept flying out to a brushy river bank where yesterday morning a young man's body had been discovered in an uncongenial grave. *How can God allow such things?* she asked silently, almost angrily. *I know he doesn't* cause *them, but he* allows *them. Rather than interfere with one person's agency—a murderer's!—he allows another person to suffer and die needlessly.*

In the case of Delia's friend Cynthia Harper, the consequences were perhaps even more tragic. Her two little boys were left motherless and fatherless. By the time Sunday School ended, Delia, a squirmer by nature, wasn't sure she wanted to sit at attention for yet another hour. Susan seemed to sense Delia's disquiet, but didn't say anything. She introduced Delia to a tall, broad woman who was principal in a local high school, and went off to meet her Laurel class.

The Relief Society lesson, as it turned out, was on grief and solace. Delia's thoughts, winging west yet again, landed at her father's funeral that June day just months ago in Smithville. She could see his still form, not lifelike at all, not as if sleeping, but chalky white, despite his perennial suntan, and very dead, stretched stiffly in a closed casket beneath the pulpit. Above him the speakers described someone who had nothing to do with the cold shell lying there. At the time, Delia didn't seem to know either of them, the shell or the subject of the appreciative eulogies. She had felt suspended somewhere outside his life, adrift in a galaxy of grief.

What came back to her now, with almost startling clarity, were the two songs he had years earlier indicated that he wanted sung at his funeral, whenever that might be. They were songs long since displaced from the official church hymn book, but they had brought her father solace in life. Perhaps he intended for them to bring his wife and daughter solace after he left them.

> . . . Does faith begin to fail, is hope departing,
> And think you all in vain those falling tears?
> Say not the Father hath not heard your prayer;
> You shall have your desire, sometime, somewhere,
> You shall have your desire, sometime, somewhere.

It was not the voices of her brother Paul and his wife Marcia in the funeral service that played through Delia's memory, but her father's mellow, diffident tenor, as the little girl of her past sat above him on the back steps, listening, while he worked on his boots with saddle soap, or mended a bridle. And if the task lasted long enough, she was sure to hear the other song.

> Not now, but in the coming years,
> It may be in the better land,

We'll read the meaning of our tears,
And there, sometime, we'll understand.
Then trust in God thro' all thy days;
Fear not, for He doth hold thy hand;
Tho' dark thy way, still sing and praise;
Sometime, sometime, we'll understand.

Delia realized that her father had never expected everything to work out fairly in this life. If we could count on absolute justice here, we wouldn't need a whole lot of faith, now, would we? she could almost hear him saying. She also remembered another thought, though the author's name escaped her: "There are two things in life, suffering and the end of suffering."

That evening, as Delia was studying some fifteenth century literary texts for Angie's class, all the while giving thanks for Edith Wharton and Mark Twain, her phone rang. Gordon.

"You're awfully extravagant," she chided, "calling twice in three days."

"Not extravagant at all. I charged it to *your* calling card. Just wanted to make sure that you're sitting home pining for me on a Sunday night."

"It's the only entertainment in town. The bars are all closed on Sunday. It's a darned shame."

"Look, I know you're preparing for classes tomorrow, so I won't keep you long."

"*My* classes are all set. It's Angie's I'm sweating over. Her last treatment knocked her for a real loop, and I'm teaching for her tomorrow."

"Will I get to meet the Turners when I come out?"

"Probably. Angie should be doing better by then. I hope so, anyway. One day of Thomas Malory is about all I can handle."

"Aha! King Arthur and his merry knights of the round table."

Delia was stunned. "You're right. How did you know that? Nobody knows that except a few nutty English teachers."

"And a nutty cowboy or two. I think it's wonderful stuff. Very romantic, all that chivalry."

"Everybody I know thinks Arthur was invented by Lerner and Loewe, or maybe Rodgers and Hammerstein. If you were here, I'd make *you* teach the class. Then I'd sign you up as a contestant on a quiz show. Start memorizing the rest of the encyclopedia."

"I've already got the encyclopedia down. Give me an assignment that's challenging," he joked.

"Okay, try this for size." Delia's voice dropped. "Why would anyone kill a young man—a boy, really—and bury him by the river?"

Gordon grew immediately serious. "One of your students?" he asked quietly.

"Not mine, but very likely somebody's. He's the right age."

"It's bothering you quite a lot, isn't it?"

"You mean it shows?"

"It does to me."

At that point, Delia's composure broke. "Oh, Gordon! I might have seen the men who did it! I was near there, and I haven't told anyone!"

"Whoa, hold on a minute. Tell me about it. You were where?"

With the barrier dropped at last, Delia poured out the events of that Monday night two weeks back, when she had first seen the pickup truck near the river and then seen its occupants up close outside the Circle K.

"Did they see you?" Gordon asked at last, his voice thin.

"With these metal sticks I use for walking, I don't exactly fade into the woodwork," she said.

"Are you going to the police?"

"I don't know. Maybe I'll wait until the coroner sets the time of death. If it's more recent, then there's no connection."

Gordon was silent for a moment. "I'm sorry on two counts," he said finally. "Sorry someone died like that, and sorry you were alone out there at night. Why do you take chances like that?"

"Don't lecture me. I don't need a lecture right now."

"What you need is a spanking."

"You sound like my mother. And by the way, don't say anything to her about this. It's bad enough having you on my case."

"Well, somebody should be on your case. You scare me, m'love."

Delia could hear the frustration in Gordon's voice and was relieved when he dropped the subject.

"Speaking of your mother," he said, "I went by the old homestead last night and got your books."

"Did she seem all right?"

"Not very talkative, but all right." Gordon didn't mention Polly McGrath's visitor from Cheyenne.

The balance of the conversation related to Gordon's arrival on Thursday. Yes, he received the map she had sent and thought he could find her place, if he could tell which way was north. He would rent a car at O'Hare airport and drive up to Jefferson. "If it's a three-hour drive, you can ignite the rockets around six," he said.

"I'll send Begonia out in her balloon-print shirt to flag you down," Delia laughed. "I haven't told her yet that I have a 'gentleman friend' coming from the West. She'll be so excited when she meets you that she won't be able to sleep. She's worried I'm going to be an old maid."

"So am I. That's why I'm coming."

"Hey! You're closer to being an old bachelor than I am to being an old maid."

"See? We can save each other from a horrible fate."

"Oh, it's not so horrible when you contemplate the alternatives—being saddled to some truck cowboy for the rest of one's days, for example."

"I can see how a man might object to that, yes, but for a woman? Nothing short of heaven on earth," Gordon chuckled.

The late news on channel three Sunday night was still full of the story about the body found at the river. Jefferson had its share of auto thefts and student pranks and protests, but all in all, it was not a violent town. A murder caught everyone's attention, and this was an especially ugly and puzzling one. It wasn't the upshot of domestic violence, and so far it hadn't been linked to other criminal activity.

The body had been tentatively identified through student photo ID records as that of a sophomore at Jefferson who had registered but had not turned up for classes. The name would not be released until the parents confirmed the identification, the announcer said. Precise time of death was difficult to establish, but the body had apparently been buried well over a week. The parents, who reside in a wealthy suburb on Chicago's north shore, were expected to arrive from abroad tonight. They hadn't missed their son because they had been in Europe on business.

Delia flipped the television off and tried to review her notes for Monday's classes. Concentration was difficult, and when she finally went to bed, sleep wouldn't come. Every time Delia closed her eyes, the dark river and the faint strip of road leading to it sprang to the surface of her mind. She could see a young man's face frozen in terror, blood oozing through his Ralph Lauren shirt, a tan deck shoe protruding from a huge black mound. Then a big pickup truck would lunge toward her, and a hoary head would screech at her from a sagging doorway.

Delia knew she should have called the police, and frankly wondered why she hadn't. Could she in all honesty attribute it to fear for her safety, or was it moral laziness—aversion to entanglement in the case and the disruption it could bring to her life? In any event, the delay in reporting what she had seen would look bad. At last, Delia threw off the comforter that served as both blanket and bedspread and crossed the bedroom to the sliding glass door that opened onto her small second-story balcony.

Leaning heavily on her crutches, she flung the door wide to the moonless night and breathed deeply. A slight breeze rustled the aged forsythia bushes by the alley, and a shiver rippled across her bare arms. This was going to be one of those nights, she could tell, when her thoughts became a maze of frightening dead-end passages, and her mind couldn't find an exit. Sleep finally came, just minutes, it seemed to her, before National Public Radio clicked on to inform her of the latest crisis in the Middle East.

Nine o'clock found Delia in front of her first flock of students, an advanced writing class. By nine on a good day, the students were at least semi-awake, and so was their teacher. But on Mondays, even though the young people generally arrived before the bell sounded, they slouched dully in their seats until Delia got things going. Expository writing was a required course, and nowhere near their idea of a good time. Delia told Angie, whose only class began at eleven this term, that she was the anti-Folger for this batch of students—the *worst* part of their waking up.

It was obvious when Delia swung in on crutches with her loaded backpack that today was not an ordinary drab Monday. The student newspaper carried the story of the presumed murder, under a large banner headline, and Delia's class was humming with it. Dan Marstein had attended high school in a north shore suburb of Chicago and was speculating about the victim's identity.

Many of the students were upset, a few were outraged. Some sat in stunned silence, while others were ready to write off both God and the human race. Delia listened for several minutes before entering the conversation. Then she encouraged the group to pursue the subject, to think about what had happened and its implications. She foresaw some impassioned writing coming out of this tragedy, and some soul-searching.

"There can't be a God!" a boy in a Save the Whales cut-off sweat-shirt cried. "How could there be, and this kind of garbage go on?"

"There might be one, but he gone on vacation. Ain't nobody safe on this green earth," a girl in the second row responded.

An older student, who clearly regarded himself as more sophisti-cated and wise than his younger classmates, spoke up. "We are all vermin," he declared in a superior tone. "How could God possibly care about us? We are incapable of absolute virtue. We are driven by instinct and self-interest, and God made us that way."

"How about the rest of you?" Delia interrupted. "Do you agree with what's been said?"

"No . . . no, I don't," protested a boy who so far had never uttered a word in class. He seemed embarrassed at having spoken up, but Delia urged him to continue.

"Well," he said, "I just don't like blaming God for the bad things people do." He paused and the others waited, shocked. "We can do good, too, you know," the boy added, looking at the floor.

Delia's mind seized the phrase. That was it. The boy knew better than all of them. She remembered her own angry meditation yesterday. In her disappointment and grief, she had wanted to assign blame—for the student's death, for her father's death, for all of it. If not on God for allowing terrible things to occur, then on the prin-ciple of agency (which God authored), human choice, that virtually guaranteed murder and mayhem. But the boy had something: "We can do good, too," he had said. The other side of agency. Delia moved to the chalkboard and wrote his words.

"That's your subject for an impromptu theme. Take out pen and paper and start writing," she said.

By the end of the school day, Delia was physically exhausted and emotionally drained. She called Angie in the late afternoon to report that Angie's students had survived the ordeal of being taught by someone who didn't know what she was talking about. "The only thing that saved me was the crutches," Delia said. "I told them that anyone who complained or poked fun got smacked with an aluminum lance or kicked with an armored leg, and they were good as gold." Angie reported that she was already feeling some better and could pick up the pieces on Wednesday.

"Don't rush it. I like your kids better than mine. Mine refuse to be intimidated any longer," Delia said. She purposely didn't bring up the boy's death—neither of them had the energy to deal with it, she knew.

At about nine that evening, as Delia was sipping apple juice from a bottle and studying for Tuesday's classes, the doorbell rang. Thinking it was probably Begonia, Delia hopped to answer the summons. Her standard study attire these days consisted of baggy gray sweats with the elastic removed from the right ankle to accommodate her cast. Cooler weather brought the snuggly comfort of sweats, and Delia avowed she could never live at the equator, unless she lived at ten thousand feet. In spring, it felt just as good to shed the thick fleece and haul out the cutoffs and T's. Instead of Delia's plucky little neighbor, however, there stood her visiting teachers, Mary Beth Archer and Susan Fines.

"Sorry we didn't call," Mary Beth said. "This isn't an official visit. We took a chance you'd be home." Mary Beth looked at Susan. "It was Susan's idea. She's been worried about how you get to school, among other things. Do you need help?"

"C'mon in. I'll take you whenever I can get you," Delia smiled. "And no, I manage with the bus just fine. But it's family home evening tonight. You never come on Mondays," Delia said. "I thought I'd be safe in my sweats on Monday for sure."

"We have our 'event' quite early—so the younger ones can get to bed," Mary Beth said. "Susan called me, and here we are. And we brought treats, concocted by our children. Multi-colored Sugar Smacks, fused by melted chocolate and marshmallows, is the house special at the Archers' tonight," laughed Mary Beth.

"Not so at the Fines," said Susan. "I didn't dare bring what we had. It was build your own burrito night. There were no limits. All I can say is that it's a good thing we were out of dog food."

"We won't stay. We just wanted you to know we haven't forgotten you," Mary Beth said.

"I'm glad you came. I could use some company tonight."

"We were shocked at the death of that student," Mary Beth said, sitting on one end of the sofa. "Has his name been released yet?"

Delia shook her head gloomily. "Not that I know of."

"Is that what you were thinking about in Sunday School?" Susan asked quietly. "You seemed preoccupied."

"What I was thinking about was the injustice of it all—the evil, the suffering, the dying, and God supposedly watching over all of it and allowing it."

"He has to," Mary Beth shrugged. "We inhabit mortal bodies, and we have agency."

"But what about justice? Does agency preclude anything resembling justice in this life?" Delia asked.

Susan, who was generally less talkative than Mary Beth on these visits, entered the discussion. "But *I* can act justly," she said, pausing, "and *you* can act justly."

When Susan said that, the student's words from this morning, Gerard Mannion's words, reverberated in Delia's head: "We can do good, too, you know."

"You're right, of course," Delia said. "You're absolutely right. In mortality, we are the authors of justice, if there is any justice—in our individual lives and in the institutions we create and sustain. God is the author of eternal justice, but he leaves the business of mortal justice to us."

"He inspires and instructs us when we let him, but he requires us to choose. Have you a Book of Mormon handy?" Susan asked hesitantly.

"Sure, hardly used—*yet*," Delia confessed with a wry smile. "I'll get it." She went into her study and returned with a quadruple combination, a gift from her parents some years ago.

Susan opened the navy blue leather cover and turned to Alma, to the chapters of Alma's counsel to his erring son, Corianton. "Alma promises us eternal justice if we practice personal justice in mortality," Susan said. "Do you mind if I read a little?" She seemed a bit embarrassed to be leading out this way. With her head bowed over the text, she read softly the fourteenth verse of the forty-first chapter of Alma:

> Therefore, my son, see that you are merciful unto your brethren; deal justly, judge righteously, and do good continually; and if ye do all these things then shall ye receive your reward; yea, ye shall have mercy restored unto you again; ye shall have justice restored unto you again; ye shall have a righteous judgment restored unto you again; and ye shall have good rewarded unto you again.

Delia remembered something Albert Schweitzer had said along these lines in his *Memoirs of Childhood*. She excused herself briefly, found the volume in the den, and read it to her visiting teachers:

> Does my behaviour in respect of love effect nothing? That is because there is not enough love in me. Am I powerless against the untruthfulness and the lies which have their being all around me? The reason is that I myself am not truthful enough. Have I to watch dislike and illwill carrying on their sad game? That means that I myself have not yet completely laid aside small-mindedness and envy. Is my love of peace misunderstood and scorned? That means that I am not yet sufficiently peace-loving.

Mary Beth and Susan nodded. "Yes," said Mary Beth, "he could have added that if I see too much injustice in the world, maybe I myself am not sufficiently just."

"Schweitzer, like Alma, saw the power inherent in the righteous behavior of one person. And if many righteous 'ones' combine, the world can be transformed," Delia said thoughtfully.

Susan signalled to Mary Beth, then stood. "It's late, and you still have work to do. Thanks for teaching us."

"It's you who have taught me, as always," Delia smiled, moving with them to the door. Each of the two women hugged her, and they left. Delia stood a long time, gazing at the dim glow of manufactured light emanating from the small lamps spaced evenly along the Morningside walkways.

CHAPTER FIVE

It was after six p.m. Thursday, and Begonia Slopek had taken it into her head to check the condition of the nylon top she was counting on to cover her venerable Pontiac convertible and herself now that fall had made its annual appearance in Jefferson, Wisconsin. Not that she intended to close the car in for good just yet, but she liked to get the jump on things. Night riding was pretty chilly these days, even with the heater going full blast.

After all, she told herself, *the lid has been down since before I got busted and spent three years in the hoosegow. And me innocent as a newborn babe the whole time. And here this poor vehicle sat under a canvas tarp in storage, without a top to its name. A person would think someone would've had the presence of mind to remove the boot, charge the battery, push the button, and raise that sad sack of a top before throwing canvas over the whole works.*

Begonia was standing tiptoe on her left foot and stretching across the right rear fender, trying with all her might to free the top's protective vinyl boot from its mooring above the trunk when a dark green Chevy Lumina with Illinois plates eased into the guest parking space next to her. On the other side of the Pontiac sat Delia McGrath's Subaru hatchback, gathering grime. Begonia was torn between curiosity over the newcomer and reluctance to lose her hold on the stubborn boot. With a sigh, she slid to the ground and steadied herself with the four-footed cane she had left leaning against the car door.

"Can I help you with that?" The most gorgeous man Begonia had ever seen this side of the movies and the Sears catalogue stepped around the front of the green Lumina. By gorgeous, Begonia didn't mean *pretty*. She meant robust and healthy-looking, sort of Robert Redfordish, only bigger and younger. She hadn't seen him around here before, but she hoped she would see him around again. Not that he was her type. Elmer Roy was more her type. But she could see right off that he was her neighbor's type, yesiree. She'd like to snare him on the spot and hand-deliver him to Delia.

"Why yes, young man, if you don't mind. I seem to be a foot or two short for this job."

"So this is the famous Pontiac convertible. I'd have known it anywhere."

Begonia eyed the speaker suspiciously. "And just how's that, might I ask? You're not coming to repossess it, are you? It's paid for, I swear on a stack of Bibles." Begonia leaned back against the aged machine and spread her arms protectively across the side of it.

Gordon Foster laughed and began unfastening the boot. "This beauty is all yours," he said. "I have no designs on it, honest." He removed the cracking vinyl cover and set it on the trunk. "Now," he said, "what next?"

"What *was* next can wait. What *is* next is who are you, and wait'll you see my neighbor. You're not married, are you?"

Gordon laughed again. "Nope, I'm afraid not."

"Sit tight, don't move an inch. Have I got a surprise for you." Begonia left Gordon half-sitting, arms folded, on her left front fender while she made a beeline for Delia's door. After ringing the bell several times, she looked back to make sure the fellow hadn't been a figment of her imagination, like Marley's ghost. It would be just her luck to have him disappear into thin air. She grinned and waved her cane at him, almost convinced that he was indeed flesh and blood.

While Begonia waited for Delia to answer her door—those crutches still slowed the girl down some—she assessed her prize. Khaki Docker pants and long-sleeved navy polo shirt were just right for him, she thought approvingly. Even the tan canvas sneakers on his feet were perfect. Delia was going to thank her for this till the end of her days.

Finally the door opened. With relief, Begonia saw that her neighbor was actually wearing a decent pair of crinkly nylon warmups and a fresh white turtleneck. Though Delia looked smart enough when she went to work, her study attire in the evenings left a lot to be desired in Begonia's opinion. A term like "casual" was way too complimentary. Why, the Goodwill Industries wouldn't want some of that stuff, especially those beat-up sandals!

Begonia's own tastes ran to elastic waist polyester pants and colorful tops with matching canvas princess shoes from K-Mart. She liked to look cheery because she was. In fact, Begonia was probably the cheeriest person she knew, though Elmer Roy came in a close second. "Let a smile be your umbrella," her mother used to say, and Begonia had always tried to. Of course, it was harder to do when she was in the pen, but that was all behind her now, thank goodness for small favors.

"Hello, dear . . . ," Begonia began, but Delia was looking beyond her. Begonia followed her gaze to the figure leaning against the Pontiac, grinning. "There's a hunk out here I want you to meet . . . ," Begonia tried again. "Wait'll you see. I don't know his name . . ."

Delia looked down and patted her neighbor's cheek. "I know him already," she whispered and started down the walk, first slowly, then faster. Gordon met her halfway, and they stood smiling at each other a long moment.

"Do you want your hug with or without aluminum sticks in your ribs?" he grinned.

"I think I'll take it without," she said, dropping her crutches and looping her arms around his neck. He picked her up and swung her around, cast and all, then carried her to the front step and deposited her at the astonished Begonia's feet.

"What do you think?" Gordon asked, addressing Begonia. "Will she do?"

"She'll do just fine," Begonia declared, and with a pleased smile descended the steps and marched toward the waiting convertible.

"They're here," Howard Turner called to his wife as the green Lumina crunched to a stop in the first fallen elm leaves on the Turner driveway. Fully aproned in black and white stripes, the middle-aged, balding Howard was barbecuing chicken for a celebratory supper on the night of Gordon's arrival in Jefferson. Angie was inside slicing hard-boiled eggs onto the potato salad. The patio table was set for four, and the dog had been banished to his fenced-in run.

Wiping his hands on a nearby towel, Howard left the chicken and met Delia and Gordon at the deck stairs. The leaves still clinging to the elm branches were golden in the setting sun, arching over the pair like the ceiling of a cathedral, and the very air took on the ruddy color of the sky. Gone were the humid evenings of summer and the mosquitoes that thrived on them. One needed a sweater now, and it was good to feel the scratchy wool on the arms.

Gordon and Howard didn't wait for Delia to introduce them, but instead grasped each other's hands like old friends meeting after years of separation. They looked each other squarely in the eye and shook hands with a firm grip. Just then Angie came out the French doors from the kitchen, potato salad in one hand, basket of hard rolls in the other.

"Hey, you don't look like a cowboy at all! Delia promised us a gen-yoo-wine fourteen-karat cowboy. Where are your boots and spurs?" Angie cried, looking her visitor over.

"Delia told me folks out here were civilized, and that I was to try to act proper, and dress proper. I wasn't sure I could do it, but here I am," Gordon replied.

"My one chance to entertain a real cowboy, and Delia spoils it for me. I'd appreciate it if you'd at least exaggerate that western drawl, and raise your voice a little for the neighbors' benefit." Setting the salad and rolls on the table, Angie stepped toward Gordon. "Come over here. I'm not settling for a measly old handshake," she declared. "When a man arrives looking as good as you do, I settle for nothing less than a twenty-second squeeze."

She turned to Delia. "Time us," she said, "twenty seconds. If I weren't still under the effects of chemotherapy, we'd go for a record." Angie had finished her scheduled treatments, and was beginning to recover both her strength and her natural optimism. Whether the breast cancer had been permanently arrested was something no one knew. She and Howard were learning to live with the uncertainty.

Predictably, the Turners and Gordon Foster hit it off from the start. He was different from Gabe, true, but they could see that he suited Delia, perhaps in ways that Gabe didn't. He was more rough cut, but gentle inside and funny. Delia, after all, was only about one-half scholar, as she said, and one-half desert rat; whereas Gabe, whom they liked immensely, was maybe four-fifths scholar and no-fifths desert rat. Gordon was also intelligent, they could see that, too. Loaded with horse sense and full of blarney, as Howard's deceased father would have put it.

After supper, Howard turned off the deck lights and the four friends traded their chairs for patio recliners. The light from the kitchen window streamed into the night, faintly illuminating the table and deck railing. Howard spoke first.

"How safe it all seems. Sitting here, one could almost believe that the world is a peaceful place—no war, no violence, no greed, no want."

"Nights like this lull us to sleep," Angie said. "And yet, a boy in expensive shoes and a Ralph Lauren shirt can wind up in a shallow hole by the river, even in a town like Jefferson."

"Has he been positively identified yet?" Howard asked. "I haven't heard the news today."

Delia stiffened, and Gordon reached over to find her hand. "Last I heard," she said, "the parents of the missing student had been located and were coming to make a positive identification. The police still aren't saying anything about the time or cause of death."

"I suppose an autopsy will be performed, if it hasn't already," Howard speculated. "Do the police have any leads?"

"They don't seem to be saying," Delia said, wishing the conversation would turn to something else.

"My students were all up in arms about it Monday," Howard added, "but didn't know what to do. It's not as if they can march on city hall or boycott classes to let off steam."

"Man's inhumanity to man," Delia grimaced. "Why do we continue to hurt each other? Why this love affair with evil?"

"There will always be evil," Gordon said, "so long as Satan is loose in the world." He paused. "The question is, how long will we personally sidestep it? We are mighty addicted to comfort."

Delia glanced over at him. Was he prodding her, or only making a general observation?

"Well," said Angie, "I prefer not to put all the blame on the old serpent. He doesn't have any power over us that we don't give him."

Gerard's words came back yet again and lodged in Delia's mind: "We can do good, too." That's what Angie was saying.

Later, on the way back to Delia's condominium, Gordon returned to the subject. "Have you told the police what you saw?"

Delia studied the lighted windows and the closed drapes of houses they were passing and shook her head. "No guts," she said.

"I'll go with you," Gordon offered, but she didn't respond.

"Want me to make some coffee?" she asked when they reached her door at Morningside condominiums. "I don't indulge anymore, but I keep it on hand for my civilized friends."

"I'll settle for water," Gordon said, waiting for Delia to find her key. "Seems I promised a certain pair of missionaries to make a stab at giving up some of my old vices."

Delia looked at him in surprise. He hadn't said anything about this in their telephone conversations.

"I'm doing it as an example to you," he grinned, "and because I want to impress your mother."

"I warn you, she doesn't impress easily."

"And neither does her daughter," he replied, lifting her off the landing and planting a kiss on her nose while her crutches clattered noisily down the steps.

"Be careful. Begonia is bound to be watching. We don't want to start talk in the neighborhood that I'm a loose woman."

"Well, if I have my way, you won't be loose very long. I aim to hogtie you and toss you in the back of my white pickup truck at the earliest opportunity."

Inside, on the sofa, Delia leaned back against the comfort of Gordon's shoulder and stared at the spider making its way across the swirled texture of the painted ceiling. She wondered again how anything, however small, could defy gravity that way. "So you think I should go to the police," she said at last.

"It's something you *can* do," Gordon said softly. "So often we feel helpless because there seems little we can do, individually, toward making this a more just world."

"And if it were you, you'd go?"

"I'd like to think I would."

"I'm quite sure you would," she said with finality, "and I guess I will, too."

He looked down at her and pulled her close to him. They sat that way for a long time, until well past eleven. Finally, she said that she'd better get to bed or she'd be worthless in classes tomorrow. "Come for me at seven-thirty?" she asked. "Let's go make a statement before I lose my nerve. I'm glad you're staying with Howard and Angie. They're better than Howard Johnson any day."

After Gordon left, Delia sat on the sofa, her mind processing the evening's events. It seemed strange to have Gordon in Jefferson, and yet it seemed good, too. She wished she had no classes tomorrow, so they could go off somewhere and have the day to let their lives catch up with each other. Well, there was always Saturday. Nibbling at the peanuts in a wooden bowl on the lamp table, Delia picked up the TV remote control device and clicked it to channel three to catch the late news. A local police detective was talking when the screen crackled to life.

The parents of the dead man had identified the body, the detective said. The deceased was Avery Austin, a freshman at the university from Kenilworth, Illinois. Cause of death appeared to be an overdose of cocaine. There were no wounds or other suspicious marks on the body. The coroner's estimated time of death was approximately three weeks ago. Investigators were focusing on how and why Avery Austin was buried by the river.

Only when she stood did Delia realize that her hand ached from clamping around the remote control gadget. Did this information change anything? Did it relieve her of responsibility? She wished she knew. In any case, Gordon would come for her at seven-thirty a.m., and she would do her duty. There was no ducking out now.

Delia's interview with a police detective the next morning was surprisingly brief. She expected a reprimand for her delay in coming forward, but he clearly had other things on his mind. It was almost disappointing that after her painful battle of conscience, he seemed only mildly interested in the two men with the souped-up truck who had passed Delia near the river that dark night. He would check them out, he said, and let her know if she was needed further.

"I worked myself into a stew for nothing!" she complained to Gordon as they drove toward the university. "I might as well have been reporting a dogfight, for all he cared."

"If there had been mortal wounds on the body, you can bet he'd have been interested," Gordon assured her. "Then, too, maybe he already has the leads he wants. The important thing now is not that the police needed or didn't need what you told them. The important thing is that you made the decision to tell it."

"Why don't I feel noble, then?"

"If you felt noble, you wouldn't be."

Gordon pulled up behind Brandon Hall, and Delia opened the door as he came around to lift her crutches and book pack from the backseat. "What'll you do while I'm in classes?" she asked. "I'm sorry I have a meeting through lunch."

He bent down and kissed her, first on the lips, then noisily, juicily, on the cheek. "Don't worry about me. I just might look up a woman I know in town. Drives a fancy Pontiac convertible and wears a fetching balloon print shirt."

"Well, be cautious. I understand she's spoken for. You know how those southern gentlemen are. You could wind up in a duel at sundown."

"Who would you be rooting for, me or Elmer Roy?"

"I haven't decided. See you at three?"

"Three it is, if I can find my way back here. Unless, of course, the duel is at high noon and I lose." Gordon helped Delia with her backpack, and then he was off. She couldn't get used to seeing him in an ordinary sedan, against a background of ivy-covered campus buildings and a pale midwestern sky.

Delia went straight to her nine o'clock class on the second floor of old Brandon Hall, home of the English Department for as long as anyone could remember. She opted for the stairs, but it was slow going. The students behind her waited, then watched for their chance to squeeze around her. The broad wooden stairs were always crowded during class change; she should have remembered and used the rickety freight elevator, for which she had a key. As she reached the second floor, Gerard Mannion fell in beside her, offering to carry her bag and opening the door to room 220 for her.

"Uh, could I maybe . . . like, talk with you after class?" he mumbled.

"Sure. What's up?"

"Uh, nothin' much. I just thought maybe we could, y'know, talk."

"Come up to my office when we're through here. Do you know where it is?"

"Uh, yeah, I think so. Third floor, right?"

"Right, room 342."

The students in Delia's expository writing class were buzzing once again with the latest developments in the unnatural death of one of their peers.

"Take it from me, the kid's a crackhead," a tall fellow in a Chicago Bulls T-shirt was asserting loudly as Delia dropped her pack on the marred surface of the old wooden desk. She looked at him. "My cousin knew him in high school," he bragged. "Says he was on the stuff then. Rich kid, pretty boy. You know the type."

"No, I guess I don't," said Delia. "All I know is that he's dead, and he shouldn't be."

"It's a jungle out there," the student muttered.

Delia decided to stir the pot. "What has any of this to do with any of you?" she challenged. "After all, you're alive and well. Isn't this someone else's grief?"

The students stopped talking with each other and stared at her in disbelief.

"He's one of us, so we care," came a defensive voice from the rear.

"Oh, do you? And when was the last time you reported a friend for possession of drugs, or snatched a cigarette from a friend's mouth, or took someone's keys to stop him from driving while drunk? If you cared, isn't that what you'd do?" Delia demanded.

No one spoke, then finally a young woman whose coal black hair was braided in neat thin ropes all over her head entered the conversation. "It's called bein' my brother's keeper," she said solemnly, then dropped her eyes.

"No man is an island," Gerard added quietly.

"Remember what you're feeling now," Delia said, "and when you get home, put that energy, that passion, into your sentences. I once heard Ray Bradbury, the great science fiction writer, tell a group of students to write at the top of their hates. And then he paused, adding that they should also write at the top of their loves, for it was a great privilege to be alive in this world."

After class, Gerard made the slow ascent with Delia to the third floor. Taking a key from her denim skirt pocket, she opened the door to a small, cluttered office and motioned him toward the only available chair. The desk was stacked with student papers and textbook advertisements from publishing firms.

"If you don't have time, like, right now, I can come back," he offered.

"No, now is fine. I have time. Sit down, please. What's on your mind?"

Gerard sat, but he didn't relax. "Well, uh, someone told me you were a Mormon. I mean, are you?"

Delia was taken back. "It's debatable. Let's say I'm in the process of trying to be. Why do you ask?"

"Well, uh, one of the girls in my institute class says she's in your ward. I'm in the First Ward. I thought maybe, like, I could talk with you. Because, like, maybe you haven't always been active, and stuff."

"You're not thinking to follow my bad example, are you?"

"Oh, no . . . I mean, I'm not planning to go inactive or anything. I just don't know . . . like . . . if I want to go on a mission. That kind of stuff. My parents get upset, like real upset, so I can't talk to them."

The irony of someone's coming to her for counseling about a mission was not lost on Delia, and she responded slowly. "In class, you quoted John Donne—'no man is an island, no man stands alone.' Do you believe that?"

"I guess so."

"Do you want to be an island, alone, or as Donne says, would you rather be a part of the main? In other words, do you want to live only for yourself, or do you want to make a difference in this world? Do you want the world to be better for your having lived?"

"I guess maybe I want to make a difference," Gerard said hesitatingly, studying his loafers and tugging at the ragged edge of his used textbook.

"Let me tell you a story of some people I met this past summer, after I acquired this plastic box on my leg and perhaps a little sense."

Delia then began to tell about young Elders Kirk and Hochtel, about their quiet persistence and their unfeigned caring as, armed with the pure love of Christ, they courageously entered the lives of three strangers and changed those lives forever. She described Jennifer's abusive resistance and her own condescension, and she told of Gordon's kindly but somewhat distant indulgence. Lesser men would have given up, Delia told Gerard, but they never did. They kept coming and coming, and as a result three people have found their way, or are finding their way.

"And there might have been others, too," Gerard said.

"Yes, undoubtedly there were others, too."

"I never thought about it that way before. Thanks. Uh, can I shake your hand?" Gerard stood and gathered his books.

"I'd be honored if you would. I want to come to your farewell, if you go."

"Thanks, I'll let you know." Gerard gave Delia's hand another shake and then disappeared into the hall. She pushed her chair back from the desk, picked up her crutches, and swung to the end of the hall. There at the window, she leaned a long while, watching a single white sail glitter across the bay and disappear behind the mass of trees on Picnic Point. Delia knew it was time for her to take her own advice, to live for something other than herself. As she returned to her office to review the reading assignment for her next class, she felt better about the world and its future than she had just one short hour ago.

Pushing through one of Brandon Hall's rear doors, Delia could see that Gordon wasn't alone, nor was he in the Chevy Lumina. There beside him in the front seat of a familiar rusted blue Pontiac convertible were Elmer Roy and Begonia, looking as pleased as punch. Begonia sat so low in the deep old seat that Delia could scarcely see more than the top of her head and her waving hand. But there was no question about who it was. They were all in sweaters.

"Yoo-hoo, yoo-hoo!" Begonia cried, waving to beat the band. "C'mon, dear, Gordon's taking us on a picnic, if it doesn't rain. A little cool air never hurt anyone."

Delia checked the sky. Even as she looked, an ominous cloud began blocking out the sun.

"You're driving, dear. We have to preserve my hairdo, so we'll put the boys in the back," Begonia informed her. "But before we go, Gordon promised to take us to the student union building, to see the beer."

"To see the beer?" Delia asked, puzzled.

"You know, the beer people drink there. Other schools don't even allow beer on campus, but Jefferson *serves* it. That nice neighbor boy told me, and I've been dying to see it ever since. Elmer Roy says he won't believe it till he sees it with his own blue eyes."

"Well, leave the Pontiac up here with that temporary parking permit I got for the semester. There's no parking by the union. We can walk down the hill."

In all, the experience did not quite live up to Begonia's expectations. The room where the beer was served did not look at all like a bar, much less a den of iniquity. It was only a cafeteria. Still, Begonia and Elmer Roy took satisfaction in seeing that the questionable liquid was imbibed from mugs rather than from more innocent fountain glasses.

"Well, at least we can say we've seen it," Begonia said as she settled herself into the Pontiac, still puffing from her climb up Brandon Hill. "Here, Elmer Roy, you keep my cane back there so I don't bang it on Delia's cast. She has to drive with her bum leg flopped over the hump," Begonia explained to Gordon. "She's good at it, too, though she wasn't so hot at first. Her braking left a lot to be desired."

"Where to?" Delia asked, crossing her eyes and smiling at Begonia.

"Where else? Picnic Point. We've got food in the back, and two blankets, one for us and one for you. We don't intend to interfere, do we Elmer Roy?" Begonia always raised her voice a little when she spoke to Elmer Roy because he was hard of hearing. He only grinned and shook his round, white-fringed head. Delia noticed that he still wore a tie. She had never seen him without one.

Later, while Begonia and Elmer Roy dozed on their red plaid stadium blanket, Delia and Gordon made their way to the end of the point and sat on a big rock to watch the sailboats and shorebirds. She wasn't exactly attired for hiking, but wanted some time for talk.

"So this is your world," Gordon said.

"Well, it's one of them."

"It's nice, but awful wet."

"A man who lived on white water all those years ought to appreciate it."

"Desert rivers and rafts are a far cry from midwestern lakes and sailboats."

"I don't know where I belong anymore. When I'm in the West, it feels as though I could never be at peace anywhere else. When I'm here, the desert fades a bit and this seems okay."

"Do you want to teach English all your life?"

"Yes, I think I do. Teach English and hike desert canyons. And ride in dirty white trucks," she added, smiling at him.

"I can arrange the last," he said, taking her hand and kissing the end of her index finger. "It's the other part that worries me."

Just then, lightning flared in the sky behind them and they heard the rumble of thunder.

Gordon slapped his leg. "Darn, just as I was getting ready to propose."

"Propose what?"

"I ain't sayin', missy. Y'all jes' wait and see."

Delia laughed and slid off the rock. "Well, don't wait too long. I might get a better offer."

"One dressed in a beard?"

"More likely one driving a Rolls Royce, and speaking with an enchanting British accent."

Another flash and roar brought Gordon off the rock, and the two of them sprinted—if one can be said to sprint on crutches—for the blankets. Elmer Roy and Begonia were ahead of them, however, and had the car loaded when they arrived.

"Does the top work on this machine?" Delia cried as she lowered herself into the driver's seat.

"The boot's off, so try it," Begonia shouted above a sudden blast of wind. "There's the button! I couldn't make it work yesterday."

Delia pushed the button. The mechanism whirred momentarily, then went silent.

"Let's make a dash for it!" Gordon yelled. "If you go fast enough, we won't get wet even if it rains."

"Ooo, I hope it rains, and that we get a rainbow!" Begonia cried. "I just love a sky full of ribbons!"

Throwing gravel across the parking area, Delia spun off the point as the wind tore at her hair and the first big drops of rain splattered the windshield. Begonia waved merrily at several joggers leaving the point in a race against the storm. Seeing the old convertible with the lid off, the joggers sent up a rowdy cheer, and Delia honked in reply. By the time the picnickers reached the shelter of the Morningside carport, they were all somewhat damp and more than a little blown. Gordon's theory worked fairly well except at stoplights, when all they could do was sit while the rain pelted their heads and shoulders. Gordon offered to take Elmer Roy home in the Lumina, but Begonia wouldn't hear of it.

"I've got to take him in and dry him out first," she said. "What will his people think if he shows up to home looking like a drowned rat?"

"Besides," Elmer Roy grinned, "we haven't finished our powwow yet, have we, Miss Begonia?"

Begonia giggled. "As a matter of fact, we haven't. We can put away the food remains while we talk." She turned to Delia and Gordon. "Get on with you now. You young folks have more to do than sit around and jaw with us old folks. Besides," she whispered to Delia, "I think Elmer Roy's working up to something. He's agitated," Begonia added confidingly.

Inside her place, Delia turned on the gas log and found towels for herself and Gordon. She pulled a jug of apple cider from the fridge and filled two ceramic mugs. "Here, put these in the microwave, would you? I spill anything runny without a lid."

"Aha, so you need me for something, after all."

"Yep, you can be my liquid transporter. Are you good for anything else?—besides saving helpless women from flash floods, that is."

"When I was little, my mother and I had a favorite routine relating to that subject. She used to come up behind me, wrap her arms across my chest, kiss me on top of the head, and ask, 'What are you good for?' I'd reply, 'Good to love,' and she'd hug me and we'd laugh."

"Do you know, that's almost the first thing you've told me about your mother. Bring the cider mugs in by the fire and tell me more. I know your father's dead, but you haven't said much about that, either. Seems we've been all wrapped up in my calamities ever since we met."

Gordon sat on the rug in front of the sofa, and Delia leaned against a throw pillow behind him, resting her legs along the sofa's familiar cushions. While they talked, night came on, and the dancing light from the fireplace played across his profile, etching copper streaks in his windblown hair. Occasionally she smoothed his hair and touched his cheek, and sometimes he tenderly kissed the palm of her hand. Neither of them reached for a light switch.

"Well," Gordon began, "I think I told you that my father was a smoke jumper in the summers. He was going back to school, studying to be a geologist. He loved the out-of-doors, so smoke jumping seemed the right kind of summer job for him. It worried my mother, but the pay was good. I was just a twirp, and sometimes, when the fire business was slow, we went to his camp to visit him. He taught me a lot about animals and flowers. That's probably why I couldn't ever kill anything."

"He died in a fire, didn't he?"

"Yes. I was only eight. I guess the wind shifted and turned a fire back into the fighters. Four of them died that night."

Delia leaned forward and held him a moment. "What did your mother do?"

"She had worked as a full-time librarian before I was born, but while dad was in school in Boulder she clerked in a bookstore part-time. After he died, she moved back to Denver and got a job in the same library where she had worked before."

"So that's why you know so much about books, and writers like Thomas Malory."

"Yep, it's all her fault. She *ruint* me."

Delia gave his hair a sharp tug.

"Ouch! Hey, be nice, and let me continue."

"Okay, but skip the editorial comments."

"Well, you might almost say I grew up in a library. Mother didn't want me to be a latchkey kid, so I became a library table kid. After school, when I didn't have soccer or baseball, I caught the school bus to the library instead of home. That way she could keep an eye on me, and we could go home together. She never restricted my reading so long as I stayed out of the trashy stuff. My tastes ran from spaceships to King Arthur, and everything in between."

"You had quite an education. Better than mine, by far."

"No, not better. Disorganized, but lots of it. When I finally settled on forestry in college, I never really expected to do anything but run rivers and strum a guitar."

"I'm glad you decided to do something else," she said. "Something like working for the BLM in Smithville."

They sat in silence, transfixed by the restless flames and the luxury of being together. Finally, Gordon spoke. "Hungry?" he asked.

"I could use a snack of some sort. Let's go prowl the town. But first, we'd better rescue Elmer Roy from my scheming neighbor. No man is safe for too long with Begonia."

"I found that out right off; but then, who'd want to be?"

CHAPTER SIX

Saturday was one of those storybook days that in the northern middle west lull even the initiated into believing that winter is still months away, or might skip its annual assault this year. After Friday's rain, the sun arrived as if announced by royal trumpeteers, first glazing, then almost inhaling the puddles that hung around to greet it. The October sun in Wisconsin is a trickster, awaking the believer with a promise of immortal summer one day and dressing the world in frost the next.

Emily Dickinson, New England's reclusive verbal wizard, observed the same phenomenon in Massachusetts. She wrote of "the days when birds come back . . . to take a backward look." On such days, the poet said, the "skies resume the old, old sophistries of June," but it's all "a blue and gold mistake." And today, anyone with a poetic soul would confess with Dickinson that although the "fraud" of such days might not "cheat" the discerning bee, "almost thy plausibility induces my belief."

It was not a morning when even an owl cared to sleep in, and Delia was ready when Gordon called for her at daybreak. They drove east into the sun, to Door County, the spindly peninsular thumb of the Wisconsin mitten. Very like an island, the narrow piece of earth was tempered by the surrounding waters of Lake Michigan. It was a country all its own despite its Wisconsin ZIP code. Here, early Norwegian settlers had found a congenial seascape, and here they did all in their power to duplicate the sea-gnawed homeland they had left. Generation after generation fished the blue waters of the mammoth lake as their fathers had fished the waters of the Atlantic Ocean.

And in the evening, still, a few of the old-timers brought a remnant of their catch to great black kettles of water that had been harrowed to 212 degrees Fahrenheit in the open air above red hot pinewood fires. There, with knives sharp enough to cut tissue paper in one clean swipe, and with educated, instinctive hands, the men rent their slippery booty into handsize chunks and dumped it, skin and all, into the blackened chest-high pots. Then they watched while the contents worked up to a ferocious bubbling.

At precisely the moment the oily froth erupted over the edge and cascaded steaming into the spitting flames, the fish was done. The fishermen then snared their catches for a second time, standing on crude pine stools and dipping large wooden sieves deep into the cauldrons' bellies. Along with great hunks of aromatic fish, the sieves also harvested whole potatoes and onions from the seasoned brew.

After a day of trekking barefooted along white sand beaches—no easy feat on crutches—visiting shops, devouring handfuls of thick-crusted sourdough bread, napping on a sand-gritty blanket, speculating about the future, and smiling over happy things in the past, Delia and Gordon found themselves seated on a rough pine bench at a rough pine table behind a rustic old restaurant, a few scant yards from one of those steaming pots. They were eating just such a meal, served by the grizzled, hump-backed old fellow named Lars who had caught the fish and cooked it. The sweet white meat flaked deliciously in their eager mouths, and they laughed as juice ran down their chins.

Driving back to Jefferson that night, Gordon was unusually quiet and Delia snuggled against him, now and then dozing off as her head rested comfortably on his shoulder. In the backseat were a couple of smooth white rocks she had picked up from one section of beach, intending them as paperweights for her desk. Both travelers seemed reluctant to break the spell, but soon enough the late night streets of Jefferson sponged up the green Lumina and deposited it at Morningside condominiums.

Collecting herself and her things, Delia felt oddly divided. Deliriously happy at what the day had brought, she was also agonizingly sad that it was over. Tomorrow was Sunday, and her magical interlude with Gordon was already slipping into the past. He began teasing a little, trying to lighten her mood. He chided her for carrying rocks home when the whole world was full of rocks, there for the taking wherever one looked, and suggested that her crutches might need a lube job after a day of plowing sand.

She hadn't mentioned church services to him, but as he left, backing slowly down the walk, one hand extended toward her, reluctant to let go, he asked if Mormons were legal in Wisconsin, and if so, would they welcome a heathen in their midst on a Sunday morning.

"I think they can handle it if you mind your manners," she called to him. "Come for me at twenty to nine?"

"Will do, if I can wait that long. I should have brought my trusty guitar to serenade you under your window."

"The neighbor's dog would probably join in the chorus and wake the whole neighborhood."

"That's okay. My singing is worth waking up for."

Delia laughed in spite of herself. He waved and was gone, bursting through the bubble of light she inhabited into the conspiring darkness of the midnight trees and the absent moon. Another thought, a pleasant one, crossed Delia's mind as she lingered at the door, balancing between two aluminum sticks—in the borderland between night and morning, between having and losing. When she saw Gordon again, after tomorrow, she would be walking unaided on two feet. With her hands back, it would be easy to give him an unpremeditated hug, or a playful punch. She had a sudden yearning to stroll with her arm slung through his, or with her hand held tightly in his strong, supple brown one. Something as simple as that. Something she had never done.

It did not go unnoticed in the congregation of the Jefferson Second Ward when Professor Delia McGrath showed up on Sunday with a tan, broad-shouldered fellow none of them had ever seen before. He looked like a Marlboro man in a suit and tie, only better. Even though Delia spoke regularly with her visiting teachers, Mary Beth Archer and Susan Fines, he was news to them, too. It was as though he were a closely guarded secret, a surprise that she was waiting to spring on the world at the auspicious moment. Not that her marital status mattered in the least to most of this segment of the world. Two people who took particular notice of Gordon Foster's presence, however, were Mary Beth Archer and Nelson Farwell.

Nelson was a bachelor who had been in Europe much of the summer, working out the details for a merger between his company, which manufactured industrial drilling equipment, and an Italian company that made parts for such equipment. Mary Beth had broached the subject of Nelson Farwell with Delia a time or two, generating about as much interest as a hamburger stand in a vegetarian colony. Wary of matchmakers and matchmaking—for herself, anyway, though she could see that arranged marriages might have a distinct appeal for parents of today's teenagers—Delia had said she preferred not to go looking for trouble.

But that didn't mean Mary Beth dropped the matter. She blithely regrouped and went to work on Nelson. *Isn't it just like Delia,* she thought that Sunday morning, *to wait till I've got Nelson chomping at the bit and then turn up with a total stranger who could lift Nelson with one hand?* Not that Nelson was unattractive. He just wasn't what Mary Beth's oldest son would call "buff." And perhaps he was a little too smooth, even for Mary Beth's taste. In the Archer family, "smooth" meant cool gone slightly bad, like a banana left in a sunbaked car. Cool too sold on itself. Even Mary Beth's non-judgmental husband Frank, who was pleasantly bumpy himself, appeared to avoid Nelson when he could.

Frank never said anything negative about Nelson, but Mary Beth could tell he wasn't crazy about the man either. As in most wards of any size, there were in the Jefferson Second one or two "social Mormons," people who went through the motions of activity but seemed far more interested in their careers and their entertainments than in the kingdom. Mary Beth privately suspected Nelson to be one of these, but she had thought he and Delia might find things to talk about and enjoy together just the same. And he was, after all, available—a fact not to be sneezed at, in her opinion. Moreover, he played the French horn, and someone had told her he had an impressive library.

Up to her ears in family, Mary Beth could scarcely imagine an eligible adult actually enjoying single life for any length of time, much less choosing it over the preferred option. Ergo, broad-minded as she was about most things, single people over twenty-five worried her. She simply couldn't rest until she got them paired up so they could be happy, like herself. As she saw it, most unmarried people were, by definition, lonely and unfulfilled, regardless of the brave front they might put up. Mary Beth liked Delia very much, but Delia perplexed her nonetheless. She honestly couldn't tell whether Delia was happy or not, or if she even wanted to be married. (Perish the thought!)

Susan Fines, on the other hand, had once commented that living singly was probably preferable to suffering through an abominable marriage. That observation had given Mary Beth pause, but she knew where Susan was coming from. Susan's younger sister was married to a bullying, abusive man with whom she remained because she couldn't support her children on her own. She had married at seventeen and delivered twins at eighteen; then several additional children had appeared in rapid succession, children in whom their father took little interest beyond the grand moment of their conception. Mary Beth also remembered Brigham Young's statement that he had never counseled a woman to follow her husband to the devil.

Oblivious to what either Nelson Farwell or Mary Beth Archer might be thinking, Delia found sitting next to Gordon in the Sego Road chapel a different experience than attending services with him in Utah's Dixie. There, Polly McGrath had been on hand, looking sideways out of the corner of her eye at the two of them, logging and assessing every blink and cough. Polly's scrutiny didn't seem to bother Gordon at all, but it made Delia uncomfortable.

Delia knew that it wasn't for her Gordon was doing this, not for her and not for Elders Kirk and Hochtel either. Nor was it out of curiosity or a feeling of obligation. Delia could sense that a number of things had slipped into place somewhere inside this sweet, funny man, things that were beginning to round out his soul, to fill in the empty spaces. In many ways, the religious quest appeared easier for him than for her. She could see a real advantage to starting from scratch, with no backlog of guilt, recriminations, and regrets. He was not burdened by a rebellious past or disappointed parents.

She, on the other hand, was attempting to retrieve valuables she had dropped by the wayside on a long and hilly journey away from herself. For her, there was no fresh beginning, no way to escape her folly, no way to erase the hurt she had inflicted on her parents. When Gordon flew west this evening, back to Polly McGrath's Zion, what would he be thinking? Would any of Jefferson go with him, tucked in a corner of his navy cloth carry-on? And if he should join the Church, what then?

Sunday afternoon came much too quickly, and Delia stood on her front walk, leaning forward on her second set of legs, watching Gordon's rented car slide out past Begonia's vintage Pontiac. Her eyes grew blurry, and she realized, with unexpected pain, her vulnerability. He looked back to her and waved, and she blew a kiss as he cranked the wheel to the right and drove away. She stood there a long time, then slowly turned and swung toward her front steps.

Glancing up, she saw Begonia at the window, peeking eagerly from behind the drapes. Yes, she thought, Begonia could have scripted the drama—the dropped crutches, the long embrace, the tender kiss, and the tears in the heroine's eyes as the hero rides away into the sunset. Delia knew that Begonia was wild about Gordon. Who wouldn't like him, after all? Even Polly liked him, for Pete's sake. Whatever flaws lurked in the man hadn't shown up yet. At least not any serious ones. Delia decided that, in the matter of flaws, she preferred to remain in ignorance anyway, and made for her front door.

Just as Delia opened it, Begonia burst from hers. "Wait, wait, dear!" she called, waving her cane and hopping toward Delia's walkway.

Delia let the door swing shut, pulled a tissue from the pocket of her warmups, blew her nose, and faced the Slopek court of inquiry. But Begonia fooled her. She was not on a fact-finding mission, after all. Just the opposite, it turned out. Miss Begonia, as the courtly Elmer Roy called her, had a message to deliver—a message of some importance, if one judged by her manner.

"A man came by your place yesterday," Begonia panted, arriving at the bottom of Delia's steps. "Somebody official, I said to myself. Wearing a suit on Saturday, mind you. That alone made me nervous," she added. "I thought maybe I had a new probation officer and he got the wrong door. I should be so lucky. Anyways, he was too young for me and too old for you. Besides which, he couldn't hold a candle to Elmer Roy in my esteem."

Delia glanced at her watch, then back to her neighbor, who went blissfully on. "Y'see, you and your young man were off gallivanting somewheres—it was Saturday, so why wouldn't you be?—so he knocked on my door. Elmer Roy and I, we were watching the Badgers play on the TV, in Oklahoma it was. He interrupted us, and it was the fourth quarter. And wouldn't you know? They lost. Do you follow the Badgers, dear?"

Begonia paused, but not long enough for Delia to get a toe in the conversational door. "I told Elmer Roy, I says, I'm pure poison for the home team. A bona fide, certified jinx. Whenever I watch they lose; when I don't they win. The coach oughtta pay me not to watch, to turn the tube off. No Rose Bowl for the Jefferson Badgers this year, mark my words."

Finally, Delia interrupted. "The man?"

Begonia's face came to a screeching halt, then jolted forward and changed lanes. "Oh yes, . . . the man! Let me think. *Detective* somebody or other, he said." Begonia patted the sides of her red polyester pants where pockets would have been if she had pockets. "He wrote his number down—I've got it somewheres–and wants you to call him." Begonia looked up and motioned Delia closer. Then she spoke in hushed tones, stretching up toward Delia, making slits of her eyes, and glancing left and right. "If you're in trouble with the law, dear," she whispered confidentially, "I'll help you beat the rap. Believe you me, I picked up some tips while I cooled my heels in the slammer."

Momentarily distracted by a russet sugar maple leaf that spiraled down and landed at her feet, Delia smiled in spite of herself. "You can relax, podner," she drawled in a loud whisper, "I ain't robbed a stage in years."

Begonia looked absently at Delia, then knitted her brow and checked inside the open neck of her Minnie Mouse knit top. "Not down there, either," she mumbled, then brightened. "Now I remember. You wait here, dear." Begonia tripped back to her own door and disappeared.

Less than a minute later she emerged waving a yellow slip of paper. "I hope you don't mind it's a little dampish. I had it in the freezer, under the Cool Whip, y'see. I read somewheres, maybe in

Modern Maturity—does your mother subscribe to *Modern Maturity*, dear?—that anything you want to hide from prying eyes, stick it in the freezer. Hot diamonds, you can freeze 'em right with the water in the ice cube tray. Just don't forget and try to crush 'em with your margarita. Fella did that in a movie I saw and drank his wife's diamonds. Didn't know she'd put 'em there. 'Course you don't drink margaritas, do you, dear? Anyways, that won't work if you have a fancy fridge with an ice-making machine. D'you have one a' those machines, dear?"

Begonia had a way of wandering about in whatever subject happened to occupy her. Her mind was a busy road map, and whenever her thought came to a junction, it was as likely as not to divert to a secondary road. The trick was to travel with her across the potholes and through the detours until she could be steered back to a reunion with the main road. The crossword puzzle game, with a twist.

"No, I don't have an ice-maker. Just plastic trays," Delia laughed, "so I can hide any stolen diamonds you might run across. And no, my mother doesn't read *Modern Maturity*. She doesn't trust the AARP any more than she trusts the IRS."

"Why, I love the AARP, dear. Elmer Roy and I might go off to their next convention. If his daughter will let him, that is. She's real straight-laced where he's concerned. She's got a live-in boyfriend, too. Right there, with her children."

Delia remembered Huck Finn's sage observation after Miss Watson had lectured him about smoking. "She took snuff, too," he said, then added, "'course that's all right 'cause she done it herself."

"Your mother really ought to go," Begonia continued enthusiastically. "She'd love it—all that shuffleboard and dancing to Benny Goodman tunes. She might even find herself a beau."

"You don't know my mother," Delia said, dropping to the top step and stretching her legs across the lower two. "The AARP started hounding her to join the minute she turned fifty. She always resented the fact that the organization found out on its own how old she was and then tried to turn her into a senior citizen before she was halfway through middle age."

"Well, they are a little pushy at times, maybe, but Elmer Roy and I love *Modern Maturity*. Especially the ads. Why, they have everything from fancy cruises to tilty beds."

"And now, the phone number?" Delia asked.

"Phone number? . . . Oh, my yes. Here it is, dear." Begonia handed Delia the paper and leaned closer. "Elmer Roy knows a good lawyer if you need one."

Delia feigned shock. "Elmer Roy? I thought he was spotless as a lamb. Why would he need a criminal lawyer?"

"Oh, he is spotless, nobody more so. Sometimes I wish he had a sin or two. Maybe then I could tell him about the pen. But he likes to prepare for all eventualities, in advance. He studies the Yellow Pages—dentists, podiatrists, plumbers, palm readers, piano tuners, lawyers, locksmiths, insect exterminators—you name it, Elmer Roy can recommend one."

"I'll remember that. Thanks for taking the message."

Delia got to her feet, but Begonia snagged her with her cane. "The man, the detective, said to call him any time, day or night. That's his cell phone number. He said he doesn't give it out to just anybody. Do you have a cell phone, dear?"

Delia decided to let Begonia follow that byway on her own. "Nope," she said, opening the door. "I'll let you know if I get busted. You can bake me a cake with a file in it."

Delia's encounter with Begonia had derailed her thoughts from Gordon's leaving enough that she could give attention to other things—namely, preparation for tomorrow's classes. But first, a phone call that she assumed had to do with Avery Austin's death. The detective answered after two rings. He had called by, he said, to tell her what the investigation had turned up. Some pieces of the story came out when police began pressuring the boy's friends for information. A couple of the youngsters broke down under questioning, sobbing out a sorry tale of a marathon Saturday night party fueled by drugs and alcohol. It was their last weekend of freedom before school began, and they had wanted to make the most of it.

Since when is negligent homicide the ultimate weekend experience? Delia asked silently.

The boys' story went like this: Sometime before daylight, Avery had passed out and couldn't be revived. When he turned cold and showed no pulse, the others panicked. Three of them, high on drugs themselves, loaded him into his own car, stole a shovel from a Parks

Department shed, and buried him in brush by the river. Then two of them drove Avery's car to Beloit where they parked it in the lot of a large, twenty-four hour grocery store. The third boy had followed them in another car, and they returned to Jefferson with him.

"We found his car, like they said," the detective added.

Delia took a deep breath. "So my suspicious characters had nothing to do with it."

"Looks that way."

Delia felt both relief and shame. She absently wrapped the coiled phone cord around her left index finger. "Are you through with me?" she asked hesitantly.

"I think so. We'll call you if anything else comes up."

This unexpected outcome to the story left Delia feeling sick inside—sick over the senseless trashing of a young life, sick over a boy's being dumped by his so-called friends to rot like a bag of garbage. His death was tragic in Shakespeare's sense of the word, she realized. Waste. A boy with a whole lifetime to live, gone. Everything he might have been and done, lost. And his friends will have to answer for their deed, too.

Delia also had to deal with her personal culpability in the tragedy, her disappointing failure of both conscience and charity. She had not reported immediately what she had seen, and she had made a hasty leap to judgment. In her heart she had tried and condemned the men in the bronze pickup truck. Just because they looked and acted coarse, even frightening, she was ready to accuse them of murder. She, who had always prided herself on being fair-minded, discovered that she wasn't fair-minded at all.

"You can't judge a book by its cover," her mother used to say, but Polly McGrath hadn't managed to practice that piece of wisdom with much consistency either. Jedediah, on the other hand, seemed to do so simply as a matter of course. He had an uncanny way of seeing past the clothes and the masks to the heart. Delia knew it was a gift. Pure love, Mormon had called it. Gabe was like that, too. Delia felt another stab of pain. She missed him.

Delia moved from cupboards to refrigerator, opening doors and looking for something that might satisfy a craving she couldn't define. Finally she took a new crop McIntosh apple to the patio, but its cool crunch and tangy nectar failed to calm her. The beguiling breeze carried with it just the slightest hint of waiting winter. Her mind was a high-speed blender, spinning thoughts of Avery Austin into the mix with her father and Gordon and Gabe—all of whom, in one way or another, had left her.

Then her mother's image cleared her mental horizon, like the moon popping up above Lake Powell on a cloudless night, and Delia very nearly called Polly McGrath. She attributed the urge to a sense of disconnectedness, of being at sea without compass or lifeline. Something in her wanted to reach out and grab Polly's rope, wanted to be pulled into her mother's admittedly rocky, yet protective, shore.

When the golden lab next door got to his feet and came expectantly to the chain link fence that separated him from Delia, she was tempted to explain to the eager mutt that with Gordon gone, the Avery Austin thing gave her no peace. But as she had suspected, the dog's interest was in her apple, not her story. It was food, not drama, that captured the canine imagination.

"You don't know it, now, but you won't want this," she promised, and chucked the half-eaten apple over the fence. The lab raced to it, sniffed at it, nudged it, then trotted back to see if Delia might not have something more to his liking. "Just goes to show," she said half aloud. "Be careful what you ask for. You might get it, and then what?" One of Polly McGrath's sayings came to mind: "It isn't what you want that makes you fat; it's what you get."

Inside, Delia went to the bin beneath the stairs where she kept recent magazines and circulars. There was the issue of the *Jefferson Journal* that reported, under blaring headlines, the discovery of Avery Austin's body. She read and reread the account. Delia knew she was being irrational—harebrained, Polly would have called it—but she couldn't quite let go of her assumption about the men she had seen. Even though she was ashamed at having misjudged them, something in her wanted to have been right about them, longed for their complicity in the crime.

Would she, in fact, have preferred a murder to a self-inflicted death by social drugs? Wouldn't anyone? It is so much easier to assign blame and mete out punishment when there's one murderer and one victim. Almost daily since the event, she had relived that night of terror, and those frightening men were always at the center of it—those men and the ugly face in the shack's lighted doorway, and the mongrel's menacing snarls. The images had fixed themselves in her consciousness, and she doubted she would ever be free of them. She hadn't told Gordon about her obsession; she hadn't told anyone.

After classes the next day, Delia dropped into Angie Turner's office. Angie was there, grading essay exams.

"Well, has the handsome cowboy saddled his pony and flown the coop?" Angie asked grandly.

"That may be the worst mixed metaphor I've ever heard."

"Thanks. I do my best. You're not easy to impress."

Delia was heartened by her friend's improving health, and wondered how long it would continue. "What are your plans for the next couple of hours?" she asked.

"Oh, the usual. Strangle a few students, burn a few exams, shed a few tears. Maybe even march for peace. You have something better to suggest?"

"Maybe, maybe not. Care to take a spin down to the river?"

"The river, is it? Sure, why not?" Angie looked questioningly at Delia but didn't press her for reasons, and Delia didn't volunteer any. "Let me call Howard and tell him I'll be a little late getting home . . . Will I be late?"

"Maybe. Go ahead and call."

This time, Delia knew exactly where she was going, and she guided Angie to the dirt road below the beltway without a hitch.

"Can you tell me what this is about, or is it a surprise?" Angie asked good-naturedly. "Also, am I going to be required to walk? It's only fair that you prepare me for the worst."

"No, no walking," Delia laughed, "unless your machine gives out."

"This station wagon is well-schooled in dirt roads, but it doesn't swim very well."

"Well, it's time it learned."

"And this spoken by an exclusively dry-ground athlete."

Delia made a face at Angie as they pulled to a stop at an area cordoned off fifty yards from the river.

Angie put two and two together. "Is this the place where that student was found?" she asked.

"Yes," Delia replied solemnly, and climbed from the car. The going was a bit rough on crutches, but she traced the boundaries of the makeshift barrier, repeatedly tangling her crutches in undergrowth. There was nothing to be learned here, Delia knew, but she had to come. The thing was eating away inside her. A willow lashed cruelly across her face, and she thought it fitting that nature exact some form of retribution. Maybe that's why she was here—to do penance, to pay a reckoning. And all the time, Angie sat in her car, watching. *Probably wondering if I've popped my cork,* Delia surmised grimly.

"Want to talk?" Angie asked quietly when Delia at last returned.

"I guess not," Delia answered, and Angie didn't insist.

When the doorbell rang Wednesday night at precisely seven o'clock, Delia was in no mood to receive visitors. The inevitable letdown after the high of Gordon's visit, combined with a brooding despondency over the dead student and disappointment in herself, made it difficult for her to focus on her work. Only in class could she even partially free her mind of the incident. Why were her students able to get on with things while she was mired in grief and guilt? After all, Avery Austin was one of their peers, and they had been upset enough at first. The old are said to have bad memories, but it is the young who most quickly forget, Delia mused. Or maybe it's just that the young are more resilient.

Opening the door and seeing Mary Beth Archer and Susan Fines, Delia remembered. Their visit last week, before Gordon arrived, had been a drop by, to bring her a few goodies. This, however, was the Relief Society's official monthly visit. With lesson, Delia presumed. She was in her sweats—her off-duty uniform, she liked to say, from October to April in Wisconsin.

"Is this a bad time?" Susan asked. "We can come back."

"Does it show?" Delia laughed without mirth. "No, come in. Rescue me from a stack of student papers."

"Got a match?" Mary Beth offered.

"Now, that's an idea," Delia replied as she motioned the women to sit down.

"When does your cast come off?" Susan asked.

"Soon, very soon, I hope. My toes are crossed, along with my fingers, eyes, and wires," she added.

"Do you want the assigned lesson tonight, or do you want to talk about something else?" Mary Beth began.

Delia looked up. Mary Beth had never offered an alternative to the scheduled lesson before, at least not until she had covered it thoroughly. What was different about tonight?

"What's the lesson?" Delia asked.

"It's about trusting in the Lord," Mary Beth answered.

"Anything in there about self-hate?" Delia asked almost cynically.

Mary Beth looked at Susan. The latter waited, then stood and walked to the sofa where Delia was sitting with her legs stretched out. Susan sat on the far arm of the sofa and looked at Delia.

"We may seem to talk a lot," she said quietly, "but we're good listeners, too."

Delia didn't know what to say. She had already said too much, and she was not a person who easily opened up to others. "Well," she ventured, "how much time do you have, and how much drivel can you stand?"

"We have time, as much time as it takes," Susan said. Mary Beth nodded agreement.

Delia wondered why she was inclined to tell these women things she couldn't tell even her dearest friends, Angie and Howard. "Well," she began, intently examining some of the nicks and scrapes in her cast, "it all started the first Monday of classes. That night . . . well, uh . . . you sure you want to hear this?"

With their encouragement, Delia spun out the story she had so far told only Gordon and the police detective. "I think I'm a bad person," she said finally. "I assumed those two men were criminals, murderers."

"But you won't have to testify now. It's all right. It's not your responsibility," Mary Beth hastened to assure Delia.

"That's true," Susan nodded. "But that's only incidental to you at this point, isn't it?"

"How did you know?"

"I know what guilt and shame feel like," Susan said softly, "and I also know how disappointing it is to have done something we regard as cowardly or weak. To have tarnished our cherished image of ourselves."

"I know I've failed in the matter of religious commitment, but I've always thought I was fair, and tolerant, and at least mildly courageous." Delia paused and began fingering the raised seam on the sofa back. "But I'm not," she said, looking down, and tears sprang to her eyes. "I hate finding out who I really am—a weakling and a hypocrite!"

Without saying anything, Susan stood again. She touched Delia's shoulder and then walked into the den and found Delia's set of scriptures. After consulting the index, Susan turned to the twelfth chapter of Ether in the Book of Mormon.

"You're turning to Moroni, aren't you, Sue?" Mary Beth said.

"Yes, Mormon's son. One of the reasons I appreciate him so much is that like the rest of us, he sometimes struggled with self-doubt. In spite of his great devotion, in spite of all he had done and all he knew, he felt inadequate to the task of keeping the record. He thought himself so inept at writing that latter-day readers would mock and discredit the words he inscribed."

Delia looked up. "That's different," she interjected. "I'm not talking about weakness in a skill, like writing."

"No, but the Lord's reply covers a lot of territory," Mary Beth exclaimed. "Read it, Sue."

Susan looked at Delia, who only nodded. She began, "'And if men come unto me I will show unto them their weakness. I give unto men weakness that they may be humble; and my grace is sufficient for all men that humble themselves before me; for if they humble themselves before me, and have faith in me, then will I make weak things become strong unto them.'"

"'I give unto men weakness that they may be humble,'" Delia repeated. "Humility has never been very noticeable in me, has it?"

"Most of us have trouble with that," Susan offered, "but the key seems to be humbling ourselves before God, which is different from humiliation."

"Read the next couple of verses, Sue," Mary Beth urged.

"All right. 'Behold, I will show unto the Gentiles their weakness, and I will show them that faith, hope and charity bringeth unto me— the fountain of all righteousness.'" Susan paused again. "I especially like verse twenty-nine," she said, and continued reading. "'And I, Moroni, having heard these words, was comforted. . . .' Isn't that lovely? We can all find that same comfort, I think. I hope."

"Is that the end of the verse?" Delia asked.

"No, I quit in the middle of a sentence. Moroni then addresses the Lord again, with these words: 'O Lord, thy righteous will be done, for I know that thou workest unto the children of men according to their faith.'"

"That's the key, isn't it?" Delia said. "We have to have weaknesses so we'll be humbled enough to walk by faith. Instead of thinking we're so all-fired powerful ourselves."

"And in learning those things, Moroni was comforted. That's important, too, to know the source of our comfort," Mary Beth added.

"When I'm whining around about my cowardice and unjustness, what I'm really doing is displaying my injured ego, isn't it," Delia declared, standing and hopping to the window. Night had fallen, and the street light behind a small tree nearby made a halo of the slender branches bared by Friday's storm.

"It would be worse if you didn't care, wouldn't it?" Susan asked. "You have a conscience. It hurts, but you wouldn't want it not to hurt at times, would you?" Then Susan seemed to become aware of how much she was talking, and she lapsed into an almost embarrassed silence.

Mary Beth jumped into the void. "Susan's right. Why don't you think about what Moroni said and try to find comfort, too?"

Delia only turned from the window and looked at her. There was no way to reply.

Then Susan found her voice. "Well," she said softly, "it's time for us to go." She opened her large handbag. "Here's a loaf of bread for you. I hope you like whole wheat."

"Just now anything 'whole' sounds good to me," Delia answered.

The three women moved to the door. "Can we pick you up for church Sunday?" Susan asked tentatively.

Delia hesitated. "Sure. Sure, why not?"

October's remaining days sped by, and shortly before Halloween, the much scruffed, dinged, and verbally maligned cast was removed from Delia's right leg. Although she had faithfully performed the prescribed exercises while wearing the cast, the limb that emerged from its worn, dirty casing looked nothing like the one that had entered it. Scrawny, pale, covered with twisted, scraggly hair and crusty dead skin, the leg looked like a graft that had failed miserably. Delia wasn't sure she wanted to claim the leg, nor was she sure it could be reclaimed.

The surgeon warned her that she should expect some pain, that the tibia was still very fragile, that she should avoid any blows from the side, and that she should use crutches to support part of her weight for another two or three weeks. In the meantime, she was to begin an intensive therapy program. She was ready; whatever it took to get her leg back, she meant to do it.

The Turners threw a "coming out" party in honor of her shedding the full-leg fiberglass sock. Gordon attended the event by telephone, and Gabe dropped around for a few minutes. Seeing the reduced circumference of Delia's limb, Angie vowed to explore the possibilities of a total body cast for herself. And when Delia got both legs behind the wheel of the Subaru a few weeks later, for the first time in months, Howard splashed a glass of champagne over its yellowing but newly washed hood. Thanksgiving was just around the corner, and then Christmas. She would be heading west to Smithville and Gordon in a matter of weeks.

CHAPTER SEVEN

The dinner, by anyone's standards, was destined to be a huge success, at least from a management standpoint. Hannah had planned it to perfection, right down to the last marinated broccoli floret on the crystal relish tray. In terms of customer satisfaction, however, the results were more difficult to assess. An opinion poll of those present that late November day at the yellow frame house on Spring Road would yield a wide range of responses.

Anyone asking Effie McGrath, after the fact, how things had gone Thanksgiving Day would be apprised that, although the affair hadn't started out so hot, it turned into a stellar event. And not because of the food or the glazed cornucopia centerpiece, not by a long shot. On the other hand, a person making the same query of Hannah McGrath Simonsen would be told something different, quite different.

The dinner began with every instrument in the symphonic feast entering at precisely the right moment and blending beautifully with every other instrument, just as Hannah had determined it would. The gravy did not turn lumpy while the potatoes were being whipped, and the rolls remained obediently warm in their napkin-lined basket. Moreover, for the most part, Ilene kept out of Hannah's way, having learned long ago that when Hannah was in charge, to express a differing opinion, or offer an innocent suggestion, was tantamount to insurrection. Besides which, it was futile. Even Polly, who rarely held back her views with anyone except the Lord—and only then when she was certain he was dead serious—judiciously kept her preferences and prejudices to herself when Hannah assumed the controls of whatever enterprise was unfolding or threatening to unfold. At least, Polly usually did. Sometimes the strain was too much.

But not today. Both Polly and Ilene held their tongues when Hannah scooped the marshmallows and at least half the brown sugar and butter off the sweet potatoes Ilene had brought, substituting more benign pineapple tidbits, apples, and unsweetened juice. Nor did they protest when she retrieved the dishes of cranberry sauce from the table set up in the parlor and sliced the chilled lumps of jellied fruit expertly into slippery individual servings. Nor did they so much as cough, either, when she sent her husband Lester to Albertson's to buy avocados that were just slightly softer than the ones Polly had bought yesterday.

After all, this was just Hannah. They had all learned long ago to live with Hannah. Hannah's father used to ask his wife how two such opposites as Hannah and Delia had been created from the same gene pool. Hannah's idea of roughing it, Jedediah once remarked, was sleeping in sheets ironed on only one side.

In one thing connected with this occasion, however, Polly had prevailed. Over Hannah's carefully phrased objections, Polly's sister Dorothy and Dorothy's senile husband Timothy had been invited. The Brittels' children were all out of state, Polly had declared, and Dorothy could not be expected to take Timothy on an airplane where she would have to hide him or expose his limitations to every Tom, Dick, and Harry who crossed their path.

Polly didn't blame Dot one bit. She wouldn't want to take him out into a bustling airline terminal either, or onto a jam-packed airplane, even if he was a dear—and he *was*, Polly had reminded Hannah. What's more, he enjoyed riding in a car, even though he didn't know whether he was in Rome or Timbuktu, or whether it was summer or Thursday. So, Polly had gone ahead and persuaded Dot to come and bring Timothy, who had a hearty appetite, and the pair had driven down from Logan.

Only two of Hannah's four children were still living at home and therefore theoretically obligated to attend official family gatherings. The oldest of the four, a daughter, had escaped such command appearances by marrying and moving to California; and the next oldest, a son, had recently proclaimed himself madly in love with a woman twice his age who had run off to Florida last month and joined a post-hippie commune. Which temporary aberration Hannah preferred not to discuss, though it accounted for his absence. He was in Florida was all she said.

The absence of her other two, both in their late teens, was harder to explain because they had been in the state two days ago but left. They were spending the holiday with cousins on their father's side, Hannah said, though why she could not for the life of her see when there would be a perfectly acceptable meal in Smithville. Lester, Hannah's faithful spouse, was there, of course.

Despite desertions left and right, Hannah didn't seem to notice that in a popular vote, she couldn't tally even a third of the Thanksgiving dinner electorate. She had the only vote she really needed: her own. Hannah was not a tall person, and she fought valiantly to maintain the figure that had turned heads when she was in high school. Her oval face was reminiscent of paintings of the British royalty, a bit too delicate and too exquisitely made up for casual comfort. Her thinly painted eyebrows never relaxed their arch, and her forehead was beginning to show perennial lines of tension below the medium brown of her mid-length, stylish hair. Delia always said that Hannah should have sold cosmetics, that she had that "look."

Dinner, as Hannah had conceived it on this nationally sanctioned day of gratitude, was grandly elegant (she had brought her own china, silver, crystal, and linen) and hopelessly boring. Like most of Hannah's productions, including at least three of her children for the first seventeen years of their lives, it was boring because nothing was left to chance. There was no latitude for the unexpected, for spontaneous combustion, Jedediah McGrath would have said.

Jed had always favored the element of surprise. Even Polly, predictable as she was in most things, surprised him sometimes; and he had liked that. In his view, which he had expressed on occasion, minor temporary calamities, so long as no one was killed or maimed, added a little chili pepper to the meat loaf of life. And indeed, he had had the last word on the subject, fooling them all by dying one cloudless June day.

Without consulting Hannah, Ron had invited Gordon to come, even though Delia, as Hannah had predicted, would remain in

Jefferson until Christmas break. Gordon declined the invitation, indicating that he had company from out of town. Gordon also said he wasn't any worse for the wear after his quick trip to Jefferson, but didn't volunteer any more information than that. All of them were aware that Delia had shed her cast a couple of days before Halloween, and Gordon described her therapy regimen to Ron, who had repeated it to his family.

Only Wilson and Effie were impressed. Wilson wanted the battered artifact to hang on his bedroom wall as a trophy, but Sabrine said that was "gross." From all appearances, the Delia-Gordon "thing" was alive and well, though with Delia, Ron and Ilene admitted to each other, one never knew.

Thanksgiving Day was one of those bright, mild days that almost persuade Smithville residents to forgive and forget July. Almost. A few harmless white clouds hung loosely around the mountain peaks north of town. The heat of summer had long since migrated south of the equator, and Smithville had experienced a little rain a day or two earlier. But as rain was wont to do in southern Utah, it passed quickly, leaving the desert refreshed and as full of smells as a mockingbird is full of song.

Even in November, the wet creosote gave off its pungent aroma. A blind person from this part of the country, transported around the world multiple times, would know that heady fragrance from all others, would know when she had arrived home, so long as she came after a rain, or in the early morning when the dew still hung on the spindly branches and small, waxy leaves. There was the smell of sagebrush in mountain country as well as in desert, but creosote was the desert's olfactory stamp. The nose can be a powerful testifier.

The moment Hannah's culinary masterpiece collapsed into chaos was precisely the moment nine-year-old Effie began to take an interest in the proceedings. From that point, it was all House of Horrors for Hannah and all Disneyland for Effie. The reversal in both their fortunes occurred just after Hannah entered the kitchen to slice more turkey for second helpings. Hannah had, of course, brought her own electric carving knife from her perfectly appointed home in Provo. Just as she raised the synchronized twin blades to make her first measured cut on the bird's systematically mutilated carcass, she heard a car outside on the gravel drive.

Turning to the window, she saw a rather tall, somewhat older man climb from the driver's side of a light gray sedan. He was wearing a brightly flowered blue Hawaiian shirt and an islander's white straw hat with a rainbow band. Hannah watched with agitated curiosity as he opened each of the rear doors of the late model vehicle and helped two elderly little women to their feet. The women were dressed identically in yellow muumuus imprinted with large red, orange, and white tropical flowers. The women's hair, Hannah saw, was tightly permed in tinted lavender curls all over their heads.

The man seemed to ignore the fact that there were three other vehicles in the yard. He parked smack dab in the middle of the gravel driveway, blocking anyone else's passage in or out. As the women straightened their muumuus and patted their thinning hair, the man opened the car's trunk and extracted a large plastic bag containing an Hawaiian lei. Setting it on the car, he fitted two smaller, somewhat faded, pink floral leis over the heads of his companions and donned a large, browning white one himself.

That accomplished, he ushered the women to the back stairs—they looking like technicolor mushrooms and he like a many-flavored popsicle—and knocked twice on the screen door. Hannah, electric knife still poised in her right hand, found her legs and moved mechanically toward the door to the back porch when Anthon Clemmer burst through it and into the kitchen.

"Aloha!" he shouted, and reached back to draw the Plumm sisters in with him.

Polly was on her feet and into the kitchen in an instant, her face blushing crimson. Effie was right behind her, and Wilson, too, had left his chair. Thirteen-year-old Sabrine tried to appear uninterested, and fifteen-year-old Miles looked at his dad with a big question on his face. Ron only shrugged.

"Mr. Clemmer!" Effie cried, running back to the parlor door. "Mama, it's Mr. Clemmer! You remember, when we had bread! Daddy, it's Mr. Clemmer! Grandma's boyfriend!"

Sabrine's curiosity got the best of her, and she craned her neck toward the kitchen. Dot quietly took Timothy's hand and led him to the screened front porch, grabbing a sweater on the way. They were staying for the weekend unless Timothy became too agitated, but she didn't want him in the middle of this party, whatever it was. Polly or Ilene could fill her in later.

"Come here, Effie," Ilene said firmly, "finish your dinner." The agony was visible in Effie's face. All the action was in the kitchen, and there was plenty of action.

"What brings you here? Don't you know it's Thanksgiving?" Polly demanded of the intruder. Hannah, speechless, looked from her mother to Anthon, then back to her mother. The slicer was still raised, ready to strike, its cord stretched to the limit from where the plug clung for dear life to the wall socket. Wilson lingered in the doorway, and the Plumm sisters adjusted their leis.

When Anthon reached out to put the fresh lei around Polly's shoulders, she backed away angrily. "Of course I know it's Thanksgiving," he laughed, "and I'm giving you something to be thankful for, this ring of flowers and my presence. The Plumm sisters and I bring greetings from paradise." With that he made a grand, swooping bow. "At your service, ma'am."

"Hmmph! The only service I care to see you at is my burial," Polly said, more composed. "Or yours," she added. Polly looked over at Hannah with a threatening "don't forget, I'm still your mother" look, then turned back to Anthon. "This is my daughter, Hannah Simonsen," she said evenly, looking straight at Anthon. "Hannah, meet Mr. Anthon Clemmer from Cheyenne, Wyoming. He professes to be a printer, though it appears spendthrift vacations are more his line."

"Anyone bearing McGrath blood is a friend of mine," Anthon said jovially, stepping forward to shake hands with Hannah. She merely gestured in his direction with the meat slicer and forced a tight-lipped smile. Knowing how Hannah made mountains out of molehills, Ron and Ilene had said nothing to her about their mother's new "friend." "Let sleeping dogs lie," Ron had advised. But now this particular dog was awake and on its feet, barking its head off.

"Have you been to call on the Widow Plimpton yet?" Polly asked pointedly, knowing full well that Anthon was not the least bit interested in her neighbor Arva, except as a woman with some acreage to sell.

Before he could answer, Golda Plumm stepped forward, and the presence of the Plumm sisters—still pear-shaped and perky as ever—

seemed to register with Polly for the first time. There they were, covered from stem to stern in what looked for all the world like badly-rigged floral tents. "Remember us, Polly?"

"Remember that day in Colton?" Rosa chimed in.

"When you took us to Ogden?" Golda prodded.

"To Cousin Archibald's funeral?" Rosa finished.

Polly was distracted by Hannah's gasp, but she remembered, all right. How on earth could she forget? It was just one episode in a series of disasters she let herself in for when she started out for Logan that day in her old Chrysler Imperial. The trouble was, Polly hadn't told anyone about that episode or any other episodes, of which there were several. Least of all had she told Hannah, who would first work herself into a lather over it, and then perform the same service for the rest of the family.

It appeared to Polly that the Lord was punishing her, both for her indiscretion and for her deception. He had punished her in advance for some of her sins by giving her a daughter like Hannah in the first place, and then one like Delia in the second place. And now he was pouring it on. Polly loved her daughters, but they didn't exactly fit the specifications she had laid out when she engineered their howling entrances into the world. Hannah, who had cried loudest and longest of Polly's babies, wouldn't rest now until she knew every last jack detail about Polly's adventures with Anthon Clemmer and the Plumm sisters. *Well,* Polly thought, *she'd better learn to sleep standing up, because she'll have a long wait.*

"Sure, you remember, Mrs. McGrath," Anthon nudged her teasingly while the family waited in astonished silence.

"I'm trying to forget!" Polly snapped, backing out of range.

"We got rich since we saw you last," Golda boasted, straightening her lei.

"Hush," said Rosa. "These folks got no interest in our good fortune, all brought about by Providence with a capital 'P.'"

"You mean Providence with a capital 'A,' for *Anthon,*" Golda said. "It isn't as if we got the money on our own, y'know. Anthon give it to us, don't forget. And Merinda give it to him."

"Don't I know it? And don't I thank my lucky stars every livin' day for such as him? But it don't do to carry on. Didn't Jesus say 'blessed are the poor and needy'?"

"Poor in spirit. What he said was 'blessed are the poor in spirit,'" Golda corrected.

"Did he now?" Rosa took up the challenge. "Well, he meant the other too, what I said, and that's that."

"Well, I for one don't see anything blessed about being poor and needy." Golda turned to Polly. "Take Polly, here, living alone in this old house, driving that old car, and bereft of her dear, departed husband. She's poor and needy, all right. Now show me where the *blessed* comes in."

Polly visibly bristled.

"Here's where it comes in," declared Anthon, deftly looping the large lei he had brought around Polly's neck.

"If it makes me sneeze, you can just take it right back where you got it," was all Polly said.

It took Ron to rescue the situation. With Effie in tow, he entered the kitchen and introduced himself. Then, to Polly's horror—and Hannah's—he invited the newcomers to share dinner. Ilene quickly set three places and dished up more food while Ron found some folding chairs. Much too excited to eat any more, Effie took up her station behind Anthon, now and then touching the fragrant chain of flowers resting on his shoulders while he ate.

"In my unbiased opinion, this food beats poi and raw fish all to pieces," Golda said as she chewed on the meaty part of a turkey wing. "Give me the good old U. S. of A. any day."

"Hawaii *is* the good old U.S.A.," Hannah said dryly.

"You know what I mean. It ain't always been," Golda replied. "It's different."

"But we loved the beaches and the ukuleles and the hula," Rosa said. "And the singing, didn't we Golda?"

"Sure we did, but I don't know as I'd care to live with all that wet all the time. Makes a person feel limp and rusty."

"Not to mention the cockroaches and geckos," Anthon chuckled.

"Oooo, don't remind me!" Golda shuddered. "I near went through the roof when that gecko dropped on my bed with me in it. Right off the ceiling!"

"Just the same, I'm glad we went," Rosa asserted. "It isn't every day you go to Hawaii."

"Lucky for the Hawaiians," Hannah muttered to Lester, who was his usual silent self at family gatherings.

"What brings you to Smithville?" Ilene asked as she moved toward the kitchen to cut the pumpkin pies.

Hannah intercepted her. "No, you stay here, Ilene. I'll serve the pie."

"Pie, is it?" Anthon cried. "Looks as if our timing couldn't have been better."

"Or worse," Polly said, looking right at him, but giving silent thanks that Jed Junior and Paul weren't here, too. And Delia. Especially Delia. She'd probably treat this gaudy trio like long-lost friends. Delia didn't always practice the tolerance she preached, but when she did, she practiced it with a vengeance. And sometimes Polly wound up paying for it. Torry–Jennifer, that is—was a good example.

Anthon winked at Polly, and Effie looked up at her mother and grinned. Anthon turned to Ilene. "Since you asked, I'll tell you why we're here," he began.

"When we landed in Los Angeles," Golda interrupted.

"We thought, why go home yet?" Rosa finished.

"After all, Las Vegas is right on the way."

"Almost."

"So we changed our flight. After all, money was no object."

"Hush, Golda, you're bragging again," scolded Rosa with a pleased frown.

Anthon broke in. "And then when we got to Las Vegas, it was only a jackrabbit's blink to Smithville. Since we're all three friends of Mrs. McGrath, we decided to come, take a chance on finding you home, and take a peek at some property I'm looking to buy."

"Friends!" Polly exclaimed. "I hardly know any of you, and what little I do know is too much."

Rosa and Golda looked at each other. It was the first inkling they had that they weren't welcome. But they brushed it off. "Some people just don't like surprises," Golda whispered to her sister. Rosa nodded and happily dug into her pie.

An hour or two later, the three vacationers were back in their rented vehicle and on the road to Las Vegas. As they pulled away, waving merrily to the gathering in the yard, everyone looked at Polly, even Miles and Sabrine. All but Effie. Effie was busy admiring Anthon's faded lei that hung nearly to her knees.

"Some people don't have the brains they were born with," was all Polly said and walked back into the house, leaving the others outside.

Polly's children knew her well enough to know that there would be no explanations forthcoming. They could draw their own conclusions. Polly had no doubt, however, that Hannah would be on the phone to her absent siblings at the crack of dawn. *Well, let them stew,* she said to herself. *They could use some excitement in their lives.* She felt a bit lightheaded and as a precaution, she returned to the kitchen and covertly took a little oval pill, yellow on top and white on the bottom, that the doctor had prescribed for her occasional dizziness.

She still took half an aspirin daily, too, for insurance. Dorothy, who had brought Timothy into the house when the Wyoming guests left, may have seen Polly set her glass down and place a brown pill bottle on the second shelf of the cabinet to the right of the sink. If Dot noted it, she didn't say anything.

Occupied with cleaning up and packing Hannah's dinner things, no one mentioned the unscheduled visit of the colorful delegation from Cheyenne, though the subject hung in the air like an overripe nectarine waiting to be picked. By all counts, it was with no little relief that Polly watched Hannah and Lester roll away at dusk. After the Simonsen Buick disappeared down the drive, Polly wearily mounted the back stairs, one step at a time, depending heavily on the railing. She opened the sagging door and slowly crossed the back porch.

The tall stack of old newspapers that had been collecting unread since Jed's death was gone. Hannah had seen to that, and Polly hadn't been surprised in the least, nor had she objected. Lester, the agent of removal, had been more than ready to do something useful, away from the house, while Hannah was running things in the kitchen.

Polly didn't mind Lester; at times she even pitied him. She just wished he'd stand up to Hannah once in a while. But then, maybe he was so used to Hannah that he didn't notice how she was anymore. Or maybe Lester was one of those people who were happy to turn their personal lives over to someone else, someone who enjoyed running things. Perhaps he was a person who couldn't stand to be in charge of anything; just possibly that's why he married Polly

McGrath's older daughter. Even Polly got tired of being in sole charge of her own house these days.

Given Hannah's natural affinity for the driver's seat, Polly was surprised that her daughter actually let Lester drive the car when she was present and perfectly able to do so. One sticky little blob of residue from the days of fascinating womanhood, Polly decided. One tiny leftover from the "Honey, I'm home" syndrome. Jed never went so far as to say Lester was henpecked, but he did remark casually to Polly once that he thought it something of a physiological miracle that his only son-in-law could walk around minus a backbone. Polly had noticed, however, that her husband watched over Lester without seeming to, asking him questions about his work as an accountant, taking him to the barn to see a new saddle, asking his opinion on a bill up before Congress.

Ron and Ilene stayed to set the parlor to rights while the children fed and watered the horses and chickens, then they, too, left. Polly went outside to see them off. As her father slowly drove toward home in the family Suburban, Effie McGrath leaned her head against her mother and asked sleepily, "Can grandmas have boyfriends?"

Ilene pulled Effie to her and answered softly, "Sure, why not?"

In the backseats, the three older children looked at each other and said nothing, though Wilson muffled a snicker.

"Well, then," Effie asked, "how many girlfriends can a boyfriend have?"

"Men like Mr. Clemmer can have many friends who aren't special 'girlfriends,'" Ron explained.

"I don't mean Mr. Clemmer, Daddy," replied Effie. "I mean Gordon."

Ron and Ilene exchanged glances. "What makes you think Gordon has more than one girlfriend?" Ron asked gently.

"'Cause I saw him with a lady by the river yesterday. Throwing rocks in the water and laughing. When Jill's mother took us to ride our bicycles on the river trail."

"You ask too many questions," Miles interrupted brusquely. "Gordon can do whatever he wants. Aunt Delia doesn't own him."

"I didn't say she did," Effie retorted.

"Then hush," said Miles angrily.

"That's enough," Ilene said. Sabrine and Wilson sat silent, and Ron began to whistle a lullaby while his headlights pointed the way home.

Having seen the last of her brood off, Polly banged into the kitchen from the back porch and dropped heavily into a ladderback chair at the big oak table. Dorothy, who had been putting Timothy down for what she hoped was the night, was descending the stairs into the parlor. Dorothy was not a prying sort of sister, but she and Polly had been so close as youngsters as to very nearly speak each other's thoughts. When Dot walked into the kitchen, Polly was sitting there with Jed's favorite pocket knife in her left hand, methodically opening and closing the tightly sleeved blades and tearing the thumbnail on her right hand in the process. She didn't even look up when Dot spoke.

"It's none of my business what happened here today, but if you want to talk, I'll listen," Dot offered, taking a chair across from Polly.

Hannah, Polly could put off, and Ron and Ilene, but Dot knew her too well. "Where's Timothy?" Polly asked at last, still staring at the knife.

"I wish I knew," Dot said quietly. "Timothy, the real Timothy, the man I married and built a life with, left a long time ago."

Polly looked up, but remained silent. Dot had never voiced her anguish to Polly before. And Polly had never fully imagined herself in Dot's place, tending the husk that remained when her beloved departed. Dot arose and stood behind Polly's chair, resting her hands on her sister's shoulders.

"I know a little about grieving, myself—how it wrenches us from our moorings and whirls us into emotional territories we have never visited before," Dot said quietly. "I find myself behaving in ways I wouldn't have thought possible before Timothy got so bad."

Polly's shoulders tensed and the cords in her neck tightened. Everything in her resisted exposure. Then, her mind rewound its reel of memories and stopped on the day after Labor Day when she was five years old. She had begged to go to school, but there was no formal kindergarten in Smithville in those days. Dot, a third-grader, was in a flurry, with a new school dress all ready and a lunch pail all packed. But Dot had seen Polly's tearful disappointment, and secretly washed and dressed her little sister for school.

While their mother was busy in the kitchen, the two girls slipped out the front door. Polly could not simply leave without her mother's knowledge, so when she reached what she deemed a safe distance from the house, she called back at the top of her lungs, "Good-bye, Mother! I'm going to school!" And she went. The school wasn't crowded in those days, and birth date policies could be set aside if a child was mentally ready.

Polly set the knife on the table, then reached up with her lean, long-fingered right hand to pat Dorothy's slightly plump one. "I wouldn't know where to begin, or how to end," she said.

"Start in the middle, if you want. We have all night if we need it."

"Sometimes . . . ," Polly began hesitantly, staring at the knife, "sometimes it feels as though someone else has taken over my body. As though I've gone off somewhere, and this person in my clothes is acting out my life while I watch from the wings."

"Doing things totally out of character."

"Yes! How did you know?"

"I've been there, my dear. I also knew when you came to Logan that something was terribly wrong, that you were not yourself, that you needed something—time, perhaps. Some of us grieve that way, and we don't even know we're grieving. We just think we're losing our minds."

"Sometimes I'm certain I've lost mine. And that clown Anthon Clemmer is only part of it."

"He's the one who came today?"

"Yes, and this isn't the first time. I can't get rid of the man! He keeps turning up. And now he's talking about buying Arva Plimpton's place. I'll have to move to another planet, or die, to get rid of him."

"Do you want to get rid of him?"

Polly's head jerked toward Dorothy. "Of course I want to get rid of him! He's a felon and a tramp, and his chief occupation is tomfoolery."

"And the people with him?" Dot asked gently, moving around to the chair nearest Polly.

With the forefinger of her right hand, Polly methodically traced the swirls in the table's woodgrain. "More trouble, only more trouble. You do a good deed, and what does it get you? Misery, with a capital 'M.'" *And 'M' also stands for Merinda,* Polly added silently.

"I take it this fellow is nothing like Jedediah?"

Polly threw her hands up. "The reverse! Absolutely the reverse! He couldn't be more different if he were the devil himself." She paused. "At least I've thought so," she added, lowering her head.

"Are you looking for another Jedediah?"

Polly hesitated a moment, then declared, "I'm not looking for anybody. What I'm looking for is a little peace and quiet!"

"Peace and quiet isn't all it's cracked up to be, believe me."

Polly looked up. *Dot still has some good years left,* Polly realized, *and they are being bled dry by the demands of caring for Timothy. And he doesn't even know it. He just plods along in contented oblivion while her life drains away. She can't leave him for more than an hour or two, and if he begins to wander far, she'll be on twenty-four hour watch.* When Jed died, Polly had envied her sister the comfort of a breathing man in the house; but she now wondered how Dot stood this living death. Maybe I am the lucky one, after all, she thought. At least Jed left with his personality intact.

"You must be afraid for the future," Polly said.

"Afraid? No, I wouldn't say I was afraid. Apprehensive, maybe. All I pray now is to be equal to it, and to live one day longer than he does. I'm not yearning for fun and excitement. I know those days are gone. I feel fortunate even to have made this trip, and I do want to come again for Christmas. It's a bonus. Talking with you is a bonus."

"Here you are, comforting me when I should be comforting you. I've never been very good at comfort, except when my children were small and needed me. Now they don't need me, I'm a dried-up well."

"What makes you think they don't need you?"

"Hmmph! Isn't it obvious?"

"Who shut the gate, you or them?"

Not wanting to pursue that question, Polly stood and walked to the sink. "Care for a drink?" she asked.

"No thanks. Come back and tell me about this man who keeps turning up—what's his name again?"

"Clemmer, Anthon Clemmer. He's from Cheyenne—and the Arizona State Penitentiary," she added with some satisfaction.

Dorothy let the reference to the penitentiary pass. "Do you like him?" she asked pointedly.

The bluntness of the question caught Polly off guard. "No," she said. "No . . . of course not. How could I like a loser like him?"

"I just wondered. Something keeps him coming back."

Polly recovered herself. "I'll tell you what keeps him coming back," she said crossly. "Stubbornness and the inability to take no for an answer. He's a worn-out needle stuck in the crack of a broken record."

Dorothy chuckled. "Okay, have it your way, but at least tell me the story of his entry into your life. I could use a good laugh. And don't forget all the subplots, either, including the penitentiary."

Polly eyed her sister and hesitated, then dropped resignedly into her chair. "It's the stuff out of which soap operas are made," she sighed, and began.

Dorothy listened, attention glued on her sister, interrupting only to comment on what she had seen in the papers or to ask a question. The ornate wooden clock above the big oak table ticked away, its pendulum swinging in time with the inflections in Polly's voice. When it struck the hour of midnight, Polly glanced up and said there was no more to tell, at least not tonight. Dot stood and stretched, stiff from sitting in one position.

"My, it's late," Dot said, "but I'm glad you told me. That's a lot to carry bottled up inside. Come, give me a hug and send me off to my Timothy."

Polly rose stiffly from the chair, crossed her arms over her chest, and rubbed her upper arms. "I don't know what possessed me to spill all that sewage on you," she said, "but I feel better for it. Likely, you feel worse."

"No," smiled Dorothy, "I feel better, too." She embraced her sister lovingly, kissed her leathery cheek, and pushed a loose strand of hair behind her ear. "Good night," she said. "I love you."

Polly watched Dorothy turn toward the door. "I love you, too," she said to the departing form. "I love you, too."

CHAPTER EIGHT

"Well, fry my gizzard. Will you look at that!" Begonia emerged from her condominium, all smiles on the Saturday before Thanksgiving, as Delia's Subaru coughed to life while Howard and Angie Turner applauded. "I do think that's a sinful waste of good champagne, if that's what you're using, though," she said, hop-skipping down the walk in her bright pink ski parka with the fur trim. "That poor vehicle wouldn't know champagne from Mountain Dew."

"And I suppose yours would?" laughed Delia from behind the wheel.

"Darn tootin' it would. It may be old, but it's aristocracy through and through," Begonia cried. "Anybody can see that."

"*Decadent* aristocracy," Delia amended. "C'mon. You're invited along for the maiden voyage."

"Are you sure it's safe?"

"What do you think, Howard?"

"Don't ask me. My knowledge of automobiles ends with the ignition key and the gas cap. Ask me something about waterfowl."

"Let's go show Elmer Roy!" Begonia sang out.

Delia turned to Angie and Howard. "How about it? Want to go show Elmer Roy?"

Angie waved off the invitation. "You don't have a shoehorn large enough to get one of us into that backseat, much less both of us. Besides, we have errands to run and laundry to do. It is Saturday, you know."

"Okay, Begonia, it's just the two of us, then. Off we go to Elmer Roy's. Look, ma, a limb of flesh." Delia knocked on her right thigh.

"Of course, this limb is only half the diameter of the other one, and it's the color of a frog's south side, but it's all mine and I love it."

Delia's crutches were in the backseat, just in case, but the cast was off, and her stiff right knee and ankle had loosened enough with therapy to let her try driving a vehicle that required two legs to operate it. Braking with the weak leg would be the trickiest part of the operation. Nonetheless, she could wait no longer. Frank Archer, Mary Beth's husband, had come over earlier with a new battery, some motor oil, and a lot of mechanical knowhow. The Subaru's lengthy sabbatical was over. To have her own wheels again was like a pardon from the governor. Delia felt liberated from a long imprisonment.

Later that afternoon, as Delia was studying for the next week's classes and doing her laundry, the phone rang. She was surprised to hear Gabe's voice on the line.

"Well, stranger," she said, "fancy hearing from you." Her voice seemed always to have an edge on it when she spoke with Gabe these days.

"Hi, stranger yourself. Got a minute?"

"For you, sure."

"How's the leg doing?"

"It's coming. I actually drove the Sube today, for the first time. I'm a free woman!"

"You were always a free woman. I think you were a free woman in your mother's womb."

"Ha! Any other woman's womb, maybe, but not Polly McGrath's. What's on your mind? Denise giving you back to me?"

"What's on my mind, smartypants, has nothing to do with Denise. Remember that fellow I told you about—the one who was working with some metal plates found in Arizona?"

Delia perked up. "You've heard from him?"

"Sure have. I hope you don't mind that I went ahead and told him about your plates. He got pretty excited when he heard."

"Well, it's nice that somebody did."

"In fact, he's coming to see the rubbings I made, if it's okay with you, and to talk about where and how you found your plates. I didn't give him details, or tell him about the pouch."

"Sounds good. Fine."

"I told him we couldn't send copies without compromising their integrity. And, of course, he can't send copies of the ones he has because the plates don't belong to him."

"When's he coming?"

"He wants to come the day after Thanksgiving. Will that work for you?"

"I don't see why not."

"You're not going anywhere for the holiday?"

"Not me, how about you?"

"I'll be around. Denise and the kids are going to her parents' place in Minneapolis for a big family gathering. I don't think I'm up to that crowd just yet."

"I know the feeling. Maybe next year?"

"Maybe next year."

"Well, I'm invited over to the Turners' for Thanksgiving dinner. Why don't you come? I'll tell them you're being abandoned, and they'll gladly set another place."

"I just might do that. Sure it'd be okay?"

"Come now, need you ask?"

"I guess not."

Hector Gabrielson sounded tired, maybe even discouraged. Delia supposed it had to do with his changed circumstances—two teenage children to supervise and an ex-wife who was steering him back to the altar. Gabe hadn't said much—Delia hadn't seen a whole lot of him since early September—but she sensed that Denise was more enthusiastic about the whole business than he was. Gabe was one who would do what he thought was right for his children, regardless of what it cost him personally. It crossed Delia's mind that it was a shame Polly McGrath never gave Gabe a chance, never allowed herself to discover that he actually was her kind of man. Honorable, self-sacrificing, and totally reliable.

"Do we need to look at the rubbings and your notes before your scholar comes, just to refresh our memories?" Delia asked.

"Probably wouldn't hurt."

"We'll have time Thanksgiving night. Want to come over then, after we leave Angie and Howard?"

"Will do. Hey, and thanks."

She knew he meant the thanks sincerely, and that it was for many things, past as well as present. She knew he meant thanks for caring. And she did care, still.

As Delia and Gabe stepped into the blustery late November air after feasting with the Turners, they were both a little pensive. A skiff of snow had made walks and drives icy, and Delia clutched Gabe's arm for safety. She intended to baby her newly emancipated leg until it was good and strong. In many ways today had been like old times, she and Gabe sharing food and conversation with the Turners. Something in Delia wished they could return to those times, erase the summer, and take up where they had left off before she went west for spring break last April.

Life was so much simpler then than now. She and Gabe enjoyed an easy, affectionate friendship, Angie's cancer didn't exist because no one knew about it, Cynthia Harper was alive, Delia's right leg was whole and matched her left one, Gordon Foster had never been heard of, Delia's awakened conscience about the Church was still under wraps, and Jedediah McGrath was very much alive. The only serious ripple on the pond of her mental serenity in those days was the matter of gaining tenure, a permanent teaching position at the university. Today that problem was only one of many ripples—more accurately, tidal waves.

Delia pulled her Land's End squall jacket close around her throat and bent her head into the perennial Wisconsin wind. Neither she nor Gabe spoke as they drove to Morningside in his familiar Pathfinder. At her condo, Delia switched on the gas log and put cider with cinnamon sticks and cloves in a pan to heat. The prospect of another winter in the northland made her shudder, just as some people in Smithville dread July and August. It crossed her mind that Gordon might call while Gabe was here. He was overdue, and she tried to block it from her mind.

When Delia brought out the rubbings Gabe had made of the Chinta Canyon plates, she remembered fondly his absolute trust in her and his painstaking work to clean and interpret them. Her feelings for him quickened, then merged with other equally complex emotions. Seeing again the faint etchings in a strange, pictorial language reawakened the thrill of finding the metal sheets deposited perhaps centuries ago in a sandstone wall above a deep desert canyon. She remembered the awe she felt in first touching them, and the snug heft of them on her back. In a real sense, finding that decaying pouch changed the whole course of her life, made business-as-usual out of the question forever.

Gabe sat at what Delia called her "outdoor-indoor" dining table and read through his notes from some months back about the sketchy inscriptions he had found on the plates. "This fellow who's coming should be able to correct some of my erroneous assumptions about our diarist and her message, if the plates are indeed the work of one woman," Gabe said.

"For some reason, I've never thought of the writer as male. My gut tells me the writer is a woman," Delia responded.

The evening flew by, easing naturally into conversation, study, and even laughter. At last, Gabe pushed back from the table, stretched his arms high above his head, yawned, and looked at Delia. "Time for some shuteye. Shall we leave this stuff as it is and bring the specialist over here to compare notes tomorrow?" he asked.

"Sure. What time shall I look for you?"

"My guess would be around four or five. He flew into Chicago a couple of days ago, and will drive up here in the afternoon."

"Sounds like a deal. Will we need to feed him?"

"Maybe later on. He plans to stay in Jefferson tomorrow night and return to Chicago Saturday. He has relatives there."

Gabe tidied the table while Delia found his jacket, and they walked together to the door. "Want some more hot cider before you go?" she asked.

"I guess not." Then unexpectedly, he turned and pulled her to him, kissing her with both passion and tenderness. She was too surprised to resist, and let him hold her close a long time. "I love you," he whispered at last in her ear. "I've never stopped." Then, abruptly, he opened the door and disappeared into the light snow that had begun to fall while they pored over Delia's messages from a faraway past.

Gordon didn't call that night or the next day either, and Delia thought it was just as well. He had been indecisive about his plans for

Thanksgiving last time they had talked, and she wondered if he had gone to see his mother in Colorado. The next day, Gabe and his new friend and colleague, Samuel Ornstein from Duke University, appeared just before five o'clock. Delia liked Samuel immediately. She guessed him to be about Gabe's age, though grayer, shorter, and balding; but he wasn't the stuffy scholar she had expected. Before he was inside the door, he had presented her with a box of Jewish pastries from his aunt in Chicago.

"She insisted," he said, "so what could I do? She isn't a woman who takes no for an answer."

"My kind of woman," Delia laughed. "I'd like to return the favor, but my domestic talents run from limited to non-existent. I could send her some red desert sand in a bottle, however."

"Nothing she'd like better, that aunt of mine. The desert in a bottle is all the desert she wants. 'What would I do with all that space?' she asks. 'Chicago is west enough for anyone with a Jewish surname. A city girl, she should stay in the city,' my aunt says, and she does."

Delia took their jackets while Gabe led Samuel to the table, where he became instantly absorbed in what he saw. Samuel's thick "coke bottle" eyeglasses were framed in heavy black rims, and they kept sliding down his nose as he bent over Gabe's rubbings of the Chinta inscriptions. "Hmmm," he murmured without raising his head. "Maybe we have some similarities. Let's take a look."

Samuel opened the small briefcase he had carried in under his arm. Inside were his own rubbings of the Arizona plates. He arranged the four Chinta copies across the upper edge of the table and his own below them. There were four also. He picked up Gabe's magnifying glass and began shifting his sheets around, turning them one way then another while Gabe and Delia watched from a respectful distance.

"Holy Methuselah!" he cried after several minutes. "They're a match!"

Even now, two hours later, Delia couldn't believe what her eyes had told her and what the eyes of two ancient language scholars had confirmed. The so-called "Arizona" plates were the very plates she had discovered in a high recess and carried out of Chinta Canyon on her back. The question now was, how did they arrive in the hands of wealthy collectors, the people who had engaged Samuel Ornstein to attempt a translation of them? And how many hands had the metal sheets passed through since the night someone had stolen them from Gordon's truck in Juniper?

It was a lot to untangle, and no one knew quite how or where to begin. Samuel asked Delia to describe how her plates were found, and how they were subsequently lost. He nodded repeatedly as she talked, and never once questioned or disputed her account of what happened. She didn't mention the small protective casing of stones, nor the pouch.

"I know Max Blohm," Samuel said at one point. "He's as skeptical as he is honest. Too bad he didn't take time to study the plates before passing judgment on them. They're authentic, all right. No question about it." Then he turned to Gabe. "Lucky you got to see them and make rubbings before they were stolen."

"Yes, wasn't it?"

Delia was dying to call Gordon and Ron with the news, but forced herself to wait. Gabe suggested they go somewhere for supper and calmly discuss the appropriate steps they should take. Delia had little choice but to agree, though she felt too excited to eat. She picked at a crisp chicken salad, mainly rearranging it rather than eating it, while Gabe and Samuel gobbled veggie burgers and considered their options. Should Samuel call his patrons first? How much should he tell them? Or should one of them call the FBI? Would the FBI give two hoots about this? Should they themselves try to track down the sellers, and maybe the thieves, before notifying authorities?

It was all too much cloak and dagger for Delia. "I say we call someone like Nevell Becker at the Chapin Mesa Museum and let him run it through channels," she said. "He has all the information on the matter, and copies of all the reports. He'll know what to do, or the woman who arranged for him to go into Chinta with us will."

Gabe and Samuel, who had been talking a mile a minute, stopped and looked at her. "Delia's right," Gabe said. "We're getting ahead of ourselves. Let the appropriate investigators take what we can tell them and run with it."

"In the meantime, aside from all the fun and games," Delia said a bit irritably, "I'd like to know what those plates say. Can you tell me, Samuel?"

"Not everything, but perhaps a few things. Let's return to your place, and I'll verbalize some guesses for you while you sample my aunt's pastries. She'll want a full description of your unbridled ecstasy."

Back at Morningside, Samuel took a yellow legal notepad from his briefcase and began thumbing through several pages of notes. "It's nearly impossible to put together anything resembling sentences from the inscriptions," he said. "Whoever engraved them didn't go very deep, and they are scratched and weathered, though surprisingly free of tarnish."

"Well, sure," Delia declared. "Gabe spent hours cleaning them."

Samuel looked up at Gabe. "You didn't tell me that."

"It didn't seem significant. We thought we were dealing with two sets of plates."

"Oh, yes, of course." Samuel picked up one of the rubbings. "See this symbol at the top? This could be the first page. I think the writer is introducing herself—or himself."

"Do you think the writer is a woman?" Delia interrupted.

"I'd almost bet on it."

"Can you find any storyline?" Gabe asked. "It suggested a diary of some sort to me."

"And it does to me, too," Samuel replied. "A much abbreviated life story, but not necessarily in an historical sense."

"More like the account of a spiritual journey?" Delia pressed.

"Yes, something like that."

"Did you find what might have been references to Deity?" Gabe asked.

"I think so, especially at the end. How about you?"

"I thought so, too."

Samuel picked up another sheet. "There seem to be a few historical references on this page—references to wars, maybe, or other conflicts. But their significance still appears to be personal."

"Is a word-for-word translation possible?" Delia asked.

Samuel shook his head. "Unfortunately, no. Not only is there the problem of only partially or vaguely familiar symbols, but there is the further difficulty, as you know, of tracings too faint to be deciphered at all. There are a few curiosities, however, that intrigue me."

"Such as?"

"Such as several detectable references to 'the fathers,' in the plural, and their practices or traditions. As if some ideas or teachings were formalized into a written code of conduct and handed down from generation to generation."

Delia leaned forward, intensely interested. "Was the writer respectful of those traditions?"

"Hard to say, though it seems she came to some sort of affirmation at the end. The religious allusions suggest that."

Delia sat back, tilting her chair on two legs and propping her feet against a low chest. She didn't say anything.

Gabe shuffled through his own notes, then broached a new subject. "Have you been able to date the plates?"

"Not yet, but we're talking about a good many centuries, I'm sure. The metal content would have to be analyzed, and for now, I've returned them to the people who hired me. They intend to enlist someone who can help with the dating. I gave them a few names." Samuel turned to Gabe. "Like you, I'm a language person, mainly Mediterranean, though I know something about early native American languages. The seeming blend of the two in the plates is rather hard to decipher, and it may be a kind of shorthand. Why don't we go through the thing sheet by sheet, and I'll attempt a little direct translation of some of the clearer symbols."

"Good idea," Gabe agreed.

Delia dropped forward onto all four legs of her chair and turned to Samuel. "Another question first," she said. "Were the plates in a container of any sort when you got them?"

"Just a flannel wrap and a canvas briefcase. Could have been K-Mart specials."

"Did you ask the owners about a container?"

"Yes, and they said this is how the plates came to them. The antique dealer claimed there was no original cover. His information was that the inscriptions were buried in sand, in a small makeshift stone vault. Were they?"

"They were in a stone box of sorts, yes, but they were also in a leather-like pouch. I carried them out of Chinta Canyon in that crumbly old pouch. And there were other things inside the pouch, too, as Gabe knows."

"Yes," Gabe said, "something that looked like a stylus, and the remains of what was probably a papyrus scroll."

"A book of some sort," Samuel nodded.

"That's what I think," Delia said.

"So, the thieves, or someone else along the line, kept the extra things," said Gabe, "probably hoping to cash in on the find a second time."

"Wouldn't surprise me," Samuel said. "Any more questions, Delia?"

"That should hold me for the time being. You talk, and I'll follow along on Gabe's sheets."

It was at least three a.m. when the two men drove away from Morningside and Delia climbed the stairs to bed. Weary as she was, she did not expect sleep very soon. Fatigue often manufactures and inflates worries, and her mind found plenty of food for insomnia. The peace she had won earlier with regard to the plates was gone, shattered by these new developments. Her brain wouldn't let the matter rest. In the first place, she wished she had insisted on seeing the plates herself, as soon as possible. Samuel would simply have to arrange that with his artifact collectors. After all, her mind argued, the metal sheets were more hers than anyone's, weren't they? Her mind didn't stop there, either, but went to rehashing and second-guessing the plan.

The three of them had decided that Samuel should break the news to his collectors first. Those people needed to know that the plates were stolen—the evidence was indisputable—and that Samuel was obligated to notify appropriate authorities. He would do so through his university's legal staff. BLM officials in Washington, and in the Denver regional office, were at the top of his list, along with the FBI. Delia agreed to make the less formal contacts, to alert the appropriate local people in southern Utah. It was too much to absorb all at once, and Delia wanted to shut her mind down. She donned her pajamas and crawled into bed without so much as brushing her teeth.

If Begonia Slopek had chanced outside her door to check on the weather, or on the lingering presence of the Pathfinder belonging to Delia's gentleman friend, she would have seen lights burning at her neighbor's place far into the night. Earlier that evening, Begonia had admitted to Elmer Roy, over the phone, that the girl had fooled her. Here she thought she was going to have an old maid on her hands, and now Delia had two men on the hook. It's feast or famine, she said. Curiously, Begonia never thought of herself as "an old maid," though she readily applied the term to others. She herself just didn't happen to have married along the way is all. And it wasn't that she hadn't had her chances.

Begonia had met Hector Gabrielson a time or two, but thought he was too tall for Delia. She did admire his vehicle, however, and found his beard quite dashing. Until she met Elmer Roy, who wore what he called a goatee, she had always been partial to full beards. Beard or no beard, she hated to see a tall man wasted on a woman who didn't need all that height. A tall fellow sweet on a girl who was short, or medium-sized like Delia, was an unfortunate extravagance, in her view. It took him off the market and left some deserving tall girl to do without. For that and other less objective reasons, Begonia was still pulling for Gordon, though she well knew the adage that absence makes the heart grow fonder—for somebody else. It was none of her business anyway, she explained to Elmer Roy no more than seven or eight times.

The next morning Begonia awoke with a start. It was Saturday. She rushed to the window to see if that tall fellow's car was still keeping the Pontiac company. It was a distinct relief that the vehicle, one of those intimidating SUV's, was nowhere to be seen. It had been sitting there when she woke up in front of the TV well after midnight and turned off "Larry King Live." The show was a repeat from earlier, so it wasn't live at all. They should change the name, she had complained. Call it Larry King Redux, maybe.

Well, in any case, the fellow hadn't stayed *all* night, she told herself. Just half of it. Begonia gathered that Delia had been indoctrinated since childhood against such doings, and she wouldn't want the girl to start any hanky-panky at this stage of the game. After all, she wasn't seventeen any longer, was she? What excuse would she have? She couldn't plead ignorance.

Now as for herself, Begonia was proud to say she was not a fallen woman. She was, rather, what she liked to call an "experienced virgin." But these days, heavens to Betsy, these days she and Elmer Roy could spend the whole night unwed in the same room and be perfectly safe, maybe even the same bed! They'd drop off to sleep fully clothed, holding hands most likely, and sleep like babies until morning. But this young blood! "Lead me not into temptation," Begonia declared emphatically to the mantel clock that had come across the ocean with her great-grandmother on her father's side and only got wet once.

It was all Begonia could do to stay put and not go ringing Delia's doorbell to get the scoop on last night. Besides, it was their regular grocery day, whenever Delia was available, and Delia had promised to take her. For the sake of the faint-hearted and uninsured, Delia had said. Begonia knew she wasn't the greatest driver in the world, but she wasn't as bad as Delia let on either. Still, Begonia didn't want to take any chances with her own life. If she died behind the wheel, it would break Elmer Roy's heart—not to mention leave him at the mercy of that daughter of his. Begonia liked the granddaughter just fine, but the daughter was something else. A hypocrite and bossy besides.

Begonia dearly wished Elmer Roy would come down on the side of common sense just this once and chop a few months off the acceptable courting period for southern gentlemen of breeding. She herself was ready to rustle up a preacher and be done with it. Maybe even elope, though in her heart she had always fancied a church wedding. Then after the honeymoon he could move in with her, and everything would be hunky-dory. If he could stand her antiques, that is. Sometimes she got the impression that he wasn't nearly so fond of them as she was. Well, if she had to, she'd put some of them in storage and work him into them gradually.

Two or three times that morning, Begonia and her pink parka had moseyed over to Delia's front steps and tried to peer through the mini-blinds on the bay window to the right of the door. Then she put her ear against the door and listened hard for signs of life. She reached out to ring the doorbell once, but retrieved her hand and paced back and forth across the small landing, pivoting neatly on her four-footed aluminum cane. It was cold out, and Thursday's inch or two of snow had thinly blanketed the brown early winter grass. Finally, Begonia sighed and returned to her place, blowing on her fingers to warm them.

Behind her busy front door and up the stairs, Delia began stretching and yawning shortly before ten. It had been after five a.m. when she scowled at the clock for the last time and finally fell asleep. Semi-awake now, her first thought was to call Gordon and tell him the news, but something in her resisted. What did his silence mean, anyway? "Long-distance relationships are the pits," she groaned, turning onto her stomach and burying her face in the pillow.

Lying there, Delia let her suspicions about the stolen plates settle once again on Max Blohm's graduate students. She hated to think that any students would destroy their careers this way. She thought of her own graduate advisees, every one of them hard-working and dependable. Theft of scholarly materials went against all their training. But then, life was full of surprises.

Well, if it was those two, she reasoned, they wouldn't have made the grade in a rigorous academic program anyway. But outright larceny and sale of stolen goods could mean prison time. "Justice will be served, and God will likely stay out of it," she said half aloud, raising herself up on both hands and twisting to a sitting position. Gingerly testing her game leg, she made a solemn vow: *Today, I am going for a walk, a real walk—even if I have to do it on the indoor track.* But first, a shower, and then a phone call, and then a grocery adventure with her highness, Miss Begonia.

When Delia stepped out of the shower to a ringing telephone, she assumed it was Begonia, who very likely had been sitting on her hands for the last two hours to keep them from dialing Delia's number. Delia had to give her plucky little neighbor credit. It was well after ten. Either Delia had finally convinced her neighbor that Saturdays were for sleeping late, or the pins and needles market was down today. Grabbing her terry robe, Delia hobbled dripping to the bedroom phone. The voice on the other end, however, was definitely not Begonia's.

"I'm calling for Delia McGrath," a suave male voice said.

"This is Delia," she replied, curious.

"Nelson Farwell here," the voice informed her. "I've seen you at church a time or two and wanted to get acquainted."

Good old Mary Beth, Delia thought. *That's all I need, a blind date.* "Oh . . . well, perhaps sometime. Maybe we can cross paths at church tomorrow or next week. Although with my leg freshly out of a cast, I walk a rather slow path."

He neatly sidestepped her hesitation. "There's a chamber concert over at Edgewood College tonight. Would you care to go with me? It ought to be very good."

"Oh? Well, I don't think I can tonight. I . . . I have other plans," she stammered.

"I understand. It is rather late for me to be calling. May I try again when I can give you more notice?"

"Uh, try again? I don't know. . . . Sure, sure, I suppose so. Forgive me for sounding like an idiot, but you caught me by surprise. I don't know whose voice I expected to hear, but it wasn't one attached to a stranger named Nelson Farwell."

"I understand that. Maybe I could drop by sometime and we could get acquainted."

"Uh, . . . sure, why not?" *Actually, there must be a million reasons why not,* she mused silently.

"Why don't I come by and pick you up for church in the morning? Save you the trouble of driving with that bad leg."

"You really don't need to, honest. I can manage fine, so long as I don't have to stop, that is. I can do everything except push the brake pedal."

Nelson chuckled politely, but Delia could tell he wasn't amused by her attempt at humor. "No, I insist," he said. "I'll be there at eight-forty. Unit 32 at Morningside, isn't it?"

"You got it." Delia returned the receiver to its cradle and dropped onto the side of the bed. *What now?* she asked herself. *How did I let that happen? The last thing I need is to encourage Nelson Farwell. But then again, maybe we can just be friends,* she rationalized. *Don't believe it,* she answered herself, *don't believe it for a minute. He didn't sound like a man looking for friendship. He's in the market for either a wife or a trophy. Maybe both. I must be on his trial shopping list, thanks to my overzealous but well-meaning visiting teacher.*

Delia sat for a moment, blankly contemplating the vertical blinds that closed off her glass balcony door. Scarcely aware of it, she began counting individual strips, mechanically scanning the blinds from left to right. It was an exercise in frustration because she kept losing count at around ten or eleven as her eyes, unable to hold so narrow a focus more than a few seconds, invariably expanded their field of vision. She tried closing one eye, but it made no difference. If anything, it was worse.

Still groggy from too little sleep too late, Delia shook her head and rumpled her hair to clear her mind. At last she picked up the phone, stared at the number pad a minute, and set it down again. *Later,* she decided. *I'll try him later.* She flopped back crossways on the bed, raising her right leg and forcing the knee to bend with her hands. It resisted, and she winced with pain.

Like an insistent conscience, the phone rang again. "Begonia this time for sure," Delia announced to the wall, and put the receiver to her ear.

"Speak, if you dare," she said to the mouthpiece.

"Hello, Delia? Is that you?"

Hannah! Delia sat up as if shot from behind with a dart gun. "Yes, I confess, it's me. I mean, it's *I*. That's what you say, isn't it Hannah? You use the proper case, the nominative, even in informal conversation? Most of the world, you know, ignores that rule."

"Delia, what's got into you? Are you drunk?"

"Whatever gave you that idea, Hannah? You know I drink only on weekdays between four and six o'clock. This is Saturday."

"Delia, listen to me. I haven't time for games. This is serious business."

"I'm sure it is, Hannah, or you wouldn't have called. You and Polly McGrath are the only people I know who keep a stopwatch by the telephone to time your calls. The difference is, you log your calls and check AT&T's figures against yours and she doesn't. Have you ever caught them fudging on the time?"

"Not yet, but I'm sure I will sometime."

For some reason, Delia took perverse pleasure in hectoring her sister. Hannah was so impossible sometimes. "Look, Hannah, I'm sorry for acting like a jerk. I didn't get much sleep last night, and I can't seem to get perking this morning. How was Thanksgiving? Does Mother seem okay?"

"That's why I'm calling. Mother definitely does not seem okay."

Delia jumped to her feet, landing too hard on her game leg, adrenalin pumping. "What's wrong? Is she sick, or hurt? Where are you?"

"I'm home in Provo, don't panic. She's not sick, at least not physically. But she's been up to something, and it worries me."

"Up to something? What?"

"I'm not sure, but it's shady—what's the word?—clandestine!"

"Oooh, that's a pretty big word for Polly McGrath." Delia relaxed. It was only one of Hannah's patented overreactions.

"She's been carrying on with some pretty bizarre characters since Dad died. Did you notice anything funny when you were there convalescing?"

"Not much happened that could be termed funny in those weeks, Hannah. But since you ask, I did notice a few oddballs around the place during what you call my *convalescence*—namely myself, Jennifer, Gordon Foster, and a couple of missionaries. Polly was the only sane one on the premises, now that I think of it."

"You aren't funny, Delia. Did mother ever mention a man named 'Clemmer'? Or twin sisters named 'Plumm'? All from Wyoming?"

"No, but I wish she had. Might have added a little spice to our lives. If the Plumms were pickled, that is."

"I don't know why I call you. You can't get serious about anything."

"Well, if Mother's hurting, or ill, or suffering, that's one thing. But if she's found a few friends, that's quite another. I'm glad if she has. A little bit of Arva Plimpton goes a long way."

"But these people turned up at our Thanksgiving dinner, uninvited, and took over. Simply took over. And that Clemmer person acted as if he owned the place, and Mother with it."

"Look, Hannah, there are enough troubles in the world without inventing some. Mother is old enough and smart enough to look out for herself. I trust her judgment. By the way, how's Roger doing? Still in Florida chasing his middle-aged flower child?"

Delia could feel Hannah react across the wires. "Roger is not the concern here," Hannah retorted icily. "Your mother is."

Delia repented. "Hannah," she said gently, "let's not worry until there's something concrete to worry about. We can't run Mother's life. I'll be flying out at Christmastime. We can talk then, okay?"

"Well, I'm glad to report that Jed Junior and Paul are showing some interest in this affair."

"How about Victor and RonJay?"

"They're cut from the same cloth you are, I'm sorry to say. And Ronald was there, too, at the dinner, and saw the whole thing. And he had the nerve to feed them, *my* rolls and pies, too, mind you."

"And Lester?"

"You know Lester. I can't get him to state an opinion, much less argue about anything."

"Well, my advice is to let it go, Hannah. You'll live longer; we'll all live longer."

"If this blows up in our faces, don't say I didn't warn you."

"I promise. I hereby acknowledge that I have been dutifully warned. Now, go take a cold shower and give Lester a kiss for me. Then count to ten and forget these people. Good-bye, Hannah, and God bless America."

Delia plunked the phone into its cradle, but then picked it up and dialed Gordon's number. No answer. She hung up and dialed Ron's number. After three rings, Effie's voice came on the line.

"Hi, Effie."

"Aunt Delia!" Effie squealed. "Daddy's over to Grandma's feeding the horses. Where are you?"

"Still in Wisconsin. Did you have a good Thanksgiving?"

"Boy, did we ever! Mr. Clemmer came, and brought two funny ladies who looked the same. Mr. Clemmer is Grandma's boyfriend."

"I didn't know Grandma had a boyfriend."

"Well, she does. Mr. Clemmer told me so."

"Did Grandma say so, too?"

"No way. She was real cross with him, but he just laughed."

"Did Gordon come?"

"No. He was with his other girlfriend. Jill and I saw them by the river."

Delia felt as though she had been clubbed. She sank to the bed, holding the phone receiver in both hands. At last she managed a mumble. "Thanks, Effie. Tell your daddy I called." The delivery instrument of so much bliss and so much heartache fell to the floor, and Delia sobbed out her frustration, her exhaustion, and her grief.

Periodically the doorbell rang, and she let it ring. Finally it went permanently silent. Begonia had given up.

CHAPTER NINE

Arva Plimpton had a lot to think about, and she sat in worship service in Smithville the Sunday after Thanksgiving doing it. Much as she tried to drag her mind back to serious contemplation of the proceedings, she couldn't. She simply couldn't, and that was all there was to it. And she didn't fare much better in Sunday School and Relief Society, either. Arva had received unexpected visitors late in the afternoon Thanksgiving Day—Anthon Clemmer and those odd little Plumm women, whom she had never laid eyes on before the minute they landed on her doorstep. Twenty minutes worth of them, she decided, was about her limit.

Arva did not have a twin sister, and she could not for the life of her imagine the inconvenience of having someone around who looked just like herself finishing all her sentences for her, uninvited. *If I wanted that, I'd carry a mirror and a tape recorder,* she told herself. Now, Anthon was a different story. He looked like a clown in that South Pacific get-up in the middle of the desert, but he was a real charmer just the same. And he seemed to enjoy those women, which just goes to show what a good-natured person he was, and tolerant, through and through.

Arva was beginning to think that Anthon was a real catch, but she wasn't settled on a way to snare him. He came to show the Plumms her property, he said, but she couldn't help wondering if he didn't come partly to see her. Or maybe mostly. If it was only *partly,* then maybe she should go ahead and sell it to him, get the cash in hand, and move into retirement living in town before he changed his mind. On the other hand, if it was *mostly,* she'd just as soon stay on her place, scoot over, and make room for him. After their legal and lawful marriage, of course.

She, Arva Plimpton, would never agree to one of those live-in arrangements that seemed to be all the rage elsewhere. She wouldn't exactly call Smithville heaven on earth, but those practices were not all the rage here, as far as she could tell. And the few people who did such things had the good sense to keep it to themselves rather than broadcast it around and upset everybody. This town tried to stay moral, or at least appear moral, and mainly succeeded. There was, of course, that fellow who ran off with his delivery truck full of watches and diamond rings, but even he came back, sorry as all getout. She could honestly say she didn't know a single criminal on a first-name basis. Not a one. For which she gave thanks to the powers that be.

As Arva was contemplating these matters and their attendant digressions, the small child hanging over the pew in front of her grinned as innocently as you please and dumped a ziploc sandwich bag of Cheerios on the floor at Arva's feet. They rolled every which way, including under the pew she occupied. Wheat Chex would have stayed put, but not Cheerios. They were built to roll. But since Arva's feet barely reached the floor when she sat back all the way, it wasn't a huge problem until the child left his seat and crawled under it in an effort to retrieve the spill.

Bumping and nudging along, he wriggled between her feet and under her seat, now and then squashing some of the little oat wheels with his knees and hands. Then he sat up, but it "warn't," as Huck Finn would have phrased it, "good judgment." He was still under Arva's pew, and directly beneath her when his head met wood with a resounding thwack. Arva shot off the bench about six inches, she judged, and when she returned, slightly in front of it, she met the child on his way out.

It was not a congenial meeting, from either point of view. Arva reflexively uttered a word she rarely found it necessary to employ at home, much less at church, and the child bellowed. In a split second, the child's mother, heretofore totally oblivious to the child's pranks or whereabouts, was out of her seat and into the space next to Arva. She lifted the howling toddler to her waist, scowled at Arva, and carried the tiny troublemaker out of the meeting on her hip, like an animated sack of puppy chow.

Arva managed to regain some of her composure by the closing hymn, though she hadn't appreciated the muffled snickers of her fellow worshipers one iota. She didn't mind being *entertaining* if the occasion called for it—she had enjoyed an exceptional degree of popularity as a girl, she wasn't ashamed to say—but she didn't want to be the day's *entertainment* for anybody. Not at her age, not on the Sabbath, and most of all, not at church.

Arva had hoped for a lengthy closing hymn, one that would allow more time for people to forget what had happened, or at least to stop taking so much pleasure in it. She was pulling for "A Poor Wayfaring Man of Grief"—all seven verses. Or at the very least, "The Spirit of God Like a Fire Is Burning." Just her luck, the bishop, struggling to keep a straight face, announced that the congregation would sing "Praise God from Whom All Blessings Flow," by far the shortest number in the hymnal. Hardly a song at all. More like an exit sign set to music. Arva couldn't help noting that the benediction was also extremely brief. It was as though the whole kit and kaboodle were dying to get out of the place before they exploded in gales of laughter.

This little episode broke Arva's concentration on matters of real estate and impending romance for the time being, and she settled into Sunday School class prepared to listen. It did cross her mind, however, as strains of "Praise God from Whom All Blessings Flow" echoed and re-echoed in her consciousness, that Anthon Clemmer might be a blessing God was thinking to wash into her stream. *Well,* she thought, *I'll save my praise for when and if it happens.* She sat in class, at the back, not daring to look right or left, not even looking for Polly McGrath, whom she had taken under her wing since Polly's unfortunate and totally unforeseen widowhood. Arva didn't want any credit for her kindness; it was what a good neighbor did, and a good neighbor is what she was. But today, Polly would have to fend for herself. Arva was lying low. And, she was thinking.

Orville Tatum was teaching the lesson, as always, and reading passages from the New Testament. He came to the ones on the resurrection, and then supplemented them with his own interpretations and with other scriptures on restoration. "Not a hair from our heads will be lost!" Brother Tatum exclaimed, and Arva was ready to believe him. But then, she started thinking about it. *If every hair will be alive and accounted for, we'll all look like walking bramble bushes in the next life.*

That thought led to further inquiry. *What* will *my hair look like when I'm resurrected?* Arva wondered. *Will I be my natural-born auburn again, or will I arise in glory with whatever color Beverly has given me at the time of my death? If she's heavy on purple the particular month I'm called home, will I be doomed to wear maroon hair for eternity?* Arva decided that when she felt the death rattle, she'd rush to Beverly and beg her to try one more time for true auburn. Failing that, she'd beg Beverly to lean toward the orange side, if lean she must. On the other hand, what if the maroon or orange disappeared at the moment all her parts were collected, leaving her everlastingly white on top?

And speaking of collected parts, a vision of amputated arms, legs, fingers, and toes, flying through the air to reattach themselves to their rightful owners, flashed through Arva's head. In fact, the whole subject opened wide the door of speculation in her mind, and one thing led to another. If not a hair will be lost, she wondered, how about a pound? Will every pound we've ever gained track us down and go with us?

Arva was admittedly one of those yo-yo dieters all the health nuts like to criticize in such superior tones. She used to say to people that she'd lost three hundred pounds, then she'd add with a hearty guffaw, thirty pounds ten times. She tried to envision herself lugging those three hundred pounds along with her, in a shiny white coaster wagon, down streets paved with gold. Somehow the image didn't fit with her notions of the afterlife, though her notions on that subject were admittedly vague.

Then it occurred to Arva that, as with her hair, whatever she weighed when she departed this vale of tears might be what she'd wind up with. In that case, she intended to go on a straight liquid diet for the last three months of her life, thus assuring herself a svelte figure forever. It was worth a try, she decided. No sooner had that thought been deposited in her mental day planner, to be extracted at the appropriate moment in her golden years, than another just as prickly flew in to occupy the space it had left.

If we get stuck permanently with what we had when we left—only spiffed up, of course—Arva thought maybe she should get that nose job she'd been thinking about. Which would accompany her into the eternities, she mused silently, the old nose or the new one? If the old one, she could spare herself a lot of expense. But if the new one, it would be a good investment.

The possibilities, Arva could plainly see, were endless. If hair and pounds and noses, then how about fingernails and toenails? And teeth? Would we get all our baby teeth back, and if we did, how would we fit them in? For just an instant, she saw herself with a mouth so full of teeth there was no room for either food or toothbrush. She assumed that false teeth would not participate in the resurrection any more than false eyelashes and wigs.

Before Arva could say Jack Robinson, Sunday School was over. She wondered where the time had gone and hoped none of the Relief Society sisters would say anything about that little episode with the Cheerios and the squalling child. Then Arva decided she needed to pay the water fountain a visit before Relief Society started. A case of nerves always left her with a dry mouth. As Arva reached the fountain, Polly McGrath stepped hurriedly by, without so much as a greeting. She was coughing into her handkerchief, and Arva figured that's why she didn't stop or at least give her friend and nearest neighbor a howdya do.

Widowhood certainly hadn't loosened Polly up any, Arva reflected, but she was determined not to give up hope that it might. She herself would remain an optimist to the end. With that thought, Arva marched into the final meeting of the day, intent on fulfilling her obligation to the Lord and the bishop whether Polly McGrath chose to stay or not.

Despite Brother Tatum's presentation of the Sunday School lesson, which was what Polly called interpretive speculation, the scriptures he read touched her deeply as she followed along. "I am the resurrection, and the life," Jesus had said. "He that believeth in me, though he were dead, yet shall he live." She didn't doubt that Jesus meant it, and in her head she knew that Jedediah was alive somewhere, waiting for her. But her heart hurt. "Whosoever liveth and believeth in me shall never die," Jesus proclaimed again. *But if Jed didn't die, why did we bury him?* a niggling voice inside her demanded.

And if she truly believed Jed was alive, then why did she feel so down in the dumps? Why couldn't she rejoice for him and see his death as only a short separation? Why did the days seem to stretch ahead of her like a long, empty highway with a single broken stripe down the middle? And why did she utterly dread Christmas without him? She wished she could excise December from the calendar this year. As a rule, Polly McGrath was not the sort who enjoyed feeling sorry for herself, and she didn't want to be the object of anybody's pity. But she felt the need of solace just now, and the lesson reminded her that she had a source of solace she didn't always turn to for that purpose. She hated to give the Lord any more grief than he already had. Still, "I will not leave you comfortless," Jesus had promised.

To make matters worse, Polly had been fighting a nagging cough the last day or two and wondered if she might be coming down with a cold. Rather than hack and wheeze through Relief Society, she elected to slip out and go home. A little olive oil and sugar in a teaspoon would fix the cough. Smithville was not Palm Springs by any means, and a rather nasty wind was gusting outside the meeting-house. Even so, hardly anybody wore heavy coats around town. Pulling her gray cardigan sweater tighter around her chest, Polly hurried toward the old Imperial, searching her handbag for keys as she went. But when she left the church parking lot, the vehicle turned toward town instead of home, almost of its own volition. It came to a stop alongside a park-like plot of earth where a good number of her acquaintances had been planted to await resurrection.

As if in a dream, Polly found herself walking away from the Imperial across the crunchy, faded cemetery grass toward Jedediah McGrath's grave. It was the first time she had come since he was buried six months ago. Scrupulously avoiding the place and its attendant pain, Polly sometimes drove several blocks out of her way so as not to see it. She marveled that the longest continuous Sunday School class under the same teacher in the history of the planet still had the power to move her like this. Yet here she was, cough and all, at the foot of her husband's grave, before noon on a late November Sunday.

She was startled to see her own name on the headstone, "Polly Appleby McGrath," and her birth date. The presence of the birth date, engraved for the ages, annoyed her a little, a public announcement of how old she was while she was still around. She wondered why that piece of information couldn't have been supplied when the other date was entered and she wasn't above ground to care one particle whether people knew her age or not. The only blank space on the granite block was the date of her death. Polly shuddered involuntarily, as if she had seen her own ghost. The specific day of her departure was up in the air, perhaps, but there was no question that she was going. People in the headstone and burial business had absolute security. Almost nobody escaped them.

Polly's cough started up again in the raw air, but she slowly, stiffly knelt on the cold grass and felt the full effect of her mortality. She wanted words with Jedediah and hoped he was close by somewhere, though it would be like him to be off puttering around in some heavenly version of the barn just when she needed him. Polly tried several times to explain to Jed how she felt about things, and how troubled she was, and how she couldn't face Christmas without him. She had never been one who could describe her feelings, and in any case, she thought feelings that showed were a sign of weakness. They embarrassed her. Unable to find the words, Polly buried her face in her hands, pleading in her heart for grace and peace, sobbing her need, feeling the earth's coldness penetrate to her very soul.

Then suddenly, as if prompted by a silent voice, Polly stopped and dropped her hands. Kneeling there, sitting back on her heels, all her senses alert, she heard the chimes in a distant church tower peal out. Reaching beneath her anguish, the ringing anthem lifted her to her feet and she rode its vibrations back to Jerusalem. In a bleak winter cemetery, in an arid western land, Polly McGrath took instruction from another desolate woman, one who centuries earlier had approached, brokenhearted, a fresh tomb in an arid eastern land. And what the Magdalene sought there, Polly remembered, was not a mere mortal, but her Savior and her Lord.

In Smithville that day, no tomb opened, no radiant figure appeared and spoke Polly McGrath's name; but she received the miracle nonetheless. The words of that earlier day pierced her consciousness: "Woman, why weepest thou? whom seekest thou?" Even in her agony, Polly realized that the voice in her mind was asking the crucial question—whom seekest thou? Whom, indeed, despite unequivocal scriptural injunctions, had she been seeking in her bottled-up anguish? The answer resounded in her head. Jedediah. She had been seeking Jedediah, hoping he might heal her, when, like Mary, she should have been seeking her Lord.

"Rabboni," she whispered through her tears, and raised her eyes to where the blowing cypress limbs orchestrated splashes of light to play across Jedediah's grave and her own face.

* * * * * * * *

The good news about the Chinta plates could not offset the effects of Effie's ingenuous revelation about Gordon's "other girl-friend," and Delia was not in the best of spirits when Nelson Farwell called for her Sunday morning and drove the familiar route to the Jefferson meetinghouse. Recent events—Effie's bulletin, Gordon's silence over the last several days, and Delia's failure to catch him by phone—had combined to produce more than a little anxiety. *Serves me right for falling too hard,* she thought. *Gabe would at least have squared with me, not just cut me off. Am I going with Nelson just to spite Gordon?*

If heads had turned when Delia McGrath appeared in the Jefferson Second Ward several weeks ago in the company of Gordon Foster, the stir was nothing compared to that evoked on the Sunday after Thanksgiving. After all, no one in the congregation had known Gordon, but everyone knew Nelson Farwell. And there he was, in his finely tailored, dark gray suit, escorting Delia to a seat in the center pews while the organ broadcast a hearty welcome to the worshipers.

The threatening snow had held off, and Delia wore only a navy blue blazer over a tan skirt and silk blouse. Mary Beth Archer nudged her husband and nodded toward the pair, but Frank Archer's head remained motionless. Glancing up, Delia thought she detected a trace of concern register in the bishop's face, and she wondered what, if anything, it meant. Was the concern for her or for Nelson?

They were a few minutes early, and as Delia sat down, she did a double take. The woman in front of her and to the right bore a strong resemblance to her sister Hannah. Delia had refused to be alarmed by Hannah's call the previous day, but it vexed her just the same. She believed what she had told Hannah, that she would be glad if her mother found new friends and interests, but a new male interest? It had never occurred to Delia that her mother might remarry and share her home and heart with someone other than Jedediah McGrath. Delia was learning yet again that tolerance is much more congenial in theory than in practice.

With the beginning strains of the opening hymn, "Sing Praise to Him," Delia's mind returned to the chapel on Sego Road and her purpose in being there. Nelson, she noticed, did not join in the congregational singing, and she sang without him. But even as her lips formed the words, her mind sprinted west, to services in Smithville, just months ago, when she sat next to her mother and Gordon, blending her voice with their stronger ones. Gordon, who was not even a member, always sang as though he meant every word. Delia considered the possibility that he had been leading her on. Would he do that? He certainly hadn't seemed the type.

In another instant, her mind was back in Jefferson, assimilating what her voice was singing: "Within the kingdom of his might, Lo! all is just and all is right. . . ." *But perhaps* only *within that kingdom, his kingdom, is all just and right,* Delia added silently. Then it came to her again: the degree to which justice and right prevail on earth depends largely on what mortals do. As young Gerard had said, we are capable of good. John Calvin got it wrong. We are not born in sin; we are made for good. The question is, will we choose good or not?

The hymn's third verse took her back to her father. Since Hannah's telephone call, Delia had been thinking about him, regretting that Jedediah McGrath hadn't lived to see his rebellious child moving toward the faith he had embraced wholeheartedly, the faith she had eagerly cast aside when at eighteen she was convinced she knew all there was to know. As Delia intoned the printed words this Sunday morning, half a continent away from her father's desert landscape—and from the high spiritual terrain he had inhabited as well—she asked herself the same questions over and over. Why did he have to die? Why did she wait so long to come to her senses? How did she become so hardened in resistance that only grief and calamity could humble her? Why couldn't she have swallowed her pride for her father's sake, if not her own?

Delia ached for another chance, longed to turn the clock back, bring her father to life so she could tell him she loved him, tell him she was sorry for disappointing him, thank him for not giving up on her, beg him to forgive her. And then, unexpectedly, ashamedly, she realized that it was not Jedediah McGrath's peace she sought at all, but her own. As always. Still, selfish as it seemed just now, she wished he could give her a sign that he knew what she was doing and how she felt. And that it made him happy.

"The Lord is never far away," the hymn promised, "But thru all grief distressing, / An ever-present help and stay, / Our peace and joy and blessing." For too many years, Delia mused, she had prided herself on being her own help and stay, and had blithely assumed she could hold the Lord at bay indefinitely. And even now, pitched off her high horse by events of the past several months, she had forgotten what long since should have been stamped on her soul.

Her father's own counsel on the subject, in a sermon delivered when Delia was in her teens, surfaced in her consciousness. There is only one source of true peace, in this world and the next, Jedediah had said; and we mistake if we look elsewhere instead of to Him. The Son of God. "As with a mother's tender hand, He leads his own . . . ," the hymn continued, and Delia opened her heart to its message. What was needed if one hungered for peace, Delia knew, was to become one of those valiant souls, one of his own: the spiritual offspring of the Prince of Peace.

After the invocation, Nelson brought out a book and began to read. Delia caught a glimpse of the title and saw that it was the writings of the Jewish historian, Josephus. She thought it rather curious that Nelson would read Josephus during the services, but didn't say anything. Nelson noticed her interest, and leaned toward her. "Josephus beats anything you'll hear in this meeting," he whispered.

Delia looked at him, expressionless, and turned her attention back to the pulpit.

Nelson persisted. "It doesn't pay to get too caught up in the emotion of religion," he said.

Delia looked at him again. "Have it your way," she replied flatly.

Later, as the emblems of the Last Supper were imparted to the congregation, she pondered the mystery and materiality of the Atonement. The words she needed leaped out of her meditation and wrote themselves across her mind: *Redemption is real. Jedediah McGrath lives, and I'll have another chance to tell him I love him. And to tell him I'm sorry.* The thought burst inside her like a long dormant shell, and her eyes filled with tears from the wound.

Begonia Slopek was on her front walk in her mittens and pink parka with the fur-trimmed hood snugged around her face when Nelson and Delia drove to a stop in his black Jaguar. Begonia was so distracted by the event that she nearly tripped over her cane. And when the elegant Nelson Farwell climbed out of the vehicle, all gussied up in suit and tie, she simply stopped and stared some more. This was too much for her to absorb all at once.

Delia's a sly one, all right, Begonia said to herself. *Leads me to think she doesn't have any prospects to speak of, and then all these gorgeous men start popping out of the woodwork.* And this one had real class, too, Begonia could see right off. "That car alone is enough to turn anyone's head—even mine," she exclaimed under her breath.

"Hello, dear," Begonia called, a little timidly, as Delia and Nelson approached Delia's front walk.

"Hey, Begonia!" Delia responded, stopping. "You headed somewhere? I can take you if you give me a minute. I'll need to get into some warmer clothes. Sorry I blew our grocery date yesterday."

"That's all right, dear." Begonia said. "As a matter of fact," she added hesitantly, "I was coming to see you. Your car was here, so I figured you were, too."

"We're just coming from church, as you can tell by our Sunday togs," Delia smiled. "Meet Nelson Farwell. He was good enough to give me a ride."

Nelson granted Begonia a glance and a nod, but he clearly was not impressed with Delia's neighbor. "C'mon," he whispered, "I'll rescue you from the old dame."

Looking straight at him, she said, "Thanks for the ride, Nelson. See you in church." Then she turned and walked over to where Begonia stood leaning on her cane in a state of mild shock.

"But, but dear . . . ," Begonia stammered in a loud whisper, "you can't let the man just escape like that, can you? He's way pretty—and that car!"

"He's not the one who's escaping, I am," Delia said with finality. Then she looked back at Nelson, waved, and gave him her biggest, phoniest smile. He shrugged, got in his Jaguar, and roared away.

Delia turned back to Begonia. "You were looking for me? What's up?"

"Well," Begonia began, clearing her throat and giggling a little. "What's on your docket for next Saturday?"

"Other than our usual outing at Kroger's and the A & P, plus my daily dozen on the therapy machines, my Saturday is free. Do you need a chauffeur for something?"

"Oh no, dear, we have a chauffeur already. Elmer Roy's granddaughter. The one who works at the Circle K and got robbed that night. We just want you to come."

"Come? To what? Where? And who, precisely, are 'we'?"

It was clear that Begonia thought Delia was being unnecessarily dense. "Why, Elmer Roy, of course! And me!" she cried. With that, she did a little jig, cane and all, and began singing in her best imitation of a lower-class British accent, "I'm gettin' married in the mor-or-ning. Ding dong, the bells are gonna chime . . ."

Delia laughed. "Well, I'll be. Good ol' Elmer Roy came through, did he? Tell me," Delia leaned close with mock seriousness, "did you break the news to him about your time served?"

Begonia looked from side to side, then stood tiptoe to get closer to Delia's ear. "Yes, I did," she said in hushed tones, "and d'ya know what he did?" She stepped back to give the revelation the space it deserved. "He laughed to beat the band!" Begonia slapped her leg. "I don't know when anything has tickled that man more. It was a great relief to me, I'll tell you. I sweat that one out for a long time, but thought I'd better 'fess up before we tied the knot."

"I'm glad you got that off your conscience. And mine. I want to hear the whole story of the proposal, but I'm freezing in this wind. How about if I come over later for the play-by-play?"

"Speaking of play-by-play, dear, you may have to hold off until after the Packers game. Y'see, Elmer Roy's coming shortly to watch it. You know how he loves his football. But not as much as he loves me," she added with a grin. "His granddaughter's bringing him. The one who's driving us. I'd rather give you the scoop when it's just us girls.

Don't worry, I won't leave out any of the vital statistics. I've got the whole thing memorized, word for word." Then she changed subjects without a blink. "You really gonna let that one get away, dear? Jaguars don't come along every day, y'know. If you can't marry for love, then do it for money, I always say. 'Course, me, I'm marrying for love."

As Delia stood shivering in her light jacket, the sky grew more and more threatening. A handful of crisp brown leaves whipped up into a tiny twister that raced across the parking lot toward Begonia's car. Delia watched it hit and break up on the Pontiac, then she turned to Begonia. "Is that the honeymoon car?"

"Of course, dear. What else have we got? We did get the top fixed, y'know."

"So, you have this all worked out, have you? Are you joking about the granddaughter? She's not really accompanying the blushing bride and handsome groom on the honeymoon, is she?"

"Yes she is, since you ask. Who else have we got that can go that we can stand? Neither of us can drive more'n a few miles. Wait'll I tell my Cousin Bettina the news! 'Course, she's still in the pokey and won't be making the wedding."

Delia laughed and dug her hands deeper into her pockets. "I wish the granddaughter well. Oh, and Cousin Bettina, too."

"Rachel'll love the trip, mark my words. That's the granddaughter. She was ready for a vacation anyways, and neither of us can afford to fly ten miles just now."

"Where are you going, or is it all hush-hush?"

"South. Far as we can go on three tanks of gas. We figure we can afford six tanks of gas—three down and three back, y'see–and three nights in a Motel 6, if we take lunches for the first two days. The trunk'll be our refrigerator. How about that?"

"And the granddaughter?"

"She said she'd pay her motel bills if we'd pay her food and transportation. She can get off work all right, and she'll only miss two days from school. It won't cost any more to drive a car with three people in it than to drive one with two. And it's winter rates at each and every Motel 6."

Begonia shivered just then, even in her pink parka, and Delia began backing toward her own walk. "I'm freezing," she said. "Catch you later?"

"Yes, dear, but don't put it off. I don't want you to miss any of the particulars."

Delia waved good-bye to Begonia and pulled a house key out of her jacket pocket. At the door, she fumbled with cold hands for several seconds, then gratefully turned the dead bolt and entered the warm room. Even though her Smithville worries remained unresolved, her heart was lighter than it had been earlier. Begonia was better than a sniff of laughing gas, and Delia was certain she would never hear from Nelson Farwell again. It was a relief.

She didn't find much to like in Nelson except his taste in automobiles, and her lack of enthusiasm must have been obvious to him. Even if Gordon backed out of her life, Nelson was much too shallow and urbane to fill the vacancy. Well, she thought, maybe Gabe's remarriage wasn't a done deal, after all. At least not judging by the other night. Or maybe he was just tired and worried. Maybe he missed their easy friendship and good times. Delia knew she did.

As she kicked off her dress shoes, Delia smiled to think of Begonia and Elmer Roy honeymooning, in southern Illinois most likely, with seventeen-year-old Rachel as chaperone and chauffeur. Rachel was a good sport; Delia had discovered that already. This would be a party for her, like living on a movie set—"Driving Miss Begonia." Delia wondered if Rachel would also drive her grandfather and his bride to the AARP convention. It wouldn't surprise her a bit.

Then it occurred to Delia that things might be quite different around Morningside once Elmer Roy settled in and Begonia was fully occupied with him. Delia would miss the regular chats and excursions with her delightful and unpredictable neighbor. But then again, winter would keep them all indoors most of the time anyway.

Midway up the stairs, more than ready to change into something warm and comfy, Delia heard the phone ring. Her pulse quickened, and she was almost afraid to answer the thing. She hesitated a moment, then rushed to the top of the stairs. Rounding the bed to reach the phone, she banged her right shin on the metal bed frame and cried out with pain. The bed caught her as she fell, but it was several seconds before she collected herself and answered the phone.

"Hello," she gasped.

"Delia? Delia, is that you? What's wrong?"

"Gordon? Where have you been? Why haven't you called? Oooh," she moaned, holding her leg and mourning over her ruined hose. "I'm okay, just give me a minute to get over this. Want me to call you back?"

"Naw, I'll foot the bill for your recovery time. I'm on weekend rates. Is it pure delight at hearing my voice that causes you to swoon, or something less powerful, like an earthquake?"

"Actually, it's shock," she said, grimacing, but laughing in spite of herself. "I banged my leg is all, trying to get to the phone before you hung up on me."

"Which leg, one of your hollow tin ones, or one with a bone in it?"

"The one with slightly mushy bone in it, for your information. I'm walking on two legs all the time now, but the one still leaves a lot to be desired."

"Well, I'd agree with that. I find myself regularly desiring that leg and the one next to it, and everything on top of those."

Delia was mystified. Why was Gordon talking like this if he had someone else? It didn't make sense at all. Delia wanted to tell him about the Chinta plates, but her heart was pounding too fast to talk business. She had to find out if she was losing him. "I thought you might have joined Mother and the others for Thanksgiving dinner," she ventured. The pain had lessened, but her voice still wasn't normal.

"Ron invited me, but I couldn't make it. I had unexpected company last week. Just left a few minutes ago."

"Company? Yes, Effie saw you by the river," Delia said peevishly. *With your other girlfriend,* she added silently.

"Oh ho, and the two of you put two and two together and got three."

"Something like that, yes." Delia slipped out of her pantyhose and examined the rising bump on her right shin, just below the ridge of bone marking the worst fracture.

"Well, m'love, I owe you an explanation. Do you want the long or the condensed version?"

"First, before you say anything else, have you changed your mind about us, about you and me? Are you giving up on long-distance courtship?"

"Not on your life. If anything, I'm more convinced than ever that you're the only woman I want to ride the range with in my white pickup truck. With the possible exceptions of Polly and Effie McGrath."

"Then give me the Reader's Digest version. You can fill in the details later." Delia pulled pillows under her head and leg while her heart rate returned to normal and the adrenalin pump shut down.

"You remember the woman I told you about, the one in Moab who ran rivers when I did?"

Delia's pulse accelerated again, and she began to perspire. Sitting up, she slipped out of her jacket.

"Delia? You still there?"

"Yep, I'm here. I had sorta hoped that particular woman wouldn't be the heroine of your narrative. What brought her to town? Did you invite her?"

"Me? Are you kidding? Monday afternoon she showed up at the BLM office in Smithville, and she stayed all week. The strain is really showing on me. You should see how stooped and gaunt I look. Just a shadow of my naturally brawny, virile self."

"Yeah, I'll bet. It's really hard on a fellow to have to entertain a beautiful woman for several days. And where did you latch onto a word like 'virile'? Have you been reading *Playboy* behind my back?"

"I should say not. I'm strictly *Country Gentleman.*"

"Did she stay with you?" Delia asked the question, dreading the answer.

"That was her original plan, yep, but I revised it ever so slightly. I turned my luxury shoebox mobile home over to her, and borrowed the couch of one of my BLM buddies. His wife and kids went over the river and through the woods to grandma's for the holiday week."

Delia relaxed again. "Did she want to take up with you again?"

"Well, yes and no. She came to see if she did. She has a new beau in Grand Junction, but thought she'd do a little comparison shopping. Stack me up against him. She also wanted to see this part of the desert. That's why she stayed all week."

"Was it hard to see her go?" Delia asked quietly.

"About as hard as saying good-bye to a rash."

Delia laughed. "Well, I forbid you to miss her. Did you do a little comparison shopping yourself?"

"I s'pose I did. She's fun, but there's something hard and worldly about her. When I told her I'd been going to church and might be a Mormon one day, she only laughed at me."

Delia caught her breath. Although Gordon had been attending church and talking with the missionaries, he had never told her he might join, never said the words in her presence. "Well," she said, "fancy that. I've been going to church myself, and I might be a Mormon one day, too."

Gordon chuckled. "That proves it," he declared, "we're meant for each other. By the way, is my favorite bearded scholar keeping his distance?"

"Well, I have news on that front—not romantic news, I'm afraid, though Gabe may be having second thoughts about his first wife. I have news about the plates. I've been trying to call you."

"I'll bet he'd snap you up in a minute if you'd let yourself be snapped. What's the news?"

"That fellow Gabe met at the conference came to see our rubbings and to talk with us about them. He brought rubbings of the plates he was studying, and guess what?"

"He could read them, and they turned out to be recipes for turtle tacos."

"Gordon, get serious! They turned out to be the same!"

"Well, I'll be . . . The graduate students, you think?"

"That's always been my guess, as you know. Samuel—his name's Samuel Ornstein, and you'd like him—is filing official reports through his university, but you could get things rolling out there to find those students."

"Sure will. I'll notify the sheriff's office over in Juniper, and I'll try to get hold of Max Blohm. If they're the kind of folks that would do such a thing, they wouldn't have lasted long in his program; but he might know where they are."

"I have other news," Delia said, taking off her watch and silver chain necklace.

"Good, I hope?"

"Well, it might break your heart, but I think you'll recover. Begonia, much as she loves you, has chosen Elmer Roy. They speak the vows next Saturday."

"Saturday! So soon? Nothing for me to do now but go out and hang myself from a Joshua tree."

"It wouldn't hold you. It'd break and you wouldn't die."

"That's why I'd choose a Joshua tree."

Delia laughed. "One more thing, my nutty cowpoke."

"Just one?"

"Well, this is a pretty big 'just one.' Have you ever heard Mother mention a man by the name of Clemmer?"

Gordon hesitated. "You mean Anthon? I've done more than hear of him, I've met the man."

"You have? Why didn't you tell me?"

"I figured it's a family matter, and you'd meet up with him soon enough. Unless he gets too discouraged from chasing a woman who's doing everything in her power not to be caught. But he strikes me as a persistent cuss, so who knows?"

Delia felt something shift in the pit of her stomach. "So he's after Mother? Hannah said he was, and I brushed her off. How on earth did they meet?"

"The story's too long for the telephone, m'love. Your ear wouldn't last. You can see for yourself at Christmastime. If I know Anthon, he'll turn up, and he won't wait for an invitation. And if I know Polly McGrath, she'll never extend one. What we have here is the proverbial irresistible force meeting the immovable object."

"But what's he like?"

"He loves Pogo, a sure sign of intelligence and taste. And he wears cowboy shirts with pearl buttons. Trust me, you'll be nuts about him."

When Delia finally replaced the telephone receiver in its cradle, she didn't know whether to laugh or cry. Maybe both were in order. She went over to the second drawer in her dresser, reached to the back on the left side under some scarves, and pulled out a square white box. Inside, wrapped in white tissue paper, was a carved silver belt buckle with set-in turquoise and coral. Her father had made the buckle years ago, and it was the only material thing of his, other than a few books, that she had wanted when he died. The family could have the rest, whenever her mother was ready to part with it. This buckle had been created by his hands. No one could ever replace him in her life and heart, regardless of what her mother did.

CHAPTER TEN

The week after Thanksgiving, winter arrived with a vengeance in the upper Middle West. Storms that had been merely nibbling at Minnesota, Michigan, Wisconsin, and northern Illinois, teasing the inhabitants with snow flurries and gusty winds for several weeks, dropped their benign facade and galloped in like a band of runaway stallions. Monday and Tuesday brought snow so thick and fast that mammoth plows were reduced to ineffectual toys, cutting swaths that filled in behind them in minutes. Parked cars became marshmallow lumps, airports closed, and children were sent home from school.

Jefferson University remained open Monday, but by mid-afternoon only a handful of people were left on campus. Delia stood at the window after her last class, mesmerized by the spectacle. Even nearby buildings were all but blotted out, and she watched the few students who had stayed for classes in Brandon Hall that afternoon pick their uncertain paths down invisible stairs and make their laborious ways through the ever-deepening snow. It was beautiful: the whirling fleece, the cuddling blanket of white wool, the amorphous forms bent into the merciless wind.

But now there was the question of getting home. Delia had come to school on the bus that morning because even then, snow had begun collecting on the roads and storm warnings had been posted. Just getting to the bus stop at this hour could be a problem, assuming buses were still running. Delia smiled, loving it all. She couldn't help it; the first big storm of the season was glorious. By March, the thrill was definitely gone, but now it was all new. The world itself seemed new, and she was ready to brave it. *Well,* she thought, *this will be the first major test for my new leg. I may be walking home.*

Delia stopped by Angie's office before heading upstairs to her own, but her friend was gone already. As she climbed the stairs in the old building, the lights stuttered and went off, leaving her in twilight darkness. The building took on a pleasantly eery aspect, and she hurried to collect her coat and book bag while she could see at all. With the power out, all the offices on campus closed, and the few people still around began emerging from buildings, only to be gobbled up by the storm.

Fighting her way toward the bus stop, Delia was soon cloaked with white from her cap to her boots. Snow coated her eyelashes, and she licked its cold feathers from her lips, finally turning her shoulder to the wind and wrapping her wool neck scarf around her face, leaving only her squinting eyes exposed. Miracle of miracles, a bus appeared like a magic lantern out of a misty cave on the partially plowed strip that was once University Avenue. Delia raced to beat it to the bus stop, hopping, running, slipping, stumbling in the tracks of others. Shaking herself at the open door, she panted her gratitude to the driver.

"Thanks for stopping," she gasped. "I didn't expect to see you on time."

The driver laughed. "I'm not on time," he said. "I'm thirty minutes late, just late enough to be on time for the next scheduled bus, which might not make it at all."

"I'm surprised any of you are getting through."

"So am I, though we can sometimes keep going when no one else can. We're heavy, and we have high clearance."

"Will the Monroe bus be operating?"

"I don't know. Let me try to radio and find out." He clicked the switch. Nothing, not even a sputter.

"Power's out on campus," Delia reported. "Maybe it's gone all over town. Skip it. I can walk from there if I have to."

She gazed out the window as the bus crept up the avenue, the scene punctuated only by the dim coins of headlights as a few vehicles ground determinedly toward home. Ten slipping, sliding minutes later, the bus arrived at Monroe. Leaving the lighted cell of the bus's interior and stepping out into the storm, Delia could see the appeal in Arctic exploration. People wanted to test themselves, find their limits, pit their strength and ingenuity against the fierceness of nature. She knew the feeling, but at the same time, she was comforted by the fact that home was only a mile or so away.

Delia found that crossing the avenue was more precarious than toiling along drifted sidewalks. The snow was choppy and rutted, and the road surface was slick. She went down once, but managed to land on her left hip and arm, protecting her still somewhat fragile right leg. Physical therapy was out of the question today, but she figured the mile up Monroe would more than compensate. As Delia fought her way, step by step, her mind traveled back to the red rock country where she had spent the first eighteen years of her life. Winter there—what the uninitiated called winter—brought only an occasional skiff of snow.

She smiled to remember the day in her childhood when an unprecedented four inches had fallen in the early morning, and the schools were promptly closed. An hour or two later, the sun came out, and the school children enjoyed the novelty of a holiday in the snow. Most roads were merely wet and puddly by noon, and by the next day, lawns showed through everywhere and snowmen drooped, haggard and mournful. Why, at this very moment, Polly McGrath might be scratching among the fading flower beds in her yard, wearing only her old red sweater with the elbows gone, while her daughter labored toward home in blinding, wind-driven snow. It hardly seemed possible that one country could encompass such extremes of climate.

By the time Delia reached her front steps she was exhausted, but the effort had kept her reasonably warm, except for her hands and feet, which were crackling with pain. The descending night was brightened only by the snow-filled air, and Delia knew her condo would be cold. Inside, with a flashlight, she found a large green candle—a Christmas holdover, if she remembered right. Removing her wet clothing, she dressed in warm sweats and made a cold supper of bread, cheese, and apples. Then, wrapping herself in a blanket, she curled up on the sofa with notepad and paper, stopping every so often to wander to the window and gaze into the night. Only three more weeks and she'd be off to Smithville for the holidays. It didn't seem possible.

The ringing of the telephone interrupted her reverie. It was Angie. "Just calling to see if you got home all right," she said.

"And if I hadn't?"

"I'd send Howard out with a dog team to look for you."

"Then who would rescue him and the dogs?"

"Don't press me, child. Are you going to be warm enough? We have a wood fire going. If you could get here, we'd let you sleep on the hearth."

"Just like Cinderella. Dear fairy godmother, send mice and pumpkin ASAP. Think the university will shut down tomorrow?"

"Not likely, unless the power's still off. Everyone else closes down, but not that outfit."

"Aren't you supposed to go for your blood test tomorrow?"

"Yes, but I'm canceling. That'll give me another day of blissful ignorance."

"Me too. Will you ever be pronounced cured?"

"In five years, the scientist says. Unless I'm pronounced dead before then."

Delia hated it when Angie joked about death like that, and she changed the subject to something safe, the proposed changes in the English curriculum. That topic covered, she sent her love to Howard and the dog team and told Angie she would see her Wednesday, provided they could both find where the university was buried. Angie's only class this term met three times a week.

Delia spent a miserably cold night, huddled in bed with down parka and slippers over her warmest sweats and socks. She presumed her next-door neighbor managed in much the same way. Power was not restored until Tuesday afternoon, giving Delia a full day at home, albeit a frosty one. Wearing gloves and cap, and wrapping in blankets, she was able to accomplish some work in the dim winter light, but even inside, she could see her breath. When the snow finally stopped, after the power came back, she donned boots and went to check on Begonia.

Everywhere, the hardier members of the populace were materializing from drifted doorways, like butterflies from cocoons. Snow shovels appeared as if cued by some invisible stage director, and mountains of white doubled along walkways and in front of automobiles. The carport that housed Begonia's Pontiac and Delia's Subaru afforded skimpy protection from the fiercely blowing snow.

Kicking through the ankle-deep powder that had accumulated since the maintenance man's last swipe down the walk, Delia arrived in the approximate vicinity of Begonia Slopek's front door and pushed the bell. The button was iced over and wouldn't budge, so Delia banged on the door. No answer. She banged again, louder. Still no answer. Delia wasn't sure what that meant, and her throat tightened. A day and a night without power in the middle of winter was serious business, especially for little children and older people.

Delia remembered reading of an elderly grandmother and two small grandchildren who froze to death in her tiny apartment during a power outage in Chicago just last winter. They were found huddled together on the kitchen floor in front of the electric stove. The neighbors wondered why the old woman hadn't the presence of mind to get into bed with the children and find some warmth that way. But Delia also remembered frightening accounts of people rescued in the mountains in cold weather. They reported that with intensifying cold and loss of body heat, their minds shut down. They couldn't think what to do to save themselves.

Begonia was not lacking in brains, though Delia thought she was rather too adventuresome for her own good. Witness the little escapade that had landed her in the pen. In any case, Delia determined to find the key Begonia had given her and enter the house of antiquities next door. As Delia left Begonia's front steps, the maintenance man appeared astride a miniature snowplow, making his nonstop rounds. Following him down the main walkway, Delia happened to glance toward the carport and noticed that the hood and soft top of Begonia's Pontiac were almost free of snow, while the Sube next door was plastered. Begonia's windows, however, except for a circle the size of a small saucer on the driver's side, were frosted over. It didn't make sense.

As she neared the car, Delia heard a dull thunking sound, but couldn't place it. She stopped a moment, then turned to go. The thunking persisted, accompanied by muffled noises of another kind.

Delia concluded that she was either going mad or receiving messages from another sphere, like Joan of Arc. Then she realized that the sounds were coming from the Pontiac. "I knew it was old, but I didn't dream it was haunted," she joked under her breath.

Pushing through the drifts in front of the car, Delia moved toward the slightly foggy circle on the door window. There, two mittened hands were working frantically to stay ahead of the frost, and then Begonia's eyes and nose appeared. Delia tried the door, but the latch was stuck and the door was frozen shut. She signaled to the eyes and nose inside that she would find a way to get the door open—*even if I have to use a crowbar,* she added to herself—and returned to her own door.

Armed with a hair dryer and the long orange extension cord that in sub-zero weather she attached to the engine heater in the Sube, Delia was ready to begin her search and rescue operation. She remembered only too well what life was like in Jefferson before she discovered the boon of the automobile engine heater. Dead batteries and frigid pajama and parka excursions to start the car and warm the engine were the order of the day—more accurately, of the night. Of course, nobody in Smithville had ever heard of such a device, much less used one. In fact, the last time Delia's car was serviced there, the mechanic had asked what the box with the plug was for. That box, she should have told him, was better than melatonin. It brought peace of mind and uninterrupted sleep.

As Delia blew a cone of hot air onto the Pontiac's door handle and worked around the edges of the door, she could see Begonia's smiling eyes following the hair dryer's path. Once, Delia kissed her mittened hand and delivered the kiss through the glass to the tip of Begonia's nose. She could see the delighted Begonia chortling even as she shivered on the other side. Finally the latch gave, and with Delia pulling and Begonia pushing, the ice-encrusted door popped open.

"Oh, thank you, dear! I thought I'd never get anyone's attention," Begonia cried, plucking her cane from the passenger's seat and climbing stiffly out of her vehicle. "Unnnh. The man doing the walks never looks beyond the front of his nose. I could have been in there all winter, like a leftover Christmas goose hung in the freezer and forgotten till Easter."

Delia laughed, and helped Begonia through the drift to the walkway. "Which raises the question, what on earth were you doing in there in the first place? And how long have you been there?"

"Well, dear, it all makes perfect sense. To a point."

"Convince me."

"Well, y'see, I was cold all yesterday evening and all night. So this morning, I says to myself, I says, 'Begonia Slopek, where's your smarts? You've got a heater sitting out there in the carport that's not dependent on any municipal power system. Go use it.'"

"Aha, the Pontiac! Now that you mention it, the critter does resemble a furnace."

"Don't be silly, dear. Ever see a furnace built like a boat? So, y'see, I take myself out to give it a try. But I can't get in. The latch won't budge, and there's frozen snow all around the door."

"The plot thickens."

"That's not all that thickens. Wait'll you hear the rest of the story."

"I'm all ears."

"Pardon me for saying so, dear, but not *all*. You're not letting me finish."

"Well, if it's going to take an hour or two, we'd better go inside. You're shaking."

"Two minutes is all, two minutes." Begonia held up one mitten, and Delia had to imagine two fingers extended inside. Then Begonia rubbed her mittened hands vigorously together and stamped her feet. "But maybe we should go in. If the heat's on, that is."

"The heat's on, and you're going to need something warm in your tummy. C'mon over to my place, and I'll burn some cider."

"Cider! I'm reduced to cider, when what I need is hot buttered rum. What's the world coming to!"

Delia ushered Begonia into her condo, where the gas log was humming and the flames were jumping. "Now, sit down and thaw out while I get the cider, for which you should be extremely grateful, young lady. If it weren't for me, you'd still be in the Pontiac staring out the porthole."

"Well, don't I know it?" Begonia called toward the kitchen. "Sometimes I wonder where I've dropped m' brains."

A few minutes later, Delia returned with mugs of steaming cider. "Now, let's have it."

"Have what, dear? Oh, you mean the story. Well, as I was saying, I couldn't get the door open on the Pontiac, y'see, and after I'd tromped through all that snow to get there. So I says to myself, I says, 'Begonia, how'll you melt that door loose?' And it comes to me. 'Hot water! The water in my double insulated hot water heater's still warm, so I'll use that.' So I fill a gallon jug and haul it out to old Betsy."

"Oh, no! You poured water on the handle and around the door!"

"Let me finish before you go into paroxysms, dear. Yes, I did, and it melted that ice pretty as you please, and quick as a wink I opened that door and hopped in. After a little coaxing, the car started, snow and all; and before you could sneeze thirty times, the heater was pumping out the heat. It was lovely, sitting there, toasty warm, in the middle of a snowstorm. So lovely that I decided to stay for a while. Get warmed up, turn Betsy off until I get cold, and then crank her up again. I even dozed a little in between times, and the windows frosted up inside."

"But you did keep a porthole open."

"I did that later, dear. I was desperate. Y'see, when I decided to get out and go back into the house, see if the power was on yet, the door was stuck tight as a raft on a lake of glue."

Delia laughed. "You mean your hot water froze everything up? What a surprise!"

"Well, I didn't think about that part until I was sealed up inside, like a genie in a bottle."

"Now that I've let you out, do I get three wishes?"

"You already got your first. I'm alive and kickin'."

"You're right. How long were you in there, anyway?"

"Half the day, I'd judge. Lucky the old gas tank was full."

Delia didn't reply. It was just occurring to her how narrowly a tragedy had been averted. If Begonia hadn't been discovered before nightfall, and if she were to have run out of gas very long before anyone noticed her . . . Delia didn't want to think about it. Bitter cold typically followed severe snowstorms in Jefferson. Begonia Slopek, Delia realized, was much more than a comical little neighbor, a bright songbird in Delia's tree, someone to chuckle with and over.

She had become one of the absolute essentials in this part of the world.

By Saturday, things were almost back to normal, winter normal, that is, in Jefferson, Wisconsin. A few flurries had moved in again Friday morning, but the roads were salted and most parked cars had been dug out. Strict parking regulations were in effect to accommodate snow removal. In the days since the big storm, mammoth trucks had hauled great heaps of snow from along Jefferson's narrow streets and dumped the stuff on the now frozen Lake Winauka.

The latter was a phenomenon Delia had never seen in the Mountain West, where streets were more typically wide and piles of snow interfered only minimally with traffic. Then, too, in the West, periodic winter thaws conducted the disappearance of whatever snow accumulated in cities. Not so in Jefferson, where no major melting could be banked on until spring, and where snow from one storm had to be removed to make room for the next onslaught.

The wedding, Begonia had announced Friday afternoon, was still on. And it was going to be a church wedding, at the Baptist Church, naturally, where Begonia and Elmer Roy had met at a bingo game. For the widowed groom, it was the second time around; but for Begonia, it was a first, and as she said, they weren't sparing the horses.

When Delia offered her services, Begonia informed her that "the ladies at church" were taking care of everything. One of them was lending her a wedding dress, another was fixing her hair, another was playing the organ, and several had planned refreshments for the guests before the ceremony at noon. The Baptist minister was officiating. Delia didn't ask what Elmer Roy's daughter was contributing to the occasion, or who was giving away the bride; but she knew the granddaughter would be there, with her travel bags in the trunk of the Pontiac along with those of the nuptial pair.

As a matter of policy, Delia avoided any and all events on Saturday that required her to wear a dress and pantyhose, but for Begonia she made an exception. She was there, along with the church bingo crew, several of whom had southern accents, she noticed, and so were transplants like Elmer Roy. Delia wondered why on earth they had migrated north when most of their set judiciously followed the birds south.

When she arrived, the church bells were ringing jubilantly, and the Pontiac sat in front of the vaulted building, bedecked with streamers and bows. Rachel had drawn the line at strings of cans tied to the back because she herself had to drive the vehicle, and her younger siblings acceded to her greater authority. The front bumper displayed a wrinkled sticker that read "Jesus is coming. Act busy." Begonia and Elmer Roy had bought the placard at a yard sale over in Elmer Roy's neighborhood in October, and Begonia had installed it herself.

It turned out that a cousin, Bettina's brother from Green Bay, was on hand to escort the bride down the aisle. When the organist launched into the measured cadence of the bridal march, Begonia appeared, walking slowly, one hand on the cousin's arm, her cane dangling from the other. From her concentration, Delia could tell that Begonia was trying to reproduce the step-pause-step gait of graceful brides in flawless weddings in dazzling movies of a bygone era. Overhead the chandeliers vibrated, and Delia was caught up in the grand emotion of the occasion.

Begonia was indeed having her day, and Delia allowed herself to be swept along. She had expected a small, unpretentious affair. After all, the thing was put together in less than two weeks. But she had underestimated her neighbor and the interest of her friends at church. Begonia, Delia decided, could plan and carry off a small circus in twenty-four hours if she put her mind to it. The ceremony itself was solemn yet simple, and when Begonia looked into Elmer Roy's eyes and said, "Yesirree sir, indeed I do," Delia smiled tenderly, as though she were the mother figure instead of the other way around.

Begonia had known from the start that Elmer Roy was the man for her, and Delia marveled at her certainty. Delia herself had entered and exited serious relationships without ever knowing, nothing doubting, that this was the one. Gordon? Well, it was different with Gordon. She knew she loved him, but something in her still held back. Perhaps she was afraid of being hurt, or of trusting his feelings—and her own—completely.

And then there was Gabe. For some reason, she hadn't quite let him go. Was she holding onto him, in her head, for insurance? And was she holding onto Jefferson the same way? Watching Begonia and the surety she had found with Elmer Roy made Delia almost envious. So what if it wasn't fired by the passion of youth and wonder, Delia could feel the goodness and durability of it. There would never be a question of loyalty or caring with Begonia and her new husband. They were getting a late start, but they were sound. They had a lot of give to them.

Delia's thoughts then flew to Polly and Jedediah McGrath, who had all the loyalty and caring Begonia and Elmer Roy had found, but who also had all the passion and wonder and devotion, not to mention the labor and heartache and faith, that a lifelong love had demanded of them and blessed them with. They went deep, and they were unshakable. Delia wanted that even more.

After the ceremony, she walked through the massive wooden doors in almost a dream state, apprehending the excitement around her, but feeling shut out from it, too. As the wedding guests lined the cold steps and walkway leading from the church to the Pontiac, Delia realized that she hadn't thought to bring rice to shower upon the bride and groom. While those around her more than made up for her lack, she said a silent prayer, invoking the glad gifts of heaven to rain down upon this precious pair.

At home again, Delia stripped off her pantyhose and climbed into flannel-lined jeans and chamois cloth shirt. Downstairs, she hit the playback switch on her telephone. The first voice was Gabe's, thin and a little tired. Call him, he said, he had heard from Samuel. Ron's voice was next, asking her to call when she got a minute. *Ron I can call later,* she thought, *but Gabe must have news.* Much as she hated to ring when Denise might be there, Delia punched the familiar numbers and waited. Relieved when only the answering machine responded, even though it meant she had to converse with plastic and metal, Delia announced that she was off to harass a few ice fishermen on Lake Winauka. She would call him when she returned—if he was lucky, she added.

Delia's recreational options on a winter Saturday in Wisconsin were markedly different and more circumscribed than those of someone in southern Utah. Not only was magnificent high mountain skiing readily available for desert folks who happened to live in

Smithville, but someone like Gordon might, at this very moment, be trekking along a sand and sandstone trail in a flannel shirt and jeans, or wandering freely on slickrock.

By contrast, in Jefferson, unless one had snowshoes, the best nearby hiking in winter was on frozen lakes. The hard freeze that followed Monday's storm had transformed glacial water into thick ice. On Friday Delia had noticed two or three little tent shacks out on Lake Winauka, poised over what she knew were sizable holes in the ice. And inside those tents were incurable fishermen—superhumans immune to cold, oblivious to storm, deaf to reason. She had seen them out there with temperatures at twenty below zero. This was their sport, and they loved it.

Driving to a parking area routinely cleared for these unshrinking souls, Delia stopped the Sube next to a weatherbeaten gold Dodge truck. She guessed that the owner would match the vehicle, which was more than a little dented and rusty but undoubtedly still going strong. Most of the men and women she had seen fishing in winter were old-timers. Not enough action and too much silence for the young, she supposed. Delia herself allowed as how there were more satisfying ways to get frostbite than huddling under tiny canvas shanties watching water through a hole in the ice, but she applauded the hardihood of those who threw the dare to winter like this.

Delia had left her crutches home, bringing instead cross-country ski poles for balance. They might save her a fall or two on the sometimes tricky ice. Zipping her parka up over her chin and tugging her wool cap down over her ears, she donned mittens and set out along the boot-stomped path to the lake. Her eyes, protected by sunglasses, scanned the huge expanse of the now solid, whiter-than-white lake surface.

The day was typical winter pasty, but the glare was blinding just the same. She headed into the wind, knowing it would give a welcome assist on the return trip. As Delia stepped gingerly along, half-walking, half-sliding, stabbing sharp poles into the lake's slick crust, she began wondering if this would be her last winter in Jefferson. One part of her almost hoped so, but another part was in no hurry to lose all this frozen wonder.

Of course, since the book that was to have brought her scant fame and a permanent position at the university was still in her head instead of on paper, it probably wouldn't be her choice to make in any event. Her department chair, Lyle Parry, hadn't asked about her progress toward the upcoming tenure review, and she hadn't raised the subject with him either. After all, what was there to hold her here? she asked herself. The lake and the woods? Ah, yes. And the university.

As for people who were more than casual acquaintances, these days the Turners and Begonia were pretty much it. "Being a loner has its advantages," Delia muttered under her breath. Fewer folks to leave behind. And now Begonia had Elmer Roy on a full-time basis. For that matter, Angie might not be around much longer, a possibility that made Delia ache inside. She couldn't imagine living in Jefferson and teaching in the English Department without her dear, nutty, and oh, so wise Angie. As for Gabe, her relationship with him could never again be what it was. Too much had happened, and besides, good old Denise wasn't about to disappear. Mary Beth and Susan were her friends, yes, but not her soul mates.

As Delia wandered farther from shore, her thoughts seemed to go in one direction and her feet in another. She avoided the deep middle of the lake, her instincts guiding her along the wide, relatively shallow stretches nearer land. Even as Delia walked, her mind refused to clear, perhaps because fall semester at Jefferson was well past the midpoint, and two stacks of papers waited for her at home, with a third due Monday. In addition, she had a couple of exams to write and some committee work to finish.

All too soon, this batch of students, in the endless parade called education, would claim their credits and walk out of her life. They got on well, she and her students, and she always felt a little sad on the last day of class, watching them load up their backpacks and stroll through the door. Most of them she would never see again.

But then there was Gerard Mannion, whom she might see in another setting, though he hadn't said any more to her about a mission for the Church. An unusually quiet fellow, Gerard was serious without being overtly pious or self-righteous. Delia wondered if he had made a decision. A sudden slip and a near fall delivered her back to the moment, and she paused to contemplate the pale rose strips that were subtly splitting the grayish clouds at the far horizon. Winter days were short everywhere, but especially so in northern climes. It was time to head back. The temperature was sinking with the dying day, and Delia's toes and fingers were complaining even in insulated boots and mittens.

Drawing closer to the shore where the Subaru waited, Delia saw a dark figure approaching across the ice. Another loony ice hiker? she wondered, or maybe a fisherman picking a more remote spot for tomorrow's contest with line and lures? It was neither. The space between the two walkers closed, and Delia recognized the tall, slightly stooped figure of Hector Gabrielson. He had come looking for her. She waved a greeting and he picked up his pace, leaning into the ever-stiffening wind.

"Hey," she called at last, "what brings you out on a day like this?"

"You do. What else? Are you frozen stiff?"

"I'm getting there fast."

"Looks as though you're practicing ski-less skiing. Makes sense to me. Must be a lot easier on the bones and ligaments." Gabe reversed directions and fell in step beside Delia.

"And easier on the pocketbook, too. You said Samuel called. Your news couldn't wait?"

"Oh, it could wait, all right. I just wanted to see you outdoors again. It's been a long time since we tramped a winter lake, or did anything that required two good legs. How does the limb feel?"

"It feels as though it's had a long, debilitating leave of absence—way too long. Let's get back while it still works."

The two stepped silently over the ice, caught in the spell that winter had cast over the polar scene. It was like walking through an imaginary land made entirely of ice and snow. Gabe stopped and faced Delia, taking her dark glasses off so he could see her eyes.

"You're leaving, aren't you, tenure or no tenure?"

"What makes you think so?"

"I can feel it. You're gathering in images to take with you. That's why you're out here today."

"Nothing has changed in my circumstances, if that's what you mean."

"But something has changed in your head."

"Maybe it has. Begonia's marriage has got me thinking about Mother, and what I owe her. And what a rotten daughter I've been."

"No worse than most, I suspect, and probably a lot better than some. At least you have a conscience."

"If there's any justice in this world, I'll have two or three hard-hearted daughters of my own."

"Don't be too rough on yourself." Gabe paused, then took her face in his gloved hands. "I can't help wishing those hard-hearted daughters could be mine, too."

Delia looked down, then lifted her eyes. "No daughters could be luckier than to be yours," she said.

"I'll miss you terribly," he said softly.

"I miss you already," she replied, half smiling.

Gabe stepped forward and enfolded her in a long and tender embrace, but it was the embrace of dear friends who just missed being lovers and lifemates, who in another place and another time might have built something splendid together.

As the two silhouetted figures crossed the final stretch of ice toward their separate vehicles, Delia asked about Samuel's call.

"He just wanted to say that he's broken the news about the plates to his collectors. He's also notified the legal people at Duke. Once they review his letters to the authorities, he'll send them. He wants to know if we think he should call Max Blohm."

"Maybe so. Gordon said he'd call him, too, thinking the nasty professor might know where to find the students who were at the dig near Rabbit Bluff."

Gabe winced slightly at the mention of Gordon's name. Delia hadn't said anything about Gordon for some time, but Gabe realized that she and the BLM man probably communicated regularly. *Well, why not?* he asked himself. After all, he talked with Denise almost daily, didn't he?

Watching Delia toss her poles into the back of the Subaru and slide in behind the wheel, Gabe smiled in spite of himself. *She doesn't belong in this two-toned country, white in winter and green in summer,* he told himself. She could never live permanently, either, where granite mountains make no backdrop to daily life, where no towering red rock cuts great spires and domes out of the sky, and where the sky itself makes no discernible statement. Hector Gabrielson stood motionless until the Subaru taillights disappeared, then slowly entered his Pathfinder and drove home to prepare supper for James and Marcie. It was Denise's night to play bridge with her friends.

CHAPTER ELEVEN

It was just a week until Christmas, and Arva Plimpton was finally getting around to hanging her Christmas wreath on the rusty nail by the peeling front door. She had her tree up already, an imitation Scotch pine, and its shaggy drooping branches turned every which way. Ever since Arva's husband died several years ago behind the lawn mower, she had valiantly clung to the traditions they had established together. The tree being the most important. Leonard loved a Christmas tree. Of course, when he brought it down in its box from the attic and assembled it, the thing had what he called *symmetry*—a word that sounded too much like "cemetery" to suit Arva.

He seemed to have a knack for poking the stiff, twisted branch wires into the pre-drilled holes in the glorified broom handle that served as a trunk. When he did it, Arva reflected, everything came out nice and even. Of course, she by herself wasn't about to take the thing apart every year and stash it in the attic. The best she could do, being a short woman to boot, was jam it still assembled in the closet in the spare bedroom, behind her wedding dress and honeymoon knickers. The newlyweds had gone to Bryce Canyon.

The wreath, Arva was sorry to say, was in no better shape than the tree; but it, too, had sentimental value. She had made it in Relief Society one summer, she couldn't remember when, of thin willow branches coiled and wired together. Pine cones and cotton angels that had seen better days were attached at random to the circle of branches. At the top was a crooked green felt bow with most of the felt rubbed off. *Been felt too much,* she haw-hawed to herself.

Arva had just placed the wreath on its accustomed nail and stepped back to admire her work when she heard a car coming up the lane. She was glad she'd got the wreath hung so her company, whoever it was, could enjoy it too and get in the holiday spirit. She fully intended to get in the spirit, even though none of her children had inconvenienced themselves to come this year. Since Arva didn't particularly care for the spouses they had chosen without inviting her opinion, she concluded it was just as well.

What she had thought was a car turned out not to be a car at all, but a large van, and an ugly faded green one at that. Normally, Arva wouldn't be pleased to see such a monstrosity on her property, but she smiled when she saw this one. She knew who was behind the wheel. None other than Anthon Clemmer, coming to see her, Arva Plimpton. Maybe with marriage on his mind. She had always hankered for a holiday wedding, and maybe she was going to get one at last. If she played her cards right. Anyway, there he was, climbing out and waving to her. She waved back, trying to curve her wave seductively, the way beauty queens in formals on floats waved. She succeeded in looking like someone washing imaginary windows.

"Why, I thought you'd have that new Lexus by now," she called in a coquettish southern accent copied straight from Scarlet O'Hara as he approached the front steps.

"I've grown attached to this old buggy, it seems," he said. "But one of these days, I'll surprise you."

"Well, you surprised me turning up today, all right. What brings you to Smithville?" *As if I didn't know,* she said smugly to herself. *After all, isn't he here at my door instead of at Polly McGrath's, and her within spittin' distance?*

"I needed an excuse to get out of Cheyenne, now that winter's set in. Taking another look at your property seemed as good as any. What's your asking price?"

"Well, just bring yourself inside out of the cold, and we'll talk turkey," Arva replied, thinking to herself that if he took her in the deal, the price would drop to zero. If she played her cards right, she'd get a man and a Lexus in one fell swoop. Already she could picture herself parking in front of the church in such a vehicle, turning heads right off their necks. Maybe Polly wouldn't be so uppity with her if she had a Lexus. But then, Polly was hardly the sort to be impressed by anything on wheels. Look at that lopsided battleship she drove. Even so, Arva would be glad to take Polly for a spin now and then. Arva wondered if she shouldn't make the car part of the deal. "If you want me and this here property," she'd say, "you gotta get rid of that unsightly van!"

Arva watched with satisfaction as Anthon wiped his boots on the mat outside the door, a mat that read "The Plimpton's." Obviously, this groom would come already trained. As for the mat, Polly had once remarked to Arva that as far as she could tell, none of the personalized mat-makers in the world knew the proper position of the apostrophe for the plural possessive. Every mat she had ever seen with a family name on it, Polly said, put the apostrophe before the "s" instead of after it. The thing made more sense in the plural form alone, anyway, "The Plimptons," with no apostrophe at all. So Polly said.

Arva herself was one of those people who wouldn't recognize a possessive, plural or singular, if it batted her over the head, and furthermore she didn't care. The mat was on *her* porch, and it stayed. She hoped Anthon wouldn't notice, though, and think she was illiterate. She'd be willing to remove it if he married her and moved in. Of course then she'd have to remove it because it wouldn't be the Plimptons anymore; it would be the Clemmers.

The thought brought a little catch to Arva's throat. She had been a Plimpton for a long time. Could she ever think of herself as Arva Clemmer, even though she had already practiced saying it? She glanced at her reflection in the door window. The whole thing hit her like a ton of bricks. The image in the glass looked like a Plimpton. It didn't look like a Clemmer at all.

Arva blew her nose in the embroidered hanky she pulled from her apron pocket and ushered Anthon into her front room. No, she hadn't had the place appraised, she told Anthon when he asked, but she supposed she could do that this week, if he was serious. He said he was. When would he want to move in, she asked him, and he said in the early spring, probably, if they agreed on a price. He said he'd hang around town a few days until the appraisal was done, and then maybe they could talk again.

It all seemed so final that it threw Arva for a loop. Furthermore, Anthon wasn't talking marriage or even acting like marriage, and maybe that was okay with her after all. Seeing her Plimpton mat on the porch and her Plimpton face in the door made the retirement center in town look better and better. She could take the mat with her.

It was with mixed feelings that Arva watched the Ford Econoline rumble out of her yard and head down the lane. If a woman were hungry for a man, he was a temptingly delicious morsel, in his cowboy boots and leather jacket, she had to admit. Life could be pretty lonely at times, especially out here away from town, and something in her wanted to corral him permanently. On the other hand, she wondered if she could ever get used to him. He laughed a lot, and she didn't trust a man who laughed too much. Not that she herself was not a cheery person. It was just that Leonard Plimpton had laughed the right amount for her degree of cheeriness.

She entered her bedroom, looked at the brass bed with its two pillows and the wagon wheel quilt that served as a spread, opened the closet and stroked two or three of the neckties that hung just inside the door, then moved to the dresser. There on top, in a 5 x 7 tarnished brass frame behind dimpled glass, were two young people, he in jaunty stiff-brimmed straw hat and she in plaid knickers, arms flopped around each other, smiling for all they were worth from the rim of Bryce Canyon. She picked up the enlarged snapshot, huffed on the glass, and rubbed it with her apron. Then, with a wistful smile, she left the room.

Miles McGrath, age fifteen, had just walked in the house from basketball practice over at the church when the phone rang. No one seemed to be around, so he picked it up in the kitchen, hoping it wasn't Mitzie Morgan inviting him to her Christmas party. He wasn't supposed to date yet, and he knew some of the older kids would be there in pairs. His parents were sticklers about no dating or driving before sixteen, and that hadn't been a problem until Mitzie moved to Smithville from Texas this fall. He thought he liked her, and she had seemed especially friendly lately, seeking him out in the school cafeteria a time or two and sitting by him in Biology. Not being a Mormon, she might not understand his parents' rules about dating.

"Hullo."

"Hey, Miles, how goes it?"

"Aunt Delia!" His relief was boundless. "When are you coming home? Will you take me skiing?"

Delia laughed. "Hold on there, pal. I'm coming in a couple of days, and if you could see my scrawny leg, you'd know I'm not ready for skiing quite yet. At least not downhill."

"How about cross-country? Like, you promised to teach me."

"Maybe we can try it, if I wear a brace and we stay on the level. Choose a spot."

"Awright! Is Dad picking you up?"

"Not this time. I'm flying into Las Vegas, to avoid any bad weather delays. Gordon will come down for me."

"Gordon! Cool!"

"Is your dad home? He called a while ago, and I never got back to him. Is everybody okay out there?"

"Nobody's home, but we're cool. I guess Grandma's kinda sick, though."

There was a pause on the other end, and Miles heard the worry in Delia's voice. "What's the matter? When did she get sick?"

Miles sat on a padded kitchen chair and began unlacing his basketball shoes, crunching the phone into his shoulder with his chin. "Like, she's not in bed or anything, just coughs a lot, Mom says. And lays on the couch a lot. Mom and Dad are a little worried 'cause she's not getting better."

Delia bit her tongue to keep from correcting him, even as her mind automatically intoned *lies* on the couch a lot. "Has she been to the doctor?"

"I dunno. I don't think so. Says you don't go to the doctor for a little cough." Miles pulled off his damp tube socks, rolled them together, and tossed them through the laundry room door and into the clothes basket. *Two points, yeh!* he cheered to himself.

"Well, I'll take her when I get there. We might have to give her knockout drops and carry her, though."

"That's for sure. Should I have Dad call you?"

"If he wants to. Otherwise, I'll just see the whole gang of you when I come."

After he left Arva Plimpton, Anthon Clemmer drove down to the county clerk's office to do a little research on property values in the area around Smithville. He hadn't stopped at the McGrath place because he didn't want to be pushed for time when he saw Polly, even though she was sure to usher him out the door with all due haste. Besides, she was more placid in the evening, he had noticed, if one could apply the word to Polly McGrath at all.

When the county offices closed, he stopped at Shoney's for supper and then drove to the overlook north of town before heading to Spring Road. The December day had shut down early, and the sky ranged from deep blue-violet at the horizon to pitch black overhead. Not a cloud blocked out so much as a single star, and the lights of Smithville were an upside-down galaxy, a bright mirror image of the sky. He left the van and walked to the edge of the bluff, pulling his jacket closed as he went.

Could a man like me be happy in a place like this? Anthon asked himself. *He could if he had a woman like Polly McGrath beside him,* that self answered. In her he saw the harsh land, the brittle vegetation, the dynamic sky, the clashing of horizontal and vertical rock. But he also saw the soft blowing sand, the high-floating hawk, the dazzling spring wildflowers, the enduring cottonwoods, the melodious canyon wren, the joyous river. *She is this place,* he conceded, *and I am here, suspended between a vast expanse of cosmic and earthly lights, because she is here.* He shook his head and chuckled. *I must be out of my mind.*

Bemused and perplexed, Anthon walked slowly back to the green Ford Econoline and cranked the engine. Then he sat for several more minutes, hands folded together, wrists slack at the top of the steering wheel, and merely looked. When a pair of teenagers—the girl sitting so close to the boy that they looked like two heads on one body—pulled in ten yards away and shut off their Corolla's engine, Anthon turned on the van lights and left the winter stars and the silent city in their custody.

Anthon had never given Polly advance notice of his arrivals in her part of the world. That way she couldn't forbid him to come, except in a general sense. When he crunched down the gravel drive on this occasion, he saw a Jeep Cherokee there ahead of him. For a moment, he considered backing out and returning tomorrow. Then he remembered how much he enjoyed watching Polly McGrath try to explain him, and he shut off the ignition. The people inside had probably heard the van anyway.

No one responded to his knock on the outside door, so he opened it and crossed the back porch to the kitchen door. In the light from the door window, he noticed that Jedediah's levi jacket and cowboy hat still hung in their places above the washing machine. *Not yet,* he thought, *not yet,* and shook his head. At last Ilene answered his knock, with Effie peeking out from behind her.

"Mr. Clemmer! Mommie, it's Mr. Clemmer!" Effie cried, tugging on her mother's sweatshirt.

"That it is, in the flesh," Anthon replied, bending toward Effie. "Is your grandmother home?"

"She is, but she's sick!" Effie announced importantly.

Anthon straightened and looked questioningly at Ilene.

"She's had a cough for a few weeks that won't seem to go away. So far, we haven't convinced her that she needs to see a doctor. Says she's never gone to the doctor with a trifling cold in her life, and doesn't intend to start now."

"What do you think?"

"We're a little worried. She used to be quite watchful of her health, before Granddad died. But since then, she doesn't seem to care much whether she lives or dies. Come in, please. It's cold on the porch."

Anthon remembered Polly's little dizzy spell on their journey together up Interstate 15, but supposed there was no connection, except for the stubborn denials, of course. On the big oak table he noticed a tray containing the remains of someone's supper, Polly's he presumed, prepared and carried to her by Ilene. Polly herself was apparently in either the parlor or her bedroom, and Anthon hesitated.

"Can I see her?" he asked softly.

Since Effie had already run ahead and announced Anthon's arrival, Ilene merely shrugged. "Why not?" she said. "Maybe it'll cheer her. Ron and Wilson are in the parlor with her."

"I seriously doubt that she'll be cheered by my arrival," Anthon laughed half-heartedly. "But maybe getting her dander up will make her feel better. I seem to affect her that way, as you may have noticed."

Polly was lying propped on the sofa, under a handmade brown and gold afghan, and she had been giving Anthon what could only be described as the evil eye ever since he walked in the door. "Well, look what the cat dragged in," she muttered weakly, coughing two or three times. Then she turned to Ron. "We may have to install a locked gate," she said. "Cheyenne's refuse keeps turning up in my driveway."

Anthon laughed. "Well, I'm glad to see you haven't lost your edge," he said, taking a chair near the foot of the sofa. "I was afraid you might have been glad to see me. Then I'd have known you were dangerously ill."

Ron went over and took his mother's hand. "We need to get on home. The kids are still in school." Wilson looked at Effie and made a face. "Call us if you need anything. If you're not improved in the morning, you must let us call the doctor."

Polly squeezed her son's hand. "We'll see," she said, and looked at Ilene. "Thanks for the soup. Sorry I couldn't eat more."

"We'll try again tomorrow. You get some sleep. Do you have enough cough medicine?"

"I still have some of that you brought the other day. It seems to help. And I have cough drops. Eucalyptus. They work the best." Polly looked and sounded very tired.

Anthon knew it was his cue to go also. "I'll follow in just a minute," he said to Ron. "But first, I want to deliver a short lecture to your mother on the benefits of medical science and our obligation as citizens to keep members of the medical profession in flashy cars and plush yachts. I think I left you room to get by me in the driveway."

"Good-bye, Mr. Clemmer," Effie said shyly. "Will you be here for Christmas? Thanksgiving sure was fun."

Anthon laughed. "Well, it was fun for you and me, anyway. And no, I won't hang around for Christmas unless your grandmother should go soft in the head and invite me."

Polly hmmphed and looked past Anthon to her son.

"Sure you'll be okay, Mom?" Ron asked, eyeing Anthon from the parlor doorway.

She coughed. "If you mean will I be safe with this vagabond, the answer is yes. If you mean will my ears be worse for the wear, the answer is also yes. Get on with you. He's harmless."

When Ron's family left, Anthon moved his chair in front of the sofa. "You look thin and flushed, young lady," he said, putting his hand on her brow. "And you have a fever. When are you going to do something about this?"

"I don't know," she mumbled, "maybe tomorrow." She began coughing again, hard.

"Other than the cough, how do you feel?"

"Worse tonight," she admitted grudgingly, between coughs. "I didn't want to worry Ronald Jay and Ilene."

"We're not waiting till tomorrow," he announced, standing up. "We're going to the emergency room tonight. Where's your coat?"

It surprised him that she didn't protest. "In the closet under the stairs," she replied huskily.

Anthon helped Polly to her feet, wrapped her in her coat, and led her slowly out to the van. The stars were even brighter out here in the country than they had been from the bluff north of town. He found himself reflexively scanning the eastern sky for signs of a miracle in progress. For this moment, at least, the woman on his arm had placed herself in his care. She had given him many gifts before, out of his need and her starchy brand of charity, but this was the first gift she had humbly accepted from him, out of her need.

When Ilene arrived at the yellow frame house on Spring Road shortly before noon the next day, Anthon's green van was still parked off the driveway. That alone surprised her. Inside, she found Anthon dozing on the sofa and Polly in her bed asleep. Anthon rehearsed for Ilene the events of the previous night—the trip to the emergency room, the chest x-rays, the diagnosis of well-developed pneumonia, the shot, the recommendation that Polly be admitted immediately, her adamant refusal, the compromise that sent her straight to bed with a steamer in the room and heavy doses of antibiotics and cough medications, and his search for a late-night pharmacy.

He had promised the attending physician that he would watch her through the night and call if the coughing grew worse and the fever rose any higher. The cough syrup, he said, contained a sedative, and she had slept much of the night despite a few coughing episodes.

By the time Delia and Gordon pulled into the drive two evenings later, the household on Spring Road had fallen into something of a routine. Anthon was the chief caretaker, with Ilene spelling him a little during the day. Even so, he rarely left the premises. Polly was holding her own and seemed willing to let Anthon stay, though she grumped at him for treating her, she said, like an invalid. The family physician, a gray-haired man with as brusque a manner as his patient's, had come by the morning before, after Anthon called him, and listened to her lungs. He scolded her and told her how sick she was, and she didn't argue the point.

Knowing her mother was ill, Delia was not surprised to see Ron's Cherokee parked at the house, but the faded green Econoline was a mystery. "Someone else is here," she said to Gordon, "and it can't be the doctor, not in that beat-up boxcar."

"It's Anthon," Gordon said.

Delia's head jerked toward him. "Anthon! What's he doing here?"

"Oh, he has a way of turning up at odd times, much to your mother's dismay."

"Well, one thing Mother doesn't need if she's sick is company, especially male company that expects to be entertained."

"Oh, I doubt that Anthon expects to be entertained. He's more likely to *do* the entertaining. Maybe he couldn't resist having a captive audience."

"Captive is right. Well, let's go in and issue him his walking orders. The man has nerve, I'll say that for him."

"That he does, m'love, that he does. And you're gonna be mad about him in spite of yourself."

"Fat chance. Mad *at* him, maybe."

Ron had heard Gordon's 4-Runner arrive and met his sister at the back door. He hurriedly explained the situation and helped Gordon carry Delia's bags inside.

"Try to be good," Gordon whispered to her, grinning, as she entered the kitchen.

"I'm always good," she returned, "but I'm not always nice."

It was a shock to see her mother looking so pale and helpless there among the sheets and blankets. She, who had always been strong, who never wanted to be waited on, who had no patience with illness.

"You're walking," Polly said from her pillow when Delia entered the bedroom. "Let me see your leg."

"My leg can wait. Tell me about you. Or is it too tiring to talk?"

"Talking's my only exercise these days, so I'd better do it. Did you just get here? I think I've been napping a little."

Delia looked at Ron, and he nodded.

"Yes, just now. Gordon brought me up from Vegas. I flew the southern route, and was lucky to get out of Chicago. Big storm brewing as we flew out."

Delia dragged a nearby chair up next to her mother, and stroked the creased forehead. "Still feverish?"

"Maybe just a little."

"But nothing compared to what she was a couple of days ago," a male voice said from the doorway. "Well, Mrs. McGrath, your daughter's home and the dog, horses, and hens are fed, all within the hour." He turned to Delia. "You must be Delia, the pride of the clan. I'm Anthon, Anthon Clemmer, and delighted to meet any and all offspring of the woman who brought me to my knees the first time I met her and keeps me there still, even from her sickbed. I regard it as a bonus that this particular offspring happens to like poetry and is willing to inflict it on the young."

"Hush, you old windbag," Polly said. "She's been here five minutes, and already you've talked her ear off."

But Delia noticed that her mother smiled when she said it, and the daughter was astonished. *She's sicker than I thought,* Delia mused, and wondered what it was about this man who smelled of hay and chicken feed that could bring a smile to her mother's lips even as she scolded him.

Anthon stepped forward, first shaking hands with Gordon, then pointing to Delia on the sly and signaling a thumbs-up. The younger man laughed. "You ain't seen nuthin' yet!" he whispered to the older man. "As I told you, she's a chip off you know which old block."

Delia glanced up at them, then returned to her mother.

"Looks like fresh troops have arrived, so I'll be off," Anthon said, with a sensitivity that surprised Delia. "I'm in town for a couple of days, so I'll drop by tomorrow and check on the patient." He turned and was gone. Ilene rushed out after him with one of the sandwiches she had brought for him and Ron's mother.

Later, after Polly McGrath had taken her medications and settled down for the night, the others sat in the parlor and talked.

"What's with this fellow?" Delia asked. "I can't believe he's been staying here, taking care of Mother."

"What's harder to believe is that she lets him," Gordon laughed.

"But what do we know about him?"

"I know a little, but I think you should get to know him yourself before anyone fills in the details," Gordon said.

Ilene broke in. "I like him," she said, "a lot. If he hadn't been here and realized how bad she was, . . . if he hadn't taken her to the hospital, I shudder to think what might have happened."

"Another day or two and she might have been too far gone to recover," Ron added. "Jeff Slater was the ER doctor on duty that night. He called the next day to rib me about sending 'the body' for him to revive. He said it was a close call, especially for someone her age."

"But what's the man after?" Delia asked.

"Her," Gordon says. "He loves her, and he's prepared to wait. His whole life, if that's what it takes."

Delia threw up her hands. "I can't believe this!" she cried. "Has everyone gone nuts around here, or am I the only one?"

Gordon reached over and took her hand. "Just wait," he urged. "Give it time. Don't pre-judge the man or the situation. Your mother knows her own mind, sick or well. Trust her."

"I do trust her—at least I think I do—but how can I trust him?"

"Well," said Ron, pushing out of his chair, "we're not going to solve anything tonight. Shall we go, honey?" He reached for Ilene's hand and pulled her up off the sofa. Then he turned to Delia. "You okay here tonight? You want some backup?"

"If a total stranger can manage the care of my mother, I think I can handle it," she said. "Besides, Gordon will be here for a while, anyway." She turned to him. "You will, won't you?"

"All night, if need be," he replied. "We've done an all-night watch or two with Jennifer, if you'll recall, and we're pretty good at it."

"No way will you stay all night," Delia said. "You have work tomorrow, and you need your beauty sleep."

"It's true that I have a slight beauty deficit, but I hoped you wouldn't mention it. These folks might not have noticed."

Delia pulled a face at him and he grinned.

At the door to the kitchen, Ron turned. "Love you, baby sister," he said.

Delia looked up. "Love you too, big brother."

The next day, while Gordon was at work and her mother was napping, Delia found the keys to the Imperial and drove into town for groceries and a few last-minute Christmas gifts. On an impulse, she turned into Joshua College and parked near the Language Arts Building. It was semester break, and the lot was nearly empty. Just a few faculty cars, she noted, distinguishable from student cars by their advanced age and less than prime condition. She smiled. *It will always be so,* she thought. *My undergraduates drive new Corvettes, and I drive a Subaru hatchback in its second midlife crisis.*

Delia really didn't expect anyone to be in the English Department office, but the building was open and she went in. Nothing much had changed, it appeared, since she had taken an Advance Placement English class here as a high school senior, a course that netted her both high school and college credit. Climbing the once familiar stairs was like re-entering her own past. At the time, she had been too eager to get out of Smithville even to consider attending college here. Joshua was small potatoes to a self-important eighteen-year-old. She remembered walking down the hall, feeling superior to the poor little hometown kids—her classmates, mainly—who were going to be stuck here for two years.

Strictly dullsville, she had told her father. Jedediah McGrath hadn't argued with his willful daughter—he never did—but he had looked at her a moment and then said, "You won't always feel that way." At the time, she couldn't imagine ever feeling another way, yet here she was, moving along the echoing hall with something akin to awe, or destiny, clutching at her heart. The department office door was ajar, and she stepped in.

"Anyone home?" she called.

Theron Paget, who had taught the AP class she took all those years ago, stepped out from an adjoining office. "We're closed, officially," he said, "for Christmas break. Can I help you in some way?"

"Mr. Paget? Is that you? I took AP English from you what seems like centuries ago. Delia McGrath." She stepped forward to shake hands. He had aged, but the stooped shoulders and unruly graying forelock, not to mention the reading glasses down on his nose and the eyes peering intelligently at her over them, were unmistakably those of her teacher.

"Delia McGrath? Ah, yes. You went off to fry your fish in a bigger and better skillet than we have around here, didn't you?"

"Bigger, yes, and considerably wetter. But maybe not better."

Theron Paget raised his heavy eyebrows. "Ah? Do I detect a little contrition for the rash pride of youth?"

"Could be. Have you a minute to talk? I'm in town for the holidays. I know you're busy, or you wouldn't be here today."

"It's my comeuppance for agreeing to serve as department chair. I seem always to be several laps behind these days. Here I am, reading examinations. But . . . ," he leaned forward and smiled impishly, "it beats last-minute Christmas shopping for the grandchildren with my wife. Do come in, come in. Of course I have time for you. What's on your mind?"

"I'm not sure." Delia sat in the chair he offered, and he sat behind the desk, twirling a yellow pencil between the thumb and forefinger of his right hand. "Well, let me put it straight, just to satisfy my curiosity," she said. "Do you expect to have an opening in the department next year?"

Theron Paget was clearly surprised, and perhaps even a little amused. "Well, well, well," he said, tipping back in his chair, his eyes twinkling over the tops of his glasses. "As a matter of fact, we do."

Polly McGrath improved every day, and the day before Christmas found her up and about a little. It tired her just to walk across the room, but the fever was gone and the cough had nearly disappeared. The household and all adjuncts gave a collective sigh of relief and prepared for the holiday. Gordon had brought a tree, and a luscious pine smell filled the house. Delia found the old lights and decorations right where Polly said they were, in an upstairs closet.

She discovered, almost to her surprise, that she was glad to be "home," stringing lights with Gordon and placing ornaments while her mother looked on. Polly didn't protest the festivities, but Delia could tell that her heart was heavy. Jedediah had always hung the lights, and Polly had dusted the brightly colored ornaments.

The children were allowed to place the lower bulbs, but their father, on a chair or stool, always hung one particular ornament at the top of the tree. It was there now, at Polly's insistence—a tarnished, badly faded red pendant, streaked with blotchy metallic gold paint. The ornament, Delia told Gordon, like many things associated with the house on Spring Road, had a story. Gently pulling her to the sofa beside him, he asked her to tell it and she did.

The first Christmas Polly and Jed McGrath spent together, they had bought that ornament on Christmas Eve for twenty-five cents. He had just returned from the mission field to greet his wife and the child he had never seen. He had no job, and she was down to their last few nickels. Someone had generously left a small, freshly cut Douglas fir on the couple's doorstep, which happened to be the doorstep to the old wash house on the Appleby farm. Times were hard and jobs were scarce just then, and that's where they lived when he got home. He hadn't found work yet, and they were too proud, and too jealous of their privacy, to move into the main house with her parents.

Having nothing to put on the tree, not even popcorn, they borrowed her father's truck and drove into town. The only store they found open in the little town that night had just one ornament left, a shiny red pendant trimmed with glossy gold. They looked at each other and counted their coins. It was Christmas, after all. The ornament became their gift, to give to each other and to receive from each other. Their only gift, and it took nearly every cent they had. And from then on, the pendant graced the top of every family Christmas tree they ever trimmed, each year becoming more scratched and tarnished, each year becoming more precious and beautiful in their eyes.

"Why, the older you get, professor, the more sentimental you get," Gordon teased when Delia finished. He gave her a little hug. "Know what? I kinda like you in your sentimental old age."

"That story always makes me blubber," she said, blinking away the tears. "And it makes me miss Dad all the more. It might even make Mother blubber."

"You're right, it might," Polly McGrath said quietly. Having slipped into the parlor to get a book and to peek at the tree, she had heard most of the story. Polly muffled a cough, then caught her robe closer to her throat and returned to her bedroom with as little fanfare as she had left it.

As daylight began to fade, and the western sky exchanged soft aqua for pale rose, the jingling of bells set up a clatter at the back door. It opened, and before Delia could get across the kitchen, Dorothy Brittel burst through the inside door like a little typhoon with Timothy caught in the backtow. She had a handful of sleigh bells and a bag of gaily wrapped packages. Delia welcomed her with open arms, hugging her jolly aunt and her bells and packages in one embrace. In the worry over Polly McGrath, they had all but forgotten that Aunt Dot and Uncle Timothy were coming for Christmas.

Absorbed by the bustle of unloading packages, removing coats, exclaiming over the tree, and greeting Polly, no one heard a vehicle arrive outside. Nor did anyone see a tallish male figure descend from a somewhat dilapidated van and look at the Brittels' automobile with its "Go USU Aggies" bumper sticker. Nor did anyone see that figure contemplate the house for several minutes in an attitude of indecision, as if debating whether to go or stay. Nor did anyone notice when the figure at last hoisted itself into the van, started the engine, and slowly backed down the drive with only the parking lights on.

CHAPTER TWELVE

Given Polly McGrath's condition, it was just as well that her married children from out of town were not coming for Christmas. Hannah, as always, would arrive by herself on the twenty-sixth and stay overnight. That visit was as predictable as Dickens' "Christmas Carol" this time of year, and the household on Spring Road unconsciously steeled itself for the event. Victor would come with his family New Year's Day.

Meanwhile, with the able Dorothy Brittel on hand to look after her sister, Delia and Gordon were freer to stay around or leave, as they chose. After supper Christmas Eve they went into town to the annual Christmas sing-along in the old tabernacle, and then made an informal tour of light displays around homes, churches, and businesses. It was nearly eleven when they turned into the gravel driveway at the yellow frame house. Only the yard light and the back porch light were on.

"They're in bed, I guess," said Delia.

"Looks like it."

"Want to come in?"

"Better not. We might disturb your mother, since she sleeps on the main floor."

"I hate to let you go."

"Then don't. Let's walk a little. Your jacket's warm, isn't it?"

Delia laughed. "Yes, indeed. Built to withstand Wisconsin winters."

"Is it also built to withstand Smithville hugs?"

"I'm not sure. Let's take it out for a test drive."

Leaving the 4-Runner in the yard, Delia and Gordon walked past the profusion of listless oleander bushes and into the street. Neither wore gloves—who did in Smithville when pockets were so handy?— and they held hands as they strolled away from the house toward the river. The dog came out of the barn expectantly and walked a hundred yards or so with them, then elected to return to his cozy bed in the hay.

"Well, Professor McGrath, what are we going to do?" Gordon asked at last.

"Do? You mean tonight? We're going to gaze at the river, we're going to marvel at the stars, we're going to think big thoughts, and I wouldn't be surprised if we sang 'Silent Night' as a finale."

"That I knew already. I mean the rest of our lives."

Delia paused. "We're going to gaze at the river, marvel at the stars, think big thoughts, and sing," she said.

Gordon stopped and turned her toward him, taking her face in his hands. "I'm serious, goofball." Then he shook his head, chuckled, and dropped to one knee. "There's only one way to get your attention. Do something dramatic and totally out of character. So here goes. Professor McGrath, may I have the honor of your very cold hand in marriage?"

She smiled and curtsied in an exaggerated fashion. "Why Mr. Foster, is this an official proposal?"

"As a paid, though poorly paid, official of the U.S. Government on land, on sea, in air, but mostly on sand and rocks, I certify that it is."

"Then I accept. You may have both of my cold hands." She bent down and kissed the top of his head. "On one condition."

"Uh-oh. Name it."

"That you sing 'Silent Night' and then tell me you love me, in that order."

"I'll do better than that, I'll dance 'Silent Night' with you and then tell you I love you."

He slowly got to his feet, groaning as if in pain, then suddenly spun her into his arms on the star-blanched road and waltzed her into the eastern sky. Only a great-horned owl was on hand in a nearby leafless cottonwood tree to blink and ask who.

Later, to escape the cold night, Delia and Gordon finally risked waking Polly by slipping into the parlor and carefully closing her bedroom door. With the tree its only light, the room took on a holy aspect. Elongated shadows from dusky lamps, vases, and chairs played against the walls like haunting memories from Christmases past. For a long while the pair sat silent, leaning into one another, bewitched by the glow emanating from the tree and the wonder of their own feelings. Being together seemed to erase all doubt for both of them.

Little by little, they began to talk—soft, unhurried words. Gordon slid to the floor and rested his head against Delia's legs as they planned the present and dreamed the future. Given Delia's tenure situation, plus Gordon's work and the highly persuasive argument of Wisconsin winters, they agreed that it made more sense for Delia to move west than for Gordon to move east. But arranging all of it would take some doing. She would have to teach through the spring semester in any case, she said.

That decided, they lapsed again into an awe-filled silence. Tonight something was born that they would fashion together, something that would forever bear the stamp of its auspicious beginning on this glorious night of nights in the Christian world.

Anthon Clemmer did not appear on Spring Road Christmas Day, but that didn't mean he had returned to Cheyenne. He wanted to decide once and for all about Arva Plimpton's property before he left, and if he decided in the affirmative, then he wanted to start that ball rolling. The big question mark was Polly McGrath. He didn't kid himself that she might marry him any time soon, but was there any hope at all?

If she really couldn't stand the sight of him, then his being nearby would serve only to make both of them miserable. If, on the other hand, she let on to dislike him more than she really did—and he thought he had lately detected some signs of that—then it was worth the gamble. Besides, he could tell from the looks of her place that she could use a little help in the department of maintenance. As a neighbor, he could see to some things.

Spending Christmas in a hotel, even if it was the Holiday Inn, was not a whole lot of fun. He walked a few miles, over near the golf course, and hung out a little with the luckless room service people who drew duty on the holiday and had few guests to serve. The previous night, Christmas Eve, he had sat in the lobby and contemplated the huge flocked tree decorated with brilliant peacocks and blue satin balls. The gas log threw flames high in the huge stone fireplace, while strains of Christmas carols floated from vacant counters to glowing tree and mantel before meandering down the hall to resonate off every door knob, fire alarm box, and light fixture.

Christmas night, his mind very much on Polly McGrath, Anthon found he couldn't get into the book he had bought the day before, thinking to learn something about his future neighbors. The book was Wallace Stegner's *The Gathering of Zion*. Not that it was a bad book. Quite the contrary. He could tell from the first page that it was well-written, and he liked Stegner. Restless, he flipped on the television.

There was little Natalie Wood, trying with all her might, as she had done every year since he could remember, to convince her stubborn, literalistic, unimaginative mother that Kris Kringle was no deranged imposter, but was, in fact, the real thing, the genuine Santa Claus. And all her mother's resistance was in the name of truth. *Well,* Anthon thought, *the movie's right. There are truths of the human heart that can't be proved by the scientific method. And, Mrs. McGrath,* he declared, silently addressing the woman on Spring Road, *there are truths of the heart that people try to hide even from themselves.*

Clicking off the television, Anthon absently opened the drawer in the lamp table by the conventional hotel bed, which was covered with a conventional bedspread. In the drawer lay a small pad of Holiday Inn stationery, a pencil, a local phone directory, a Gideon Bible, and a Book of Mormon. He picked up the last and began thumbing through it, wondering what power lay in it that it could snare and reform a philanderer like Archibald Plumm.

Throughout the book, someone had highlighted a number of passages in yellow transparent ink, and Anthon began to read them, dropping to the bed and sitting hunched over the scriptural text. He scarcely moved for an hour or more, skimming the pages, reading the marked passages. Reaching the book's final chapter, he wasn't ready to quit, so he read it all, the ancient Moroni's final testimony and admonitions to modern readers.

By the time he had read verses twenty-seven through twenty-nine, Anthon knew the book was no fraud. He was certain that no one, not even the most skilled literary artist, could have convincingly put words like these into another's mouth: " . . . the time speedily cometh that ye shall know that I lie not, for ye shall see me at the bar of God." Anthon felt something sweep over him, some unexpected chill that seemed made of fire, and at the same time some irrepressible urge to weep. His tear-clouded eyes pulled the words into his mind, and he read aloud, "And God shall show unto you, that that which I have written is true." Anthon read hungrily to the end of the chapter, then closed the book and sat staring at it for several minutes.

He had no idea who this Moroni was, but he knew he was no invention of some writer's overactive fancy. *This fellow is a straight-talker,* Anthon mused. *Like someone else I know,* he added, chuckling to himself. Picking up the van keys, he left the motel and drove out to Spring Road, wanting to tell Polly what he had discovered, needing to talk about this book with someone. But when he arrived and saw that visitors were still there, he lost courage.

Virtually nothing was open in town, so he meandered through gaily lighted neighborhoods for an hour or more and then returned to the hotel. If he slept, he wasn't aware of it. It seemed to Anthon that he stared at the patterns in the textured ceiling of his second-floor room all night long. He could have closed the drapes and shut out the comfortless exterior lights, but he didn't.

Hannah blew in around noon on the twenty-sixth, having driven down from Provo that morning. Within sixty seconds, she had demoted Dorothy from nursing staff to kitchen help. Within sixty more, she had diagnosed Polly's illness—forget what the doctor said, she knew bronchitis when she saw it—silently delivered her opinion of the emerald solitaire on Delia's left hand, pecked Uncle Timothy on the left cheek, and scolded her mother for neglecting her health. No one had the nerve to ask Hannah if any of her children had been home for Christmas, and she kept mum on the subject. Lester, however, could be discussed because everyone knew he had been home, where he belonged, though as always when Christmas fell on a weekday, he was back at work the next day, as was Gordon.

"Have Paul and Jed Junior called? And Victor?" Hannah wanted to know the first time she had Delia alone. They were in the big kitchen, making a grocery list. That is, Hannah was creating the list and Delia was serving as scribe.

The answer was affirmative for all three brothers.

"Now that Christmas is over, we've got to decide what to do about this Clemmer person. How to get rid of him."

"Clemmer person?" Delia asked, being intentionally obtuse and contrary. Hannah seemed always to rub her the wrong way.

"Well, that's his name, isn't it?"

"His name is Anthon Clemmer, yes, but he's more than simply a 'Clemmer person,' Hannah." Delia didn't look up from her pencil and notepad. "Anyway, how did you know he'd been here again?"

"Here?! Again?!" Hannah's voice squeaked as the words flew out, and her hand went automatically to her throat, as if she might choke. Or faint, like the heroine in a cheap Gothic novel. "I *didn't* know! And what do you mean, *more?*" she demanded.

"Well, for one thing, he took care of Mother, almost single-handedly, for a couple of days before I got here." Delia was concentrating heavily on a floral border she was methodically drawing around the grocery list.

"What?!" Hannah squeaked again. "He's been alone in this house with Mother?! He didn't stay all night, did he?" Hannah dropped into a chair at the table as if the very thought had sliced off her legs at the knees.

"I suppose he did. I doubt that he slept much, she was so bad." Delia paused, then put down her pencil and looked straight at Hannah. "If he hadn't taken her to the hospital, you might have been coming for her funeral instead of for your post-Christmas dutiful-daughter visit."

"Well!" Hannah blustered, rising to her feet on legs that had somehow miraculously reattached themselves. "Well! We have always had standards of decorum that we observe in this family. Regardless of your liberal Wisconsin views, this man, whoever he is, has breeched those standards. We'll just see what Jed Junior and Paul think."

"What about Victor? I'll bet dollars to doughnuts he'll vote with me on this one. And RonJay, too. Moreover, nobody—not you, not Jed, not Paul, not me—nobody says anything to Mother about it. Probably never, but certainly not while she's convalescing. If you want her to have a relapse, you just go in there and throw a tantrum. Me, I'm going to the store for groceries."

Delia didn't slam the pencil down, but she set it down as a period rather than a comma. Then she tore the floral-edged list from the notepad, yanked the Imperial keys from their wall hook by the table, grabbed her wallet from the cabinet, and stalked out.

Hannah took a few steps toward the door, as though she had additional things to say in defense of her position, then turned and sat at the table once again. She absently picked up her father's pocket knife, studied the handle, and set it down. Like one asleep, Hannah arose once more and stepped through the parlor toward her mother's bedroom.

Dot and Timothy were in the parlor, she thumbing through a Sears catalogue, he dozing in the platform rocker. Only if Dot had been hard of hearing could she have entirely missed the low-toned but heated discussion in the kitchen. There was nothing wrong with Dot's hearing, and she scrupulously avoided eye contact with Hannah as Polly's older daughter passed through, hesitated at her mother's door, fidgeted with the gold chain around her neck, then made an about face and returned to the kitchen, where she picked up her jacket and walked out.

Her mind in a tangle, Delia did not drive to the grocery store. The peace she had felt with Gordon and Aunt Dot and Uncle Timothy was gone. Like a sudden blast of angry wind, Hannah had stirred up a maelstrom of debris, all the doubts and anxieties Delia herself had entertained about Anthon Clemmer and his obvious affection for her mother. Things she would never admit to the tempestuous Hannah. If the man was indeed courting Polly McGrath, it was all too soon and too unthinkable. Hadn't she loved Jedediah McGrath as she valued her own soul?

Anthon Clemmer had arrived out of nowhere, an unknown and unmeasured entity, to complicate all of their lives. And yet, they owed him a great deal. After what he had done for their mother, they couldn't just turn their backs on him. And then there was the fact that Gordon liked him—Gordon, who was a good judge of character. Perhaps most troubling, there was something about the man—Delia couldn't put her finger on it—something that reminded her of her father.

No matter how convivial Anthon seemed, however, Delia knew that there were charming, conniving men who preyed on widows, looking to take advantage of their loneliness and insecurity. Polly McGrath had always been a sensible woman, and it was not likely that she would fall for some fly-by-night scam. But even if his intentions were honorable, and he was honorable, where was all this leading?

It was small comfort that Anthon, not her mother, was the pursuer, and that Polly had not invited pursuit. Delia could tell that her mother wasn't totally down on the fellow, either. If Polly were down on him, he would have been out the door, permanently, long ago. He might be persistent, but he wasn't dense by any means. And what about that green wreck-on-wheels he drove? Hardly a vehicle to ease the minds of a nervous flock of adult children.

Delia was almost surprised to find herself at the cemetery. Perhaps she needed an anchor just now, and had instinctively turned to her father. Parking the Imperial, she zipped her jacket up to her chin, jammed her hands into the side pockets, and made her way across the winter grass. A wind had come up in the last hour or so, and ever blackening clouds were bulging over the mountains to the north. Too agitated to rest on the craggy ridge tops, they cut loose and chased each other from north to south across the thin blue of the late December sky. Delia's mind traveled back to that June day when they had all gathered here and said a prayer over a cold form sealed up in a polished box. She could hardly believe, even now, that the familiar body was there, in front of her, under six feet of soil and a thick layer of sod.

The headstone testified that Jedediah McGrath was indeed there, and that one day the love of his life would lie there beside him. *If her place is beside Dad,* Delia asked silently, *then how could someone else possibly fit into her life?* Wasn't that really what Hannah was asking, after all? Delia knew she had been hard on Hannah. She always was, and she hated herself for it. But Hannah could be so exasperating and so closed-minded. And so in need of running everyone's life.

Delia thought back to that one brief moment last summer, after her father's death, when she and Hannah had found a few real words to say to one another. Sometimes, maybe, Hannah wasn't so bad. If imperturbable Lester could continue to love her, there must be something more to Hannah than a compulsion to remake the world in her own image.

Sitting cross-legged on the cold ground, Delia huddled forward and asked her father what he thought about one Anthon Clemmer and his unblushing intrusion into Polly McGrath's life. Delia reached out and touched the headstone, tracing each letter of her father's name with the forefinger of her right hand. Uncrossing her ankles and pulling her knees toward her, she folded her arms across her knees and dropped her head onto her arms. Her bowed frame began to shake, but she didn't notice the cold at all.

How long she sat there, Delia couldn't have said. When a car door slammed in the distance, she made no effort to get up or even to lift her head. *Someone else missing a loved one,* she thought. *Well, that makes two of us. A community of mourners.* A few moments later, she heard the crunch of footsteps approaching across the shriveled grass. She didn't turn until a hand touched her shoulder. Startled, Delia looked up as Hannah sank to her knees beside her. Neither spoke.

Then, as if instructed by the man who had laid claim to this particular plot of earth, Hannah stood, and taking Delia's hand, she pulled Delia gently to her feet. As if prompted again, a bit awkwardly, perhaps, Hannah embraced her younger sister, holding her close and sobbing.

"I'm sorry," she wept. "I don't know what gets into me. Please, please, forgive me."

Delia, knowing the fault was more hers than Hannah's, whispered through her own tears, holding onto Hannah as though her very life depended on it, the words of a beloved but erring Cordelia to a repentant Lear, "No cause, no cause."

* * * * * * * *

The first day of classes after the Christmas break had just ended, and Delia dropped into her office chair at Jefferson University, wondering how it was that just one day back in the traces could so completely erase a vacation. The day was gray, but at least it wasn't stormy. Snow lay everywhere, some of it new, and a January thaw seemed a distant dream. Delia smiled to remember her first post-Christmas conversation with Angie Turner.

"Well," Angie had said, "let's have it. The Smithville chronicles."

It was almost disappointing that Angie hadn't shown the least surprise when Delia told her she was making plans to become a "Foster wife" and rear a bunch of Foster children.

"Now tell me some real news," Angie had declared. "I knew from the beginning that you'd wind up marrying some straw-chewing cowboy with sand under his fingernails and a guitar under his arm. Now who'll nag me about my eating habits, and set me an example of maniacal fitness?"

"I'll find someone. You can count on it."

"That's what I'm afraid of," Angie had replied. "And now, I suppose, the Turners will have to visit that colossal sandpile you call southern Utah every year or so to check up on you."

"Yes, I'll take a sworn statement to that effect," Delia had said.

Three weeks of school remained before fall semester finals in late January. Delia sighed and thumbed through the stack of unread student papers she had carried to and from Smithville, with the best of intentions. One more semester at Jefferson. It scarcely seemed possible. What was still undetermined was if and where she would be teaching next year. However things turned out, it had been an eventful holiday.

During the week between Christmas and New Year's Day, Theron Paget had called the department hiring and promotions committee together to talk with Delia. He also took her in to meet the president of Joshua College and the academic vice president and dean. This week in Jefferson, she intended to complete the Joshua application and update her resumé. Only Gordon knew of these interviews in Smithville, and she had pledged him to silence. Nothing was certain, of course. She was one of several candidates, and she hadn't exactly shown interest in the college in the past. Nevertheless, Theron had been quite encouraging.

Delia had left Smithville before Victor arrived, and Gordon had flown to Denver to visit his mother over the New Year's holiday.

Hannah, bless her, had not mentioned Anthon Clemmer to her mother, and she had even convinced Jed Junior and Paul to wait and see what developed after their mother was fully recovered from her bout with pneumonia. By the time Delia left, Polly McGrath was feeling much better, though she was still weak.

She would recover fully, it appeared, and the household settled back to near normal operations. Before Christmas week ended, however, Timothy had taken to wandering if no one was watching him. One afternoon, when after a lengthy search Delia found him on Arva Plimpton's porch, dismantling a rusty old kitchen range while Arva was at yoga class, Aunt Dorothy announced that their stay was over. She packed him up, and off they went the next morning.

What became of Anthon Clemmer was something of a mystery, though Delia knew he had been by the house at least once more. Upon entering the Imperial to run a few errands a day or two after Christmas, she had spotted a folded piece of paper in the ashtray. Thinking it might be a note from Gordon, she opened it and realized at once it was not. The Smithville Holiday Inn letterhead puzzled her, but only for a moment. On the paper there were four lines, unsigned, in broad, surprisingly graceful script:

> Humpty Dumpty sat on a wall,
> Humpty Dumpty had a great fall.
> All the king's horses and all the king's men
> Wondered if Polly would ever give in.

Delia gathered that the verse had some significance she didn't fully understand, but thought it better not to trouble her mother with it just then. She had tucked the paper in her handbag and forgotten it. Polly McGrath had not inquired about Anthon since his disappearance before Christmas, and no one mentioned him in her presence. The subject was a loaded mine field that everyone skirted on tiptoe.

Now, in post-holiday Jefferson, Delia opened a student paper on Emily Dickinson's use of slant rhyme. Mechanically clicking the lead forward in her black Pentel pencil, Delia began to read. Glancing up, she noticed her handbag on the filing cabinet and remembered Anthon's revisionist rendering of Humpty Dumpty. She dug through one of the bag's front pockets, found Anthon's missive, and read it again.

He, too, had used a slant rhyme—"men/in"—but in his case Delia credited sloppy technique rather than clever off-balancing. Her mind was not settled as to Jedediah's possible views of Anthon and the man's various enactments of the courtship dance, but she knew that her father would have delivered the note to Polly McGrath unopened, no questions asked, if he had found it. Ashamed at her deviousness, Delia vowed to deliver Anthon's message, via telephone or Uncle Sam's couriers, within the week.

Shortly before five-thirty, someone tapped on her office door and tried the knob. A familiar bearded face appeared around the door's edge.

"Anybody home?" Hector Gabrielson asked.

"For you, yes. For anyone else, no. C'mon in," Delia smiled. "How'd your holiday go? Did you speak the vows?"

"Not yet," Gabe replied. "I think I'm getting cold feet. How about you? Anything to confess?"

"Well, it looks as though I'm going to kiss single life good-bye." Delia held up her left hand.

Gabe hesitated, took her hand and looked at the ring on her third finger. "Well," he said in a low voice, "serves me right for asking. Congratulations."

Delia could tell he was crushed. She stood and moved around the desk to him, taking his other hand. "I'm sorry it didn't work out for you and me," she said, "but what would you have done with a desert rat anyway?"

"You mean besides love her? What else is there?"

Delia squeezed his hands and pulled him to the only empty chair. "Sit down and tell me why you came over," she pleaded. "I know it wasn't to check my marital status."

"You're right, it wasn't. At least not entirely," Gabe said, forcing a smile. "Samuel called this morning. Apparently Max Blohm's students have been found and apprehended. The antique dealer who set up the deal with Samuel's buyers identified them from their pictures. Blohm's department had good photos of them."

"Have they admitted to anything?"

"I don't know, but since they're not experienced thieves, I imagine they'll crack under questioning."

"What will happen to them?"

"Who knows at this point? But aren't you more concerned about what will happen to the plates than to the students?"

"I guess I'm always concerned about students. It's an occupational hazard. Besides, what happens to the plates now isn't nearly so important as what has already happened inside me because of them."

Gabe nodded thoughtfully. "They made a believer of you, didn't they?"

"Something like that, I guess. Let's say they started the process." Delia walked to the small window. She spoke without turning. "The plates, you know, are only sheets of metal, and we have copies of them. Students are people, and they've done something stupid they'll regret the rest of their lives."

"Well, well, my dear, you have changed, haven't you? I think you've gone and got soft on me." He smiled at her. "And you know what? I like it. You haven't exactly been a turn-the-other-cheek sort of person in the past, m'friend."

Delia walked behind Gabe's chair. Putting her hands lightly on his shoulders, she said, "And you have always been that sort of person. How have you stood me?"

He chuckled and reached up to pat her hands. "Oh, you have other redeeming qualities," he said.

"Which we won't enumerate at this time," she declared, abruptly leaving him and returning to the window. "So, since you bring it up, what about the plates? I wonder who has first rights to them?" she asked.

"I don't know. My guess is you do, but the buyers put out a chunk of money for them, in good faith. Samuel has proposed that, if both parties agree to it, the plates should go to a museum."

"Sounds good to me, especially if it's Nevell Becker's outfit at Mesa Verde."

"That's what Samuel thought, too."

Delia sat on the edge of her desk. "What about the other things—the pouch, the stylus, and the scroll?" she asked.

"I'll bet the students have them and will turn them over."

"Well, maybe we can finally close the books on the case of the purloined plates," Delia said. "But ask Samuel to let me know if he comes up with a more specific translation of them, would you?"

Gabe looked absently at the bookshelves, rubbing his fingers along one row of books. Then he stood. "Sure thing. Where should he send it?"

Delia knew this was a difficult moment for Gabe, and it was hard for her, too. "I'll be here through spring semester, at least."

"Then it's off to the desert?"

Delia dropped her eyes and picked up a large paper clip which she proceeded to straighten, leg by leg. "Looks like it, I guess."

Gabe reached for the doorknob. "Tell me if the prospects of hiking and playing tennis outdoors year round played any part in your decision."

She smiled. "Maybe the thought did skitter across my mind once or twice," she said.

"Good," he replied. "Need a ride home?"

"Sure. Thanks. The Sube was so frosty this morning I got lazy and came in on the bus. I developed the bus habit last fall. It's easier than driving some days."

Walking across the parking lot with Gabe on creaky packed snow seemed to Delia the most natural thing in the world. How many nights had they done this very thing, stepping warily across icy spots, hunching deep into their thick coats? The colorless skies of Jefferson winter days became black ceilings at night, blocking out the heavens and the lights of high-flying planes. The only illumination came from the bottom up rather than the top down, in campus lights reflecting off the white, snow-spread earth.

At home, Delia ignited the gas fireplace and put cider on to heat. Giving up coffee had not been pleasant, but hot spiced cider had eased her over the hump. In summer, she had resorted to diet soft drinks and juices. All in all, she thought herself cured and accepted her fate. Her next stop was the telephone where, mug in hand, she punched the playback button. She couldn't place the first voice.

"Hello, Professor McGrath? Uh, I mean Sister McGrath, I guess. This is Gerard, uh, you know, . . . Gerard in your writing class and the other ward?"

The boy was clearly nervous, and Delia wished she could enter this one-sided conversation and calm him a little. He paused and gulped, then went on.

"Well, I've decided to go on a mission, like we talked about that day in your office, remember? and I told you I'd let you know when and if it happened and so I am, letting you know I mean," he said, running his words together and scarcely pausing for breath. Then he gasped audibly and continued. "And I want you to speak at my farewell, like, it's not until February, I just wanted you to know in advance." Gerard took another breath. "Uh, if it's okay I'll come by your office sometime next week to talk about it. Maybe, like, after class. Thanks a lot, g'bye." That was it. End of message.

Now it was Delia's turn to be nervous. She felt herself perspiring even in the chilly room, and she couldn't blame it on the hot cider. How could she speak in church? What on earth could she say? What had possessed Gerard to ask her? Delia's first impulse was to track down his phone number and call him, explaining that it was impossible. But then she realized that at least she owed him the courtesy of telling him in person.

Instead of calling Gerard, therefore, she called Angie, and instead of getting sympathy and support, she got a guilty conscience. "I think you should do it," Angie said.

Since her conscience was already on active duty, Delia decided to call her mother and confess that she had come off with Anthon's message in her handbag. Polly's voice on the line was reassuring. She sounded like herself, though she admitted that her strength hadn't quite returned to normal yet.

"Are you resting enough?" Delia asked anxiously.

"Am I doing anything else is a better question. Ilene is over here half the time. Won't let me lift a hand. I'll forget how to work if this keeps up. I see by the news that it's cold where you are."

"You saw rightly. If it's winter, it's cold." Delia took a deep breath. "Mother . . . uh, Mother, I have a confession."

No response, then, "What have you done now? Run off with that bearded professor?"

Delia laughed. "No, nothing like that. Look, Mother, I know your relationship with Anthon Clemmer is none of my business, but . . ."

Polly interrupted. "Relationship! What relationship? A figment of the man's imagination."

"Let me finish, Mother, please."

"Well, get on with it."

"He left a note for you. In the Imperial. I found it, but didn't give it to you when you were so ill. Then I forgot about it. It's a poem."

"Doesn't surprise me. The man scribbles rhymes when he should be working for salary. Just because he inherited a lot of money doesn't mean he should sit around and rewrite Mother Goose for the rest of his days."

"He has money? How do you know? And how did you know it was a nursery rhyme?"

"I assumed it. It wouldn't be the first time he twisted an innocent rhyme to suit his whim. And yes, I suppose he has inherited some money, though you wouldn't know it to look at that contraption he drives. It was in all the papers."

Delia swallowed her surprise. If Anthon had money, he certainly wasn't flaunting it. "Want me to read the poem to you?"

"Heaven forbid. It'll be bad enough having him right next door without having to get him over the phone, too."

"Next door?" Delia nearly choked on a sip of hot cider, spilling some of it down the front of her sweater.

"Seems he's planning to buy Arva Plimpton's place. She couldn't wait to tell me. Came flying in after church Sunday. I didn't feel up to going. And I didn't feel up to Arva, either."

"Arva's moving?"

"To one of those fancy retirement centers in town. She can have it, with its bean-shaped pool and palm trees."

Delia swallowed hard. "Mr. Clemmer seems quite likable."

"Hmmph. I suppose he is, in a clownish sort of way. The money hasn't changed him a bit, unfortunately."

"He probably saved your life."

"Well, that makes us even."

Just what her mother meant by that Delia didn't dare ask, but she gathered that Anthon Clemmer and Polly McGrath had a history known only to them. She decided to find another subject.

"Have you heard from Jennifer lately? I haven't talked with her in a while."

"Jennifer, as you call her, came by last night. She just got in town. She's starting school at Joshua this term. They're on a different schedule than you are."

"She is? Well, that's news. I guess she finished up her high school work, then."

"I expect so. I knew that mother of hers would smother her right out of the house. I told her she could stay here if she wanted."

Absorbing yet another shock, Delia tried not to let it show in her voice. "Will she stay with you?"

"I hardly think so. I suppose now I'll have to stop calling her Torry. Says she goes to church every week. She's cleaned up her tongue considerably, too. Even her grammar has improved."

CHAPTER THIRTEEN

When Saturday arrived, Delia realized she hadn't seen Begonia and Elmer Roy since before Christmas. She herself had been away, of course, but she had been back more than a week. Here in Wisconsin, people who didn't have to go out in bad weather, particularly older people, burrowed into their homes like groundhogs until the first signs of spring. In fact, in condo land these folks emerging from their brick and plaster dens *were* the first signs of spring. Around noon, Delia went calling on the lovebirds.

"The grocery wagon at your service, m'am," Delia announced, clicking her heels to attention when Begonia opened the door just a crack and peered out. "You want to come along, or should I just pick up some things for you?"

Talking through the crack to keep out the cold, Begonia was invisible but for one eye and half a smiling mouth. The mouth moved. "Oh, would you, dear? When did you get back? When are you getting hitched?"

"Hooold on a second," Delia said, still standing outside Begonia's door, talking to one eye and half a mouth, which, she reflected, was getting to be a habit. "What makes you think I'm getting 'hitched,' as you put it?"

"Well, aren't you, dear? Elmer Roy said just yesterday that he bet so, too. In fact, he plans to set up a little lottery on the date with the bingo group at church. They all saw you at the wedding and think it's high time you settled into marital bliss. Don't get me wrong. I'm not dying for you to move, y'understand."

Delia laughed and threw up her hands. "A lottery! How is it, anyway, that I can't surprise anybody in this town? Everybody seems to have known my plans before I did."

"Simple as falling off a horse, dear," Begonia said. "When all those men started showing up around here, I smelled a race. And I knew who had the inside track. You going out there where the tanned one was made him a sure bet. As for me, I'd have been torn between him and that slick one's Jaguar. I could put up with a lot of stuffed shirt to acquire a vehicle like that."

Begonia winked the eye Delia could see, then opened the door fast and grabbed Delia's arm. "But come in, dear, you'll freeze out here," she said, snatching Delia inside and steering her into the museum. "Wait'll I get m'list."

Elmer Roy was glued to the television, which looked oddly out of place tucked among Begonia's antiques. The Badgers, he informed Begonia without turning around, were making a comeback from a twelve-point deficit. Begonia leaned over him and raised her voice a few decibels. "Look who's here, Elmer Roy," she cried, "and look who's betrothed! We started a reg'lar stampede to the altar!" He smiled and nodded and went back to his screen. Begonia turned to Delia. "If it's not football, it's basketball," she said, shaking her head and clucking her tongue but grinning all the while.

As Delia watched Begonia review and amend her grocery list, she realized that much as she loved Begonia, saying good-bye to the Turners would be the hardest part about leaving Jefferson. Harder even than separating from Gabe, since he was already as good as gone. No more summer nights on their deck, no more winter evenings talking books in front of their fireplace, no more stopping off at Angie's office for a few laughs at the end of a long day. Somehow it had all seemed simpler when she was in Smithville and Jefferson was on another planet.

Sunday was uneventful—Delia said nothing about her changed circumstances to anyone at church—and Monday morning came soon enough. The air was the color of spent ashes when Delia trudged out to the Subaru, disengaged the extension cord to the engine heater, removed the ossified rug from the engine, and cranked the protesting machine to life. She had an early appointment with Lyle Parry, her department chair, the only time he could spare today.

"Thanks for working me in," she said as Lyle ushered her into his office twenty minutes later. "Whooh, it's nippy out there!"

"Glad you didn't mind coming in early."

"Well, coming in at this hour reminded me again why I never want to be a department chair. I can't even find my brain before eight-thirty, much less conduct business or motivate a class of groggy nineteen-year-olds."

"Early morning meetings are a negative in the job description, all right, but they're a party compared with some of the things I have to do, as you've seen firsthand." Delia dropped her cap and mittens on a table, and Lyle helped her out of her down parka. "Care for coffee?" he asked, pulling a chair forward for her.

"I guess not." She hesitated. "I've given it up."

Lyle raised his eyebrows. "For health reasons?"

Delia chuckled. "In a manner of speaking, I suppose. The soul's health. I'm a Mormon, you know—or at least finally trying to be one."

"I gather this is a recent turn?"

"Mostly since my father died, yes. And since I tangled with Mother Nature in a slot canyon in southern Utah."

Picking up a white ballpoint pen and slowly turning it back and forth in his hands, Lyle rotated his chair to face the window. "Um, yes, I sensed that you'd changed, but I wasn't sure what prompted it," he said at last. Then he turned back and looked her squarely in the eye. "You went to see Horace Rostrand when he was dying, didn't you?"

Delia dropped her eyes and locked her hands together. "How did you know I went?"

Lyle spun around once more to the window, and Delia followed his gaze. The gray dawn absorbed the light fog that all but snuffed out trees, buildings, light posts, and scurrying walkers folded up against the cold. Sky and earth blended into one ghostly hue, broken only by a slanting line of shrouded dark trees that vaguely defined the slope of Brandon hill. Abraham Lincoln, sitting unmoved on his concrete pedestal, appeared to be dissolving into the mist.

Without turning, Lyle said, "I called the hospital the night he died, to check on his condition. The nurse at the intensive care unit told me a young woman was with him. The woman was on crutches, the nurse said, but she stayed by him until he died."

Lyle spun back to face her. "She said his wife had not been in that evening at all." He paused and set the pen down. "After all he had done to hurt you, you forgave him, didn't you?"

Delia looked up at Lyle, then lowered her head. "I suppose I did. He was so alone. I'm no saint. I went for selfish reasons—to get the rancor out of my own heart. That sort of thing can destroy a person. He didn't know I was there, but I saw another side of him that night. A noble side."

Lyle rose slowly from his desk chair and scanned the bookshelves behind him. "Ah, yes," he said. "One would like to think he had such a side." Pausing, he lifted a navy blue soft cover book from a high shelf. "As you can see, I have your Book of Mormon. A graduate student of your faith gave it to me some years ago. An excellent student, and a most decent human being." He raised the book. "Do you recommend it?"

Delia didn't answer immediately. "A year ago, I might not have been able to," she said finally, "because I hadn't ever given it serious thought. Now I believe it to be true. Every word."

"Then I'll read it, and perhaps we can talk about it."

"I'd like that," Delia said quietly, "but we'll have to do it in the next few months, I guess."

Again Lyle Parry raised his eyebrows and set the book on his desk. "You're not here to discuss a date for your tenure review?"

"No, I'm afraid not. I'm here to tell you that I'll be leaving at the end of spring semester," she said, making a tent of her thumbs, "and to ask you to write a letter of recommendation for my file."

Lyle nodded his head. "You won't reconsider?"

Delia shook her head.

He picked up the pen again, paused, and then said thoughtfully, "I respect your decision, but I hate to see you go. And, yes, of course, I'll write the letter."

"I'm applying at Joshua College, in my hometown. It's a small school. They want to know if I'm an effective teacher. They don't care about the publication record."

"Well, since your student evaluations seem to go off the charts every semester, that should be no problem. But what about your research and writing?"

"Oh, I'll keep those going one way or another. How can I teach if I'm not learning?"

At home that evening, Delia heard the front windows begin to rattle. The local weather service had warned that a storm was approaching southern Wisconsin, and the surge of wind confirmed it. Within minutes, hard-driven snow splattered in sheets against the sliding door to the patio, and the lights flickered. Shuddering involuntarily, Delia took her bowl of fat-free vegetable soup into the front room and settled on cushions by the fireplace to study for tomorrow's classes. Dressed in sweats and wrapped in a quilted cotton throw, she read for a couple of hours. Finally, she closed Hawthorne and simply stared into the restive flames.

Then, as if a button had been pushed in her brain, Delia's conversation with Lyle Parry played back through her mind, especially the part about the Book of Mormon. She felt some guilt at having hinted that she knew the book better than she did. Worse still, until recently she had been one of the book's detractors, and had argued with RonJay against it.

Although she now believed the book to be authentic, she hadn't put it—or Delia McGrath—to the test. *And here you are,* she lectured herself, *spending all your professional energy and most of your off-duty hours studying, in often minute detail, the literature of the world. Isn't it about time you invested at least some of that energy in a study of the Book of Mormon?* Even as she phrased the question, she knew the answer. The question was rhetorical.

A little later, after her tuck-in call from Gordon, Delia ascended the stairs to her bedroom with her scriptures and a pencil in her hand. Hawthorne's *The House of the Seven Gables* lay closed on the front room floor. As she turned down the bed and changed into flannel pajamas, Delia's mind flashed back to her sophomore year in high school when Brother Lechter had been her Sunday School teacher. For the most part, she had dismissed him in those days as an old fuddy-duddy, out of touch with the times. He was a quiet, graying man who didn't try to be a pal to the youths in his class. He tried instead to be a teacher, a guide, someone who stood for something, someone who was serious about the gospel and serious about teaching it to young people.

Delia was surprised to find that she remembered him more vividly than other teachers who were a lot more fun. She remembered several of the things he said, but most of all tonight she saw him standing beside a scarred little table in a cramped classroom with a cracked chalkboard, reading from Third Nephi. With his image still in her mind, she sat on the bed and scanned the book's index, then turned to the ninth chapter of Third Nephi, where the voice of Christ speaks out of the paralyzing darkness to the Nephite survivors of the great cleansing cataclysm.

"And ye shall offer for a sacrifice unto me a broken heart and a contrite spirit," the voice said; and Delia knew now what she hadn't known, or hadn't cared to know, at sixteen or seventeen—that a broken heart and a contrite spirit were the very things she was lacking. She read on. "And whoso cometh unto me with a broken heart and a contrite spirit, him will I baptize with fire and with the Holy Ghost." The words stung her with a realization of her own intractable pridefulness, but at the same time they filled her with hope.

After the Atonement, ritual sacrifice of animals was no longer required of Christ's people. But that didn't mean no sacrifice was required, Brother Lechter had said. In fact, he insisted, the new sacrifice—of a broken heart and a contrite spirit—was a more demanding, a more difficult requirement than the old. And it, too, might well signify the Savior's sacrifice, perhaps especially his sacrifice wrought in Gethsemane. *Nevertheless not as I will, but as thou wilt. . . .*

All this came to Delia McGrath, assistant professor of English, as she sat on plaid flannel sheets in an upstairs room at Morningside condominiums in Jefferson, Wisconsin, in the midst of a lowering storm. She slid off the bedside and onto her knees, book still in hand. In a broken, sobbing whisper addressed to her merciful and just God, she begged forgiveness and sought infinite grace.

The next few weeks sped by, with one semester gone and another underway. The Saturday before Gerard Mannion's farewell service in the Jefferson First Ward, Delia was more than a little apprehensive. When Gerard had come in to restate his request, she simply couldn't say no. She knew, possibly even better than his parents, the anguished soul-searching that had led to his decision, and she couldn't disappoint him. "On the other hand, when I get up there and open my mouth," she chuckled grimly, "he just might experience major disappointment."

Rather than sit home and fret, she loaded cross-country skis and a light leg brace into the Sube and headed for Elbow Mountain, a euphemism for a large bump on the landscape that boasted a small ski area with the fastest, fiercest rope tow in captivity. Her leg wasn't ready for downhill skiing, and especially for the Elbow Mountain rope tow, which demanded more of the skier than the ski runs, but she and Miles had tested the limb on skinny skis over Christmas and found it at least minimally snow worthy.

In the wooded area around the base of the hill, Delia followed tracks of other Nordic skiers, and by mid-afternoon she had mellowed by several degrees. Possibly, just possibly, she might survive Sunday's ordeal. The workout felt good, better than indoor machine therapy, she attested, for the mental state if not for the leg. The workout also kept her warm, even on a raw February day.

Driving home, she found herself singing along with Nancy Griffith on tape, an hilarious song about the woman from Salt Lake City who ran off to California in a Ford Econoline. Which song inevitably brought a certain Wyoming printer to mind, and Delia dialed her mother as soon as she arrived home. Jennifer Grenville answered the phone.

"Jennifer! Is that you?"

"Delia? . . . Hey, like, long time no see."

"How goes it?"

"Good, like, real good. I'm in school, and I'm studyin'. Can you b'lieve it? Me, the big-time loser. Hey, what's this I hear about you and hunky Gordon?"

"Depends on what you hear," Delia laughed.

"Hey, he's the man. Cool. He's a keeper."

"How's your leg—and the rest of you?"

"Good, like, real good. I still limp a little, but nuthin' much."

"Thanks for going by to visit Mother."

"Visit! I'm livin' here now."

Delia paused. "Well, good for you. Good for both of you. When did you move in?"

"Day before yesterday. I was, like, in an apartment, with three other girls. But, man, they were bad news. I called your mom and told her, and she said to come on out here. So here I am. C'n you believe it? Just like old times, and Gordon came by, too. That's how I knew about you and him. Wanna talk to your mom?"

"Uh, yes, sure." Delia was still absorbing the news when Polly's voice came on the line.

"So the boarder is back?" Delia began.

"Yes, she is. I insisted. Those girls she was with stay up all night, and use drugs, and I don't know what all. They aren't in school, and they don't seem to work. I don't know what they do, and furthermore I don't want to know. Jennifer works in the college cafeteria and goes to school both. Her father got her a little car, but mostly she plans to ride a bicycle. To save money."

"If it weren't for you, she could have destroyed her life long ago."

"Hmmph. All I did was refuse to put up with her shenanigans. She did the rest. With the help of you and the missionaries. Too bad those two we had last summer got transferred. I told her if she wanted to live with me she could, rent free, provided she signed up for a class at the Institute of Religion."

"And she's doing it?!"

"Of course, why wouldn't she? They don't bite people over there. It'll do her good."

Delia carried the phone into the kitchen and took an orange from the refrigerator. She hadn't eaten since morning, and her mother was unusually talkative today. Delia wanted to ask more about Anthon and his move to Smithville, but she lost her nerve. She also elected not to tell her mother about her speaking assignment at Gerard's farewell the next day.

"You're very likely wondering whatever possessed Gerard to ask me to participate today, and then whatever possessed me to agree to it," Delia began, her voice apologetic and trembling. The pulpit seemed huge to her, and her knees felt wobbly.

A hush fell over the Jefferson First Ward congregation, and Delia saw the Archer and Fines families come to rapt attention in center rows near the front. She hadn't expected them since they were in the

Second Ward, but there they were. Probably friends of the Mannions, she surmised. When she caught Mary Beth's and then Susan's eye, they both smiled at her, warm, encouraging smiles. Delia coughed once and cleared her throat, but her mind kept casting about for words. She looked again toward the Fines family; little Amy grinned and fluttered a tiny wave at her, like a signal in the dark. She smiled at Amy and the words came, slowly at first.

"Gerard, Elder Mannion, took a class with me last semester," she said. "He didn't know it, but he changed the whole complexion of the class, and he permanently influenced my life, with two short sentences." Delia paused, dropping her head, then looked up. "You remember that student who was found dead by the river last fall? Well, it was a blow to the town, especially at first when we assumed foul play, and it turned the campus upside down."

Delia stopped and swallowed hard. Lowering her eyes and fingering the set of scriptures resting on the pulpit, she continued. "Our class was up in arms. The students seemed ready to give up on the human race and on a God who would stand back and let evil run rampant. Gerard's was the only dissenting voice from all that hatred and despair. And, believe me, no one expresses those emotions more passionately than the young."

Delia raised her eyes and went on, her voice becoming more sure. "Do you know what he said?" A young man on the front row looked up from the airplane he was making of the printed program, as though she were speaking directly to him. "Bucking the tide of a whole room full of his very vocal peers," she continued, "he said this: 'I don't like blaming God for what people do.'

"And he said something else, something redeeming, something full of hope and spiritual significance, something so simple that we might miss its profundity." Delia stopped again, looked down, then raised her head. "I've tried to make what he said a guiding principle of my life from that moment on. I haven't always succeeded, but his words hang there, bright and true, as a beacon to me. And a conscience. This is what he said. Five words: 'We can do good, too.'"

Her voice broke momentarily. "'We can do good, too.' I have only returned to church activity in the last several months," she continued, "but I recognized true doctrine when I heard it from this boy's mouth. I've been studying the Book of Mormon intensely of late, and Gerard's statement clarified splendidly for me what Nephi and others meant when they said that eternal life was ours for the choosing. It is there, but we have to choose it. We have to choose to do what will lead to it. We have to choose what is good and right and true."

Delia struggled to keep her tears in check. She held up the Book of Mormon. "This is the message he will take to the world," she said, "and he has already proved that he has the courage to do it. I am indebted to him for the rest of my life."

She turned to Gerard, who was studying his shoes, but who looked up when he felt her eyes on him. "God bless you and keep you," she said softly, and walked to her seat.

* * * * * * * *

It was the beginning of April, and the desert was blooming. In spite of developments next door, Polly McGrath smiled as she washed up her few supper dishes before the open window. The early flowers in her yard had come and gone, but the roses and bedding plants were getting started. Polly could smell the first of the scarlet climbers on the trellis beneath her window. It was after six o'clock when Arva Plimpton's Chevrolet pulled in. As she crawled out of the car, Arva looked up and saw Polly.

"Yoo-hoo, Polly!" Arva called. "How's about if I just come in without knocking? Don't even bother to dry your hands, I'm only here for a minute."

Seconds later, Arva was in the door with a small, ivory-colored vase in her hands. "Today's the day," she said. "The movers came and I'm off to the Pleasant Hours. Anthon, that dear man, said he'd take care of anything I left behind. Said he might could use some stuff. Me? I don't have room for it. It's good-bye and good riddance."

Polly wiped her hands on the dishtowel and motioned Arva to a chair. "Does that go for neighbors, too?" she asked.

Arva looked startled, then dismayed. "Why a'course not, Polly McGrath. Once a friend, always a friend. That's my motto." She set the vase on the table. "It's for you. To remember me by. My great aunt, Claudine—you've heard me talk about Aunt Claudine, the one with the Great Dane and the moustache? She gave it to me on my tenth birthday."

Just then the screen door slammed and Jennifer crossed the back porch, tossing her bicycle helmet in the laundry basket. "Guess what?" she declared, "I'm doin' it! Oh, hi, Miz Plimpton."

"Doing what, girl? My sakes how you do startle a person, doesn't she, Polly?"

"She's been here long enough that I guess I'm past startle," Polly replied dryly.

"Baptized! I'm gettin' dunked! Like, this Saturday, the day before Easter. Cool, huh? We just talked to the bishop."

"*Our* bishop?" Arva asked, then raised one eyebrow to ensure that her point hit home and added, "I don't rightly recall seeing you over at the meetings lately."

"At the campus church. I go to a campus ward, don't I, Miz McGrath?"

"That's what you tell me, so it must be so."

"We want Ron to do it. Cool, huh?"

"Oh, yes, *real* cool," Polly assented at last. "Now you get in there and call your parents."

"What if they say no?"

"They won't. They wouldn't have let you come here if they intended to say no. Who's *we?*"

"Gordon, who else?"

As the young woman walked by her toward the telephone, Polly touched her shoulder and she stopped. "Any parent would be proud of you," Polly said a little gruffly, and Jennifer looked up at Polly with wonder in her face. This was not a woman given to idle compliments, and Jennifer knew it.

Arva hadn't been gone forty minutes when another vehicle pulled into the yard. Polly was still in the kitchen, mending the torn corner on a fitted bed sheet. Jennifer had just left in her blue food services uniform. Big banquet tonight over at the college, she told Polly. Shouldn't be too late, she promised, and she'd get to fill up on the leftovers.

When Anthon Clemmer appeared at the door, Polly wasn't exactly surprised. With Arva on her way to carefree living where peeling doors were somebody else's worry, Polly figured the new owner of the old Plimpton place wouldn't waste any time getting over here. It was one of those occasions when she was glad Jennifer was gone for the evening. Polly hadn't seen Anthon since Christmastime, though she knew he had been in the area for a few days, making arrangements to move in next door. Arva kept her well informed about his doings. Arva should have been a gossip columnist, Polly had said to Ilene on more than one occasion. She missed her calling in life.

Polly felt especially awkward about seeing Anthon, not only because she was in his debt, but also because when she was ill he had seen her at her weakest and worst. Under the circumstances, she could hardly turn him out. The fact was, she had never thanked him properly for taking care of her, and she didn't know how to do it without embarrassing herself and encouraging him. Now here the man was, moving into the Plimpton place. *Well,* she declared silently, *this is a fellow made for disappointment. He brings it on himself. Please Lord,* she begged silently, *tell me I needn't be my neighbor's keeper. Not this neighbor, anyway.*

"Don't bother to get up," a familiar voice called from the back porch, and Anthon Clemmer came into the kitchen.

Polly's needle didn't slow at all. "Hmmph. So you did it, did you?"

"Is that the only greeting I get after all my trouble moving down here?"

"What were you expecting, the welcome wagon?"

Anthon laughed. "At the very least. C'mon, give your old nurse-maid a squeeze."

"I'll give my old nursemaid a black eye if he isn't careful," Polly returned, but a smile threatened the corners of her mouth.

Anthon only laughed. "Glad to see you've recovered. When you were sick, you talked so nice you worried me."

"You must have dreamed that part, or else I was delirious."

"Care to ride into town with me? I need to pick up a few things if I'm to sleep at the old homestead tonight. It's a beautiful night for a luxury ride in a van."

"I think I can forgo the pleasure. Still driving that dumpster on wheels, are you? Arva said you were getting a Lexus. She'd have married you if you'd driven up in a Lexus that day."

"I knew I was asking for trouble when I spoke the word. Arva's eyes lit up like a slot machine coughing up quarters. That van holds me and all my worldly goods. How could I move down here without it?"

"Well, if you're as rich as Arva claims you are, you could hire a mover."

"For one van load? Not me. I'm saving all my money for courting activities." He winked at her. "Plenty of merry widows around these parts, I hear."

Polly noticed how Anthon's eyes smiled along with his mouth when he teased her. It used to annoy her, how he fielded her every jab and turned it into a joke. But now, she thought it one of his more appealing traits. She shooshed him out of the room.

Upwards of two hours later, Polly heard a vehicle roll into the yard. Jennifer, she thought, but she was wrong. It was Anthon again, bearing two dripping ice cream cones in a carton.

"Vanilla," he said. "I hope you like vanilla. I'm a purist when it comes to ice cream. There's only one flavor."

Polly stared at him briefly, then fetched dishes and spoons, just in case, she said. As she set them in front of him, she didn't look up. "Jed ate only vanilla, too," she said quietly.

Occupied by the rapidly melting ice cream, the two exchanged few words. Polly finally plopped hers in a dish, but Anthon kept ahead of the melt with his tongue. He was pushing back his chair to leave when another vehicle drove up.

"That must be Jennifer," Polly said.

"Ah, yes, the reformed delinquent," Anthon replied.

"The two of you ought to get along. You have that in common."

Anthon chuckled. "Just when I think you're starting to soften toward me a little, you say something like that. Are you trying to discourage me, Mrs. McGrath?"

Before Polly could reply, Jennifer was at the door. She stopped when she saw Anthon. She knew of him from Arva, but they had never met. "Come in, Jennifer." Polly turned to Anthon. "Anthon, meet Jennifer Grenville. She lives at Joshua College, but she sleeps here."

Anthon had stood already, and Jennifer met his extended hand. "Jennifer," Polly said, "meet a friend of mine, Mr. Anthon Clemmer."

Bells went off in Anthon's head.

* * * * * * * *

From the window of the 737, Delia looked out over the patterned fields of Nebraska. It was Saturday morning, the day before Easter, and she was making a surprise visit to Smithville. She had taken a shuttle from Jefferson to O'Hare Field Friday night and caught an early-morning flight to Las Vegas. It was a last-minute decision, and flights were jammed on the day before Easter.

The plan had been for Gordon to drive out to Jefferson for Delia's spring break and then haul a load of her winter things back to Smithville in his 4-Runner. But then he had called to say he couldn't get away until late Saturday afternoon. He didn't say why. When Delia called her mother Friday afternoon, however, she found out why. She also found out where. The calm, deep pool in the river on Spring Road, the old swimming hole. And when. Two o'clock, the warmest hour of the day. It was, after all, early April still.

Delia's plane was late, and she missed the shuttle from Las Vegas to Smithville. Racing to the curb, she picked an older taxi driver and negotiated a fare to Smithville with him. He was an independent, which meant he was glad to get out of the rat race for short fares and hit the open road. Delia knew this was crazy, spending money she really didn't have, but it was important. She had to be there.

It was 1:45 when the taxi entered the McGrath yard on Spring Road. Delia dumped her things on the back porch, threatened the dog who came over to greet her with dirty paws, and ran for the road. Then something registered in her mind. She tore back to the steps, opened the screen door and looked above the washing machine. Sure enough, the cowboy hat and levi jacket were gone.

Pondering the significance of the missing hat and jacket, Delia dashed again to the road. She hadn't covered a hundred yards when a white BMW convertible pulled up beside her.

"It's an old line, but can I give you a lift?"

Delia stopped and stared. "Mr. Clemmer, is that you? In this car?"

"In the flesh. Call me Anthon. And don't be fooled by the car. My van broke down, and I rented this for the day, mostly to get a rise out of your mother. I'm on my way to a baptism; care to join me?"

She jumped in and off they went.

Several cars lined the road near the big cottonwood tree with the swinging rope. Clouds had moved in, just in the last hour or so Anthon said, overtaking some sections of sky. They now blocked the sun, dropping the temperature several degrees.

"You run, I'll hang back a little," Anthon urged as he turned off the ignition switch. "I don't want to ruin your mother's day until after the baptisms," he grinned. "Don't pray for rain," he added.

"Thanks, thanks a lot," she called, and ran to the river bank where her mother stood with Ilene and Polly's four Smithville grandchildren. The scene was like a framed picture, beatific and serene despite the turbulent clouds: Ron in the hip-deep water, and Jennifer there with him, shivering, looking only at him, beseeching him, counting on him to help her. Ron talking to her, calming her, assuring her. The two of them dressed completely in white.

Several missionaries, a group of older men, and a number of young people from the college watched from the shore, all smiling, and all watching the sky with some apprehension. As Ron prepared to lower Jennifer into the icy water, a few big splotches of rain struck his head and shoulders. He pronounced the sacred words and immersed her, then helped her to the shore where friends surrounded her with a blanket and their arms, laughing and crying.

Jennifer, too, was laughing and crying, and a little distance away, Delia's mother snuffled and blew her nose in her handkerchief. Delia stepped forward and put her arm around her mother, who had not known she was coming. Polly McGrath wiped her eyes, returned her lace-trimmed handkerchief to the sleeve of her dress, and slipped her arm around the waist of her daughter.

Only then did Delia see Gordon. He stepped forward from the group of missionaries to meet Ron at the water's edge. Delia thought she had never seen anything so beautiful as Gordon at that moment, dressed in white, the unruly breeze rippling his hair, his face shining. Ron had noticed Delia, after Jennifer left the water, but Gordon hadn't. When Gordon entered the river, Ron said something to him and pointed in Delia's direction. Gordon looked, smiled with surprise, mouthed the words "I love you," and followed Ron into the deep pool.

As Ron uttered the baptismal words and lowered his friend into the water, the clouds broke above them and a torrent of sunlight streaked into the tumbling eastern sky, flinging a multi-colored ribbon across the firmament. The rain began in earnest then, but the rainbow clung to the sky with bright fingers while Gordon Foster walked dripping and rejoicing toward Delia McGrath.

As the appearance of the bow that is in the cloud on the day of rain, so was the appearance of the brightness round about. This was the appearance of the likeness of the glory of the Lord.

EZEKIAL 1:28

READER'S GUIDE

DISCUSSION QUESTIONS FOR YOUR READING GROUP

1. *Sky Full of Ribbons* has two general settings, southwestern Utah and south central Wisconsin, and the novel's action alternates between those settings. Compare and contrast other aspects of the two worlds of the novel and suggest ways in which they reflect (and underscore) the conflict within Delia McGrath. Note, too, the ways in which weather figures in the presentation of the contrasting worlds. Consider also the use of various characters to represent aspects of the two worlds. Is the resolution of Delia's conflict in favor of the western setting inevitable, or might she just as logically have opted to remain in the Midwest? Why does she ultimately choose to return to the land of her nativity? To what degree do Hector Gabrielson's altered circumstances affect Delia's decision? How about Begonia's marriage? Angie's cancer?

2. The novel has two plots, a main plot concerned with Delia's experiences and conflicts, and a subplot concerned with Delia's mother, Polly McGrath. Are the two plots mutually exclusive, or are they interwoven in some aspects? Do you find echoes of one in the other, and if so, what are they? Do the plots present any similar themes? On the basis of your discoveries, consider whether Delia and her mother are more different than alike, or more alike than different.

3. Consider also that the two plots present two other kinds of intersecting worlds, the world of senior citizens and the world of younger professionals. Discuss the similarities and differences between these two worlds as presented in the novel. Both plots, for example, treat the growth of affection between man and woman. How was the "courting" of senior citizens viewed by people of different ages in your reading group?

4. In chapter one, Anthon Clemmer realizes that "it wasn't bragging rights that brought him to the old two-story, yellow frame house on Spring Road. It was the woman. He liked her. He suspected he even loved her. . . (p. 16)." What is there about Polly that attracts Anthon, and about Anthon that draws him to her? Why would he fall

for and pursue a woman whom others might see as a crotchety old sourpuss? Is it a mistake for him to move to Smithville? Is the children's response to him predictable? Do you foresee acceptance of him or not?

5.   What evidence does the novel give that by the end, Polly is beginning to soften toward Anthon? How do you account for that softening? What does it signify? How important in Polly's spiritual journey is the scene near the end of chapter seven when she finally opens up to her sister Dorothy? What can sisters do for each other that no one else can? Discuss the relationships between sisters portrayed in the novel, noting again how these matters play out in the parallel worlds of senior and juniors. What could Hannah and Delia be to and for each other? Are they on their way to a meaningful relationship? What will it take to get them there?

5.   Jedediah McGrath died before the beginning of this novel. To what extent is his presence still felt in the novel? Point to instances in which he is quoted or alluded to. How important a role does he play in the lives and relationships of other characters, especially those in his family? What role does he play in Delia's return to church and in her decision to return to southern Utah? What role does he play in Polly's spiritual healing? How does his grave function as a symbol of peace and reconciliation? (see chapters 9 and 12)

6.   Discuss each of the "supporting actors" in the novel and discover how each one functions in the narrative. For example, consider Delia's neighbor, Begonia Slopek. She certainly serves to add the spice of humor to the novel, as do Arva Plimpton and the Plumm sisters, but she may have other purposes as well. Does she, for example, become a substitute mother figure for Delia—a "mother" who makes few demands and fully accepts Delia as she is? Does she also set an example for Delia by her decisiveness in choosing a mate and marrying him?

7.   One of the novel's large, affirming truths is that people can change for the better. We are not locked into the persons we are at

any particular stage of our lives. Which of the characters change in significant ways in the course of the novel? Describe those changes, and discuss the events and circumstances that produced the changes. Consider Delia, for example. Several people notice the change in her, the softening and the newfound faith. She herself declares that only "grief and calamity could humble her" (p. 250). Is she right? What other things might have figured in the change as well? How important were the metal plates in precipitating the change? In what other ways do ancient writings ("plates," if you will) figure in the text and participate in changes of heart? (Consider the role of the Book of Mormon itself and its effect on Delia as her visiting teachers read from it and as she studies it. Consider, also, the book's effect on Anthon and any changes it might have precipitated in him.)

8. In literature, very often some characters are made to serve as "foils" to other characters. That is, by their contrasting natures, they serve to bring out and highlight character traits of another. In what ways might Arva Plimpton, the Plumm sisters, and Begonia Slopek be said to serve as foils for Polly McGrath? Note also how positioning in the text helps establish these contrasts. For example, Arva's inane responses to the Sunday School lesson are followed immediately by the promptings that touch Polly deeply. What characters serve as foils for Delia, and in what ways?

9. Most novels "say" something. That is, they have themes. What themes can you discover in *Sky Full of Ribbons*? One rather obvious and important theme is the question of a mortal's innate capacity for good or evil. How is that theme presented in the novel? How is the student's death important in that presentation? What is Delia (the teacher) taught about the subject by Gerard (the student)? In your experience, what have you learned from those you are assigned to teach? How instrumental is Gerard in Delia's conversion? There are other themes, some related to each other. For example, during worship service, Delia realizes that "the degree to which justice and right prevail on earth depends largely on what mortals do" (p. 249). In what ways is the theme of justice addressed and illustrated in the novel? Is the justice theme related to the matter of rushing to

judgment against another mortal? Is Delia's judgment of the men in the truck the only instance of such rushing to judgment, or does it figure in the Smithville subplot as well? Consider, too, the theme of the particular vulnerability of women to harm. Discuss how Delia's broken leg helps convey that theme. In a less threatening sense, Polly's illness also makes her vulnerable in a way that she had not been, thus underscoring the theme in the second plot. Women in your group might add their own insights and experiences in the matter of vulnerability.

10. Imaginative literature often relies on the use of images (things that can be detected through the senses—that is, things that can be seen (like a river or a rainbow), or heard (like a hymn), or touched (like a leg cast), or smelled (like a creosote bush)—to create mood or to suggest more than is said. With the latter, the image, then, is used as a symbol. In this novel, rivers have significance both at the beginning and the end. Note that the first river, a scene of terror and death, is pictured in one world while the second river, a scene of joy and rebirth, is pictured in the other world. How does that imagery contribute to the novel's basic concerns? Is there other water imagery that lends additional depth to the novel? (Consider, for example, in the latter part of chapter ten when Delia walks on the ice-covered lake, which is frozen water. Does this subtly suggest that her faith is increasing?) Discuss some of the other images that seem important or at least of interest in the novel.

11. Two Biblical passages appear in the novel, separate from the text, at its beginning and end. What is their relation to the novel itself, and to its title?

12. If members of your reading group have read the two novels that preceded this one, *Desert Song* and *Song of Hope,* the discussion could be expanded to include references to them.

ABOUT THE AUTHOR

Marilyn Arnold graduated from Brigham Young University with highest honors and earned her Ph.D. in American Literature from the University of Wisconsin at Madison. Her distinguished career has included tenure at BYU as a Professor of English, Assistant to the President, Dean of Graduate Studies, and Director of the Center for the Study of Christian Values in Literature. A nationally recognized scholar on the works of author Willa Cather and other American writers, she has written four books on Cather and has published widely in scholarly journals and Church publications. *Sky Full of Ribbons* is her third novel.

A resident of St. George, Utah, Marilyn is an avid skier, hiker, and tennis player. She has served in numerous Church positions throughout her adult life.